CELTIC ODYSSEY
Book 2

D.L. Narrol

CELTIC ODYSSEY
Book 2

DOUBLE DRAGON

Chapter One

January 1909:

The sea was finally calm. The creature lay low and out of sight. Pieces of human flesh, along with other debris, floated about the bloody surface. The vessel's two steam pipes were cracked, but still managed to expel steam in their regular fashion. The one sail was completely destroyed. It was early morning, where the day was already long and hard. Captain Colin Limmerick wrapped a wool scarf around his broad neck, while casting the nets into the sea. The ten-man crew worked endlessly at staying alert, hoping to overcome the incident from the previous night.

The Atlantic Mermaid sailed along the Irish coast, while still trying to make the catch they should have made hours ago. The sharp winds made their sail a difficult one, where the usual temperament of the sea had worsened. The crew's knees buckled with exhaustion. They stunk of ale, sweat, and the sea. They watched the scarce rays of light beam upon the hull as the morning fully set in. The distant screeching of a plump dirigible floated above them, which gave them a sense of ease. Eddy, the first mate, woke from his bunk making his way to the deck where he saw his captain hang his torso over the gunnels in the midst of rising sun.

"Captain, haven't ya slept at all?"

The towering captain turned to Eddy. "Slept?"

"Ya look awful; get some rest. We're docked at the Dublin Quays. Go, clean yar self up 'n get some sleep."

"That I can't do just yet, because I found this on the ship," the captain said, holding a gigantic tooth with both his hands.

Eddy stepped back. "It looks heavy, Captain."

"I'd say it's a good weight."

5

Eddy examined the tooth with his eyes. "It don't resemble a shark, nor a whale."

The Captain lowered it to the deck. "Surely, it doesn't. I bloody don't feckin' know what attacked us last night, but this is what it left us."

Eddy stepped closer. "The crew, Captain, are feelin' a wee bit rattled at last night's incident. Don't show them that tooth. Yar crew could quit on yaz, 'n then what?"

The captain raised his soaking cap and flicked back his lengthy forelock. He nervously tied back his long, wet hair.

"And then what? I'll sell me boat 'n move permanently to London."

"Now, yar talkin' nonsense. C'mon, let me buy ya a pint. Ya sure look like ya need it."

"Ed, we docked at Rosslare some hours ago to get the reel fixed with a new net. Why? Somethin' is still out there. Somethin' devoured our lifeboat. Ed, what's gone on here?" Colin's complexion was pale. He found himself in an endless shiver. "Our *Mermaid*, she needs loads of fixin'. She can't sail over shore; she's all broke."

Eddy gave Colin a pat on the shoulder. "Captain, yar starved; maybe we could go for some grub, eh? I remember when yaz was a wee lad workin' on yar uncle's ship. Ya always took everythin' too serious, even then."

Colin sighed. "I need to return to London. Get her fixed somehow. Just can't stick 'round here now."

"London? The weekend's not over yet. London won't give ya the answers yaz lookin' for."

Colin pulled his soggy cap from his head. The dark circles under his eyes over-powered his handsome face. He stood on the deck, drenched with the sea as blood dripped from his inner thigh. He scanned his body to below his groin, noticing his bloodstained trousers. Eddy's eyes widened with shock.

"Captain, ya need a doctor?"

"As long as me balls 'n cock are still hangin' low, all is well," Colin forced a smile and unbuttoned his trousers to check. He ran his fingers along his testicles and penis. "It's all there, thank the good lord." Eddy stood in silence and smiled. Colin smiled back at his first mate. "I bes' get to work. We's so bloody behind."

He moved several large crates of fish onto the peer. The rest of the crew reluctantly helped. After their work was done for the day they decided to relax at the nearby fisherman's pub.

Colin and his crew staggered in feeling their exhaustion and stress get the best of them. They sat at one of the largest tables. They ordered food and several pints of ale. Colin sat with his head buried in his arms. His tweed cap was pulled down over his eyes. His pint sat in front of him with the froth bubbling over top of the glass. His ears were perked, but his eyes were closed. A group of fisherman sat at the next table. They were drunk and loud.

"Three vessels went down last night," one of the fishermen said, to the others at the next table. "Three, I tell yaz…three bloody vessels!" Colin's head rose as he repositioned himself to sit straight in his chair. "It happened 'round 3:00 in the mornin'. Gone, I tell yaz – all gone. Not a nibble of debris was even found."

Colin took a swig of ale and glanced at his crew.

"What was out there?" one of the other fishermen at the next table asked. "Not a shark, nor a whale – not even the Scots' Nessie. Sometin' is out there."

Colin gulped his ale. He glanced at his crew. "Shite. What have I done? Shite."

Eddy tried to smile. "Done? Ya haven't done anythin', Captain. Yar not in charge of nature."

The crew chuckled and agreed with the first mate. Colin stared at his first mate and then his crew with a serious expression on his face.

"Ye'd be surprised. Shite, what the feck?"

***

7

That following Monday morning London was dim and chilly. Colin made his way to the Natural History Building at The London University; bound up in his vested suit, coat and bowler hat. He used his umbrella as a cane, where each step was painful. He appeared more awkward than he felt, because the umbrella was so much smaller than a fitted cane would be for a man his size. He hoped he wouldn't be noticed by anyone he knew.

He made his way into the building and proceeded to squirm up every step, which led to his office. He flopped in his chair, not bothering to remove his coat and hat. A lanky fair-haired, young man appeared.

"Mr. Limmerick, so here I find you looking not so fresh and not so professional in your so nice office. You have big drunk last night on high seas with your crew, nyet?" blurted Dr. Sasha Dimitrikov, peering through the doorframe.

Colin sat straight in his chair and fiddled with his crooked tie. "What the feck are ye goin' on about now? Shite, man, we've got us more problems. Will this mess ever end?"

"Last time I see you, you so happy man with Miss Amoli – why you so upset now? I know, you have fight, da?"

"Don't even think about draggin' Amoli into this conversation. I had a rough weekend on the *Atlantic Mermaid*. Some kinda monster is tearin' up the waters."

Sasha quickly shut the door. "What happened on your ship?" Sasha asked, searching his blazer pockets.

"I don't think we completely closed the vortex openin'." Colin blinked his eyes several times with fatigue; he had lost his usual zest. "Our last prehistoric expedition was a failure, don't ye think?"

"*Shto?*" Sasha asked in Russian, as he pulled a cigarette box from his jacket pocket. He sat down and popped it into his mouth. "What you say? Sorry, I sometimes forget my English."

"We was at sea this weekend, close to home, the Irish Sea 'n Saint George's Straight – ye know, not far at all. Somethin' shook the bleedin' feck out of the *Atlantic Mermaid*, so much so it tore away at me trawlin' nets, the reel, 'n even done away with our lifeboat." He recklessly reached for his leather *bolg* and grabbed a small flask of whiskey. He drank from it with conviction. "I haven't slept the weekend. We've got a serious problem, so we do."

Sasha puffed on his cigarette. "Why you act like all so terrible? You all survive?"

"Aye."

"Then, you not know my Russia. I leave my Russia at beginning of Revolution. You not know how we live. All workers work eleven-hour days. We have poor wages, you not know. All Russian goods very expensive. That is serious problem, da?"

Colin rolled his eyes back with a sigh. "Oh, mother of God, would ye stop comparin' everythin' to Russia? This is not Russia. We've done some expeditions through time 'n now we've opened a Pendora's box, don't ye think?"

"I walk these streets of London, I do not see so much suffrage as my streets of Petersburg. You not know, Mr. Limmerick. I think Czar will soon be in great trouble. There is movement happening now."

Ye like yer Czar?"

"Nyet! I hate him. I hate all politicals."

Colin shook his head. "How'd we get onto this topic, I don't know?"

"You mention serious problem. You not know serious problem. You are big strong Irishman. You have so easy."

"Oh, God."

"You visit my Russia and you see upheaval."

"Ye certainly know bullocks about Ireland, don't ye?"

Sasha had smoked his cigarette to its butt. "And, now, Mr. Limmerick, you sit there in comfortable university office, dressed in so nice suit, and so many women ogle for you."

Colin sat forward in his chair behind his desk. "Mate, there's prehistoric marine life roamin' about our waters. I'm feelin' rather responsible for it."

Sasha's eyes widened. "Did you see what was in water?"

"I didn't. Somethin' much bigger than any whale we know was definitely before us that night."

Sasha gazed at the floor while he lit his cigarette. He paused, and slowly scanned the room.

"You blame it on vortex?"

Colin sat back in his chair, causing the springs to creek. "Oh, feck, why wouldn't I blame it on the bloody vortex?"

"You imply something here? Shark do this."

Colin hung over the table to get a closer view of Sasha. "And…there's more. Somethin' else happened," he said, his voice trembled. "Three fishin' vessels went down last night."

"How you know this?"

"I heard other fishermen chattin' about in the pub."

Sasha pretended to be interested in the academic journals sitting on the desk. He smoked in silence. Colin was anxious, but silent. Colin folded his arms in front of him and took a deep breath.

"Sasha, I understand yer theory is beyond any scientists' comprehension, but it has a shite load of bugs, so it does."

"Bugs? What you say?"

"It's all gone wrong is what I'm sayin'. We may've destroyed the world," Colin huffed, as he rubbed the inseam of his leg. "Almost lost me tanker in the midst of the attack."

Sasha smiled, and pointed at Colin's crotch. "You lose that, you lose everything." Colin's eyes widened.

10

"If you see doctor he will say you have shark attack. All people know this."

"That was no shark. Prehistoric it was. It had to be."

"Prehistoric? Why? You not have prehistoric attack, you have big shark with so many teeth."

"That was no shark."

"Show me your wound, I tell you if it is shark attack."

"First, I'm not removin' me trousers here in me office. Second, this creature didn't touch me. It was when I returned to me vessel after bein' in the lifeboat, this monster attacked me ship almost capsizin' us in the process. It swallowed down the lifeboat. The rigging boom fell on me cuttin' the inside of me leg. I'm in pain every time I walk."

Sasha appeared to be engrossed in one of the scientific journals on Colin's desk. "A shark can do that."

"In all me years at sea I've never spotted a shark. Why would a man-eatin' shark be in these cold waters? Their primitive fish, not the most adaptable." Colin reached for his whiskey-filled flask and took a few relentless gulps, and then took a few deep breaths. "Besides, this beast lost a tooth on me ship. By the looks of it, it's no shark."

"Show me this tooth."

"It won't mean anything to yez. Yer a physicist."

"I know these things."

"Ye don't. I'll show it to Rosa. She's the archeologist, she'll be able to make heads or tails out of it."

"Fine, you think woman can examine it. Go ahead," Sasha said, with his arms in the air.

Colin slapped his hand over his face. "Oh, dear God, whatever made me want to live in two different worlds? Why didn't I just remain a fisherman, 'n only that?"

Sasha stood up. "Because you want so bad to prove how *Megaloceros* came to be extinct."

Colin ran his hands through his long crimson hair. "Aye, me thirst for the impossible got the best of me. I'm

11

a Darwinist, 'n me belief in natural selection had to be proven with me research on *Megaloceros giganteus*."

"You were bored of fishing life, da?"

"Never bored of me life as a fisherman, but I wanted more, so ye see."

"You get your degrees, and you still fisherman."

Colin chuckled. "Here I am, a workin' class fisherman from Ireland, no doubt. Me academic advisor hates me bleedin' guts, 'cause of who I am."

"You no look like scholar, either."

"Aye, me biggest problem is I stick out in a crowd, that's for sure."

"When I first saw you, I think you were lumberjack."

"I'm cursed, so I am."

"You not, but you work too much. Take vacation and relax. Rosa say me you like Portuguel coast."

A brisk shadow passed by the doorway. "Colin! In my office, please!"

Colin tensed. "Cushing, that's all I need just now."

Sasha tiptoed to the door. "You must go to your *Dr. Advisor* and please him."

"Never."

"You have bad attitude, Mr. Limmerick."

Colin hoisted himself from the chair. He clenched his teeth at Sasha and limped from the room.

"Can't ye ever address me as Colin? Why ye always so damn formal?"

"Formal? I not formal? Good luck with your advisor, Mr. Limmerick," Sasha said, as he watched Colin leave the room.

Sasha sighed and continued to smoke his cigarette. Colin poked his head in Dr. Cushing's office.

"Ye needed to speak with me, sar?"

"Colin, yes, do come in," Dr. Cushing said, placing his glasses onto his nose. "My, my, you do look dreadful."

Colin leaned against the doorframe. "I had a challengin' weekend, one could say."

Dr. Cushing showed no concern. "I'm wondering where that chapter is on your time-travels to find the *Horseshoe crab*. Is 10,000 years suitable for your geologic time-frame?"

Colin took a deep breath, rolling his eyes back. "Wasn't really plannin' on time-travelin' again, but who knows? Also, wasn't really plannin' on wastin' me time-travelin' in search of yer mate – the *Horseshoe* crab. There really isn't space in me dissertation to devote a chapter on that bleedin' crustacean."

"Speak English. Are you saying you will be time-traveling some time soon?"

Colin took another deep breath, puffing his broad chest. "Soon, sar? Aye, it may very well be, but I'll be *enroute* to find *Megaloceros giganteus*, or perhaps some of the *Irish Deer's* neighborin' community, like a large threatenin' whale. I'm afraid there won't be time for the *Horseshoe crab*, forgive me."

"Oh, yes, you will very well make time for the *Horseshoe crab*. This is where you and I can collaborate an academic paper. I think this will impress the chancellor of this academic institution."

"Ye 'n me, write a paper together?" He chuckled loudly in a deep tone.

"Are you aware we have a new chancellor?"

"New chancellor, ye sayin'? Didn't the university just get a new chancellor?"

"That was last year."

"It's not an annual position, is it, sar?"

Dr. Cushing grunted and snorted. "Oh, God, no. These positions are very valued in our academic world. They don't come along everyday, you know." Colin rose from his chair. "Do not express these outlandish thoughts to anyone on this campus, Colin. It could stand in the way of your academic reputation."

"Do I even have an academic reputation, sar?"

"Reputation? Yes, of course you have a reputation."
Dr. Cushing laughed.

Colin gave another deep chuckle. "Reputations 'n new chancellors, what's this to do with me? I don't know."

"This is extremely important to all of us who produce the work we do." He lifted one eyebrow. "But, I suppose you are too absorbed with your silly boat, when your thoughts should be here with this academic institution."

Colin placed his hand over his mouth to yawn. "If yer done chattin' with me, sar, I bes' be on me way."

"Not so fast. The concept of time-travel is astounding, don't you think?"

"Astoundin', ye put it? It has its pros 'n cons; I think I'm feelin' closer to the cons."

Professor Cushing gathered some notes and handed them to Colin. "I have created a time-travel data scroll. It will be on this that you will record the geologic time frame in which you travel, and if you run your eyes down to the bottom of the page you will see there is a section for you to record your *Horseshoe crab* findings. On the blank spaces you will write the leg count."

Dr. Cushing stood up and waved the form in Colin's face. Colin's head hung down and he shut his eyes.

"Leg count? I told ye I wasn't goin' after researchin' this ridiculous crustacean of yers. Sar, if ye could excuse me, I left me specs at me flat 'n I must really go fetch 'im."

"This is the problem with you as a graduate student – you spend too much time and energy on that damn boat of yours. You cannot afford to be rushing off here and there. This has got to stop, or I will see to it that your research funding is cut."

Colin's posture became more erect. "So, I either write about this crustacean or yer goin' to bloody well cut off me fundin'? What's this to do with me ship, I don't know? You've gone too far this time."

14

"I don't think I've gone too far, no not at all. In fact, not far enough."

"Excuse me whilst I go fetch me specs."

Dr. Cushing watched Colin exit his office in a rage.

**

"Such a strong handsome man looking so ill-kept once again," said Rosa, wearing a long cloth coat and feathered hat.

Colin glanced at her. "I'm not at me best. Ye need not look at me then 'n ye can go about yer way."

"What happened? You have a limp."

"Had an accident on the ship this past weekend."

"Oh, my, how awful."

Colin stopped walking. "Shhh, I'd prefer if we keep this one under our hats, if ye don't mind. Everyone here at the university has painted us as gods, yet nobody really knows the inner pitfalls of time-travel."

Rosa had a confused expression on her face. "Wait a minute, you said there was an accident on your ship." She lowered her eyebrows. "What does that have to do with time-travel?"

He took a deep breath. "Everythin', love, everythin'."

She moved closer to him and took a whiff. "Darling, you really must bathe; you do smell repulsive."

"I was on me way to me flat to clean meself up."

Maybe I could help you scrub your back?"

"I suppose."

"Amoli wouldn't mind?"

"Ah, um…that she would." She latched onto his arm and buried herself in his over-sized bicep. She walked while he struggled in pain. "Ye know I'm with me crew each Friday to Sunday, somethin' big 'n aquatic tore me nets off me ship 'n devoured me lifeboat. It shook us good, so it did. It put me crew at risk. Although, it seemed to have lost a tooth."

She took her time to respond. "Well, the vortex opening was never closed. Sasha doesn't know how to close it. I don't know why he claims that he knows how to fix this mess. Sasha's bright idea about that *dodecagon* was not effective. In fact, it was idiotic. I think you and Sasha are two twentieth-century men who don't know what you're doing in some far off time in the past – especially prehistoric times. Colin, think about it, was there really an opening to the time vortex?"

He noticed that it started to snow. "The vortex never had an openin'?"

"Think about it, Colin. Was it an actual opening, or was it a path through the passage of time?"

"A path, ye say?"

"Yes, a path, rather than some silly opening. You're going to fix this mess. I know you will. Do you know for certain this creature you saw was, in fact, prehistoric?"

"Quite sure of it, I am. Nothin' in our time would do that. I'm a fishin' merchant – I know marine life, so I do. I've come across whales. Their teeth are different. Also, the size of this creature was, well, unthinkable."

"I want to see this tooth." She took his hand and held it tightly where she could feel his unease. "Why don't we discuss this a little later? Right now, I think I'm going to walk with you to your flat, and see that you get cleaned up and get some bed rest."

She tugged on his jacket. When they entered his flat she drew a hot bath for him. He stood in front of the toilet to urinate. She forced herself not to take notice. She scurried out the bathroom and shut the door leaving only a crack ajar. She placed her ear near the door and was relieved to hear him make a splash into the tub.

"Darling, Colin, maybe I'll come in and wash your back."

He soaked in the tub, rubbing a bar of soap in a circular motion around his pectoral muscles. He chuckled at her comment.

"I'm someone else's gent, ye know it, so why ye so persistent to see me naked? Ye never fancied the thought of seein' me hangin' balls before."

She cringed at his comment and fluttered around his flat trying to straighten up.

"If you had yourself a real lady in waiting she would straighten your messy and disgraceful flat. Maybe Amoli is a bigger slob than you, my dear," she said, calling to him through the bathroom door.

He fondled himself in the water with a smile. "Ah, jealous, so ye are. Ye can't fathom the thought of Amoli winnin' over me manliness."

She straightened the cushions on his sofa. "Colin Limmerick, you grow more disgusting with every day that passes," she said, squinting her eyes as she heard his laughter penetrate through the bathroom door. "You better behave yourself, or I may just enter."

He continued to laugh. "Ye wouldn't, I know it."

She noticed a photograph of Amoli sitting on his table. "She would do it without a second thought. Your sweet and innocent Amoli."

"Jealous."

"Never of her. When's the wedding?" she asked, with a slight tremble.

He splashed loudly, while exiting the tub; his towel was wrapped around his lower half, to join her in the next room.

"Let's see, it's already mid January, me birthday's in a fortnight. We're goin' after the end of the year sometime, a Catholic weddin' it'll be. I'm so busy these days. It may even be in 1910 or even after that. I just don't know. She's so anxious is what she is."

She sat down where he caught her eyes scanning his body. "I'm afraid you will have to elope then. Her father would never allow it."

"I do what I damn well want. It's me bleedin' weddin' 'n Amoli will be me wife."

17

She wiped her sweaty palms on her skirt. "I do like a man in charge. However, you are making a mistake…a serious mistake."

"How's that?"

"For one, she is not your color; two, not your religion; and three, just think of what your children will look like."

He paced to his bedroom to get dressed. She entered and caught him buttoning his trousers. "You don't love her. The one you'll always love is me."

He smiled, while he slipped into his shirt. She rushed to button it for him. He watched her do up each button with care.

"Ye shant be doin' any of this for me. If Amoli were to walk in it would be another bloody battle, 'n this time to the death, no doubt."

Rosa stepped back. He pulled away from her.

"Colin, are you afraid of me, all of a sudden?"

"Never of ye, love."

"Are you that much under Amoli's spell?"

He laughed. "I just want to make sure you're doing the right thing."

"I'm a big enough lad to know what I'm doin', don't ye think?"

"You've waited this long to marry, and you think this spoiled little rich girl from India is the one for you?"

"She's the only wench whose ever understood me. Ye never did 'n I don't blame ye, not a bit."

Rosa stood directly in front of him. "You will tire of her, Colin."

"Tire of her? She's got way too much spunk for that."

"Precisely! She's half your age. You both will soon realize that you're not on the same page."

"I'll take me chances." He paced to the other end of the room and paused. He glanced at Rosa. She smiled at him. He continued to button his shirt. "Don't see yez much with Sasha these days."

18

"Don't even mention him. He's in his own little Russian world. Why did he even move to England? He still has strong ties to that country of his. He's been very secretive about the letters he receives."

Colin continued to get dressed. "Maybe they's from his parents."

"I don't think so. He's acting very strange."

"I always thought of him as a mad scientist. Ye took him over me. I'll always hate his guts for it, too."

She cleared her throat. "So, I'm here in your flat to discuss business. I think we should get started." She swirled around with her nose in the air. "Proceed, please."

"Alright, well, this creature was a size I've never witnessed. I never saw teeth like that. The power of this creature was unstoppable. Sasha insists it was a shark. That was no shark, I tell ye. A shark would have to be stark mad to be swimmin' about these chilly waters, wouldn't ye think?"

"Do you have its tooth, so I can see it?"

"Aye. It's under the bed, if ye can believe it?" he said, as he bent down beside the bed.

"Are you keeping this secret from Amoli?"

"Wouldn't want to scare the poor lass."

"I don't think Amoli would even flinch if she saw that tooth." Colin held the tooth before him, while Rosa examined it with her eyes. "Oh, my." She felt the ridges along the side of it. "Is it really what I think it is?"

Colin's eyes widened. "Do you know just by lookin' at this?"

"Could it be *Basilosaurus?* You haven't read about *Basilosaurus?* You're so fixed on *Megaloceros giganteus* and nothing else. *Basilosaurus* was an ancient whale, which had tiny hind limbs. However, it was one of the earliest killer whales. It was a giant, about 18 meters and weighed 60 tones. It lived 35 million years ago."

Colin sat on the bed, and took a deep breath. "I see. What shall I do? Millions of years ago. Feck, I don't know

19

how to deal with such a time in pre-history. This marine beast is post dinosaur era. What shall I do?"

"I'm only guessing based on this tooth. I'd have to take a closer look whilst in the lab." He sprawled back on his bed. He stared at the ceiling almost in a trance. Rosa stepped closer to him. "Are you alright?"

"I'm not. I need to get *langered* in me grave tonight."

She nestled up to his thigh. "I know you, you're going to fix this mess."

"I don't know how."

"You obtained the answers you needed for *Megaloceros giganteus*. Dear Colin, you can do anything. I know what kind of man you are, you're impressively determined."

"A stupid arse is what I am. Who do I think I am? I'm playin' God, am I?"

She stroked his thigh. "I know you can solve this problem."

"I never studied life on earth 35 million years ago. I wouldn't know where to begin. Me stupid ideas will destroy our planet. Oh, sweet Lord, please help me."

She ran her delicate fingers along his jaw. "I never stopped loving you. And I know you never stopped loving me."

"Rosa, yer a confusin' wench. And now yer goin' after confusin' me. I won't let ye do that to me, not again, no I won't."

She brought her face to his and kissed his lips. "I know you're still attracted to me." She untied the laces of her dress and let it fall below her shoulders. "You never stopped loving me."

"Oh, why did I let ye in me flat? Ye can't be here if yer doin' that sort of thing."

"Are you kicking me out?"

"I think so." He sprung off the bed. "Fix yer dress the way it was."

"Can you fix it for me? I heard you're having difficulty with Amoli."

"Heard what? From who?"

"You're relationship is in trouble." She slid off the bed to fasten her dress. "Will you ever forgive me for the time you found me with Sasha?"

"Forgiveness is what I've already given ye," he said, trying not to focus on her delicate bare shoulders. "Yer Sasha's wench."

"Am I no longer beautiful to you? Why are you resisting me?" She stepped closer to him and tugged on his suspenders. "I want to do *that* with you, now. I've thought about it long enough. I think you and I should do *that*. I'm ready."

Her eyes shifted around. He burst into laughter.

"Ready? Ready for what? Ye want me to feck ye? Is this what yer askin' me?" He pulled her hands from him. "This can't be happin'. Ye don't want to get fecked, 'n especially by me. Ye don't want this, I know it."

"I dream of you every night."

"Surely, ye don't dream of me feckin' ye silly?"

She closed her eyes with a wince. "Must you be so disgusting when we discuss the act of love between a man and a woman? You talk like a sailor."

"A sailor, so I am. Haven't ye got it from Sasha yet?"

"I'd prefer to be married. He doesn't seem that interested anymore."

"Surely he is. He risked gettin' his arse kicked by me. He's interested in ye alright."

"Yes, but I made a terrible mistake." She stepped closer to him. "I don't doubt your distrust in me. I've let you down too many times. I've come to realize there aren't too many men out there like you."

"Thank the Lord for that."

"Colin, I know you still love me."

"Don't go actin' the maggot."

"Is that all you can say?"

21

"Aye."

Chapter Two

It was a late January morning, Colin entered the dean's office.

"Excuse me, but I'd like to make an appointment to see the dean."

An older, heavy-set woman with a monocle in her eye sat at a typewriter. She lifted one eyebrow.

"Who are you?"

"Colin Limmerick is me name, good lady."

"What is your reason for this request?"

Colin held his bowler hat in his hands. "Ye askin' me to tell ye why I'm here? Well, um, I wish to make a complaint, if I may."

"About what or whom?"

"About me academic advisor."

She stared at Colin for a few seconds. She stood up and continued to stare at him a little longer.

"You must either be a member of faculty or a student at this institution, sir. Good day." She sat down and continued to type.

Colin took a few steps forward. "Ma'am, I am in the doctorate program with the Natural History Department." He handed her his official acceptance into the program. "Please, is there a way I could meet with the dean?" Colin smiled at her.

She scanned the document and removed her monocle. "You're in the doctorate program?" She walked to the door behind her, which had a sign saying *Dean's Office*. She knocked on the door. "Excuse me, but there is a doctorate student here to see you." She took a few steps toward Colin. "Please, sit down and when it is your turn, your name will be called."

Colin scanned the office. "Excuse me, but I'm the only one here."

"Your name will be called when the dean is ready to see you, Mr. Limmick."

"Limm-erick, ye know, like the city. Limerick, Ireland, surely ye know it."

"Never heard of it." She sat down and continued to type.

"Um, could ye be so kind in tellin' me how long of a wait I'll have? I don't have a great deal of time. I need to teach a lecture soon."

"If you want to see Dean Roberts you will have to wait your turn, Mr. Limmerick."

Colin slumped in one of the uncomfortable chairs and took a deep breath. The Dean's secretary stopped typing. She stared at Colin for a few seconds. "The dean will see you now, Mr. Limm-erick."

Colin smiled at the secretary. She resumed typing. Colin entered the dean's office.

"Excuse me, sar."

A meek man sitting behind a large desk appeared startled by Colin's appearance. "Yes, so you're Mr. Colin Limmerick? Yes, do sit down and tell me why you're here."

"Sar, me academic advisor has been hinderin' me research for two years, and I'd like to ask if it's at all possible to change advisors."

"Hindering? Oh, my, that's a strong word, isn't it? Who is your advisor?"

Colin hesitated with his answer. "Dr. Randolph Cushing."

The Dean coughed so violently that he spewed phlegm into his handkerchief. Colin stood before him, feeling awkward and helpless at the same time. "Is somethin' wrong? Do ye need a doctor?"

"You're cross with Randolph? How is this possible? He is such a gentle soul. How can anyone not get on with him?"

"You know him personally?"

24

"He and I are golfing pals. His wife goes berry picking with my wife every Sunday until the frost comes. They've been doing that for years."

"Well, I'm sorry to have wasted yer time. There's an obvious conflict of interest."

"Well, I mean you could have a different academic advisor, but it wouldn't look very attractive on you. You could, in deed, taint your academic reputation."

"Reputation? Do I even have a reputation? Should I even care?"

The dean sank in his chair. "Oh, my, yes, reputations are vitally important in the academic world. Yes, you should care."

Colin's eyebrows lowered toward his eyes. "Don't ye even know why I would like to change advisors?"

"I'm not interested in the reason." The dean appeared interested in the book that sat on his desk. "Do you know what this book is about, Mr. Limmerick?" The dean held the book above his head. "This is the first academic work Randolph wrote on the *Horseshoe crab*. Fascinating. Did you ever read this? It's magnificent."

"Read it? Nay, I can't really say I've read it."

"Well, there's the problem, Mr. Limmerick. A graduate student who is not well-versed in his advisor's work will have some issues to take up. It's inevitable. Read this book and I'll even lend my personal copy to you and your problem with your academic advisor will be solved." The dean grinned at Colin.

"I've read some of Dr. Cushing's work, Dean Roberts, and I can't say that I fancy it. I couldn't believe what rubbish it was."

"Rubbish? Randolph couldn't write rubbish if he tried. Oh, no, Mr. Limmerick, your advisor is natural history's answer to the prehistoric world. What is your research?"

"I'm currently writin' me dissertation on *Megaloceros giganteus*, sar. I've proven that this prehistoric mammal was sexually selected against 10,000 years ago, which led to its demise."

"Oh, I see. Well, what's Randolph's complaint?"

"He simply don't fancy me, sar. We just never got on, from day one."

"Really?"

"He's always held somethin' against me."

The dean stared at a fly on his desk. "Oh, well, that explains it, then. Well, you see, Mr. Limmerick, this is terribly difficult for me to believe."

"Not lyin' to ye, sar, nay, I'm not. I can show ye some of his unprofessional comments that he wrote on me work."

"Unprofessional? Oh, my, that is another strong word."

Colin sighed. "Does this sort of thing often occur between academic advisors 'n graduate students?"

The dean tapped his ink pen on his desk. "Often? Even that's a strong word."

"Oh, God."

"Yes, I think you better speak to God about this one. You see, Randolph is such a jovial soul he gets on with everyone."

"Well, Dean Roberts, just for the few minutes you've spent with me, what could it possibly be about me that he don't fancy?"

The dean stared at Colin for a few seconds. "You're definitely Irish aren't you? Well, that could be one small reason. I mean, I'd have to read your work."

"Don't ye think if I was accepted into this competitive program that me writin' would speak for itself?"

"Yes, you are correct about that. Yes, most definitely."

"Do you think perhaps Dr. Cushing is a bleedin' wanker who deserves to get his bleedin' arse kicked?"

"Oh, my goodness gracious…no, I don't think you're correct about that. No."

26

"Would there be someone else of authority that I can take this up with?"

The dean sniffled a few times. He pulled out his handkerchief to blow his nose.

"The only person I can think of who is above me is Evelyn Gordon. This is really not her job responsibility, but she may do it as a favour to me." The dean dipped his pen nib in his inkbottle and scratched the name on a piece of paper. "Take this; you can find her in the building next door. She's not always there, though."

Colin smiled as he took the information from the dean. "Thank-ye. What is Miss or Mrs. Gordon's title?" Colin asked, as he stepped toward the door.

The dean snickered. "She's the chancellor of the university."

"Chancellor? Would the chancellor even deal with a matter like this, sar?"

"No, but Evelyn would. By the way, Mr. Limmerick, perhaps Randolph isn't too keen on, well, the way you look."

"I can't help that, sar. I'm feelin' I'm bein' discriminated against."

"One should fit into this type of academic league, don't you think?"

"I don't think me appearance should bear any weight, don't ye think?"

"Yes, you're correct about that, however, you resemble a lumberjack, or a Viking warrior, perhaps – all in a dashing way, so to speak."

"Is there a clause written anywhere in the graduate studies rules that even suggests a Ph.D. candidate is to look a certain way?"

"Not a all. You seem like a very well spoken man, yes, indeed. Perhaps being so rough around the edges gives you color and charisma. I know Randolph is not fond of graduate students with color and charisma."

Colin forced a smile. "I'll see Chancellor Gordon, sar. Thank-ye." He scratched his head and left.

***

Rosa worked long hours at the university lab almost everyday. Sasha entered holding an unlit cigarette.

"Greetings, beautiful lady, why you hide here so much?"

She was engrossed with a sample in a Petri dish. "You don't have that much to do with me anyway. I see that you are responding to several letters from Russia. Who is she?"

"My dear, Rosa, why you ask such silliness? I have great many friends in Petersburg. Naturally, I receive many letters. My friends so impressed with this England."

"Sasha, I feel our courtship has come to a stalemate. You don't woo me anymore. I thought you were smitten with me at one time."

He approached her and rubbed her shoulders. "Why so much doubt? I only have eyes for you, so beautiful lady. You must go now; I expect Mr. Limmerick."

"Pardon?"

"I must talk business with Mr. Limmerick. Time vortex hole is problem for him."

"Colin, is my friend, as well. I will do no such thing by leaving this laboratory. Besides, I have something I would like to say to both of you."

Colin stormed through the door swinging it opened while singing *As I Roved Out*.

"And who are you, me pretty fair maid.
And who are you, me honey?
And who are you, me pretty fair maid.
And who are you, me honey?
She answered me quite modestly,
I am me mother's darlin'.
With me too-ry-ay, fol-de-diddle-day,
di-re fol-de-diddle, dai-rie oh."

28

He came to a stop and looked at Rosa standing beside Sasha. "Rosa, how'ye?" He removed his hat with a clumsy bow.

"Well, Mr. Limmerick, my dear sweet Rosa would like to say us something."

Colin paused, looking confused. "Alright, then."

Rosa primped herself tightening the blue velvet bows in her hair. "It's about the time vortex. Colin…Sasha."

"My time vortex has changed science forever, what would you like to add, my beautiful lady?" Sasha asked, popping his unlit cigarette into his mouth.

Colin stood still folding his arms in front of him, waiting for Rosa to speak.

"Gentlemen, your theory of plugging the time vortex opening didn't work. That *dodecagon* was an absurd idea. Sasha, I can't believe you came up with such stupidity."

Colin was about to respond, but Sasha stepped in front of him.

"It did work. We close opening during last prehistoric journey. We do this with great success."

Colin shoved Sasha aside. "Great success, ye say? How's that?"

"I not see your mega mammal romping along The Strand!"

"Sasha, please understand that Colin and his crew experienced something strange when they were out at sea. Something with tremendous size almost capsized the boat."

"Da, da, I hear this already from Mr. Limmerick."

"Colin is almost certain this creature was of prehistoric nature."

"He not know this. He only say so."

"Colin is afraid this prehistoric creature is the result of the time vortex."

"Mr. Limmerick spend so much time with worry. Rest him assure, no such thing exist in his fishing water."

"Maybe the problem is not an actual vortex opening, but rather something else."

Sasha stepped away holding his arms in the air. "What? What else could be problem? You are not physicist, Rosa. You are just woman."

"Sasha, Rosa 'n I've discussed this. Rosa seems to think never was it an openin', but rather a pathway. Agreein' with her, so I am at this."

"PachiMU?"

Colin appeared confused with Sasha's response. Rosa glanced at Colin.

"I think Sasha's asking why. The *dodecagon*, Sasha, was absolutely ridiculous. How could you come up with such absurdity?"

"Shto? Khvatit!"

"Shite, he's blowin' a nerve, is he?" Colin wondered.

Rosa stepped closer to Sasha. "There was never an opening to the vortex; it's a pathway, therefore a much bigger opening than you thought. This is why creatures as grand in size as *Basilosaurus* are sneaking through and they are not native to Ireland or even Europe for that matter, and furthermore, they are from the post dinosaur era."

Sasha's face turned a shade of red. He glanced at Colin.

"Can you imagine? This woman say such silliness. This b-whale of yours has to be native to Ireland."

"Why, Sasha?" Rosa asked, with a louder voice.

"Because my time-travel device does not deal with different geography. It deals only with what is in front of it."

"Oh, Lord, help this man!" Rosa shouted, with her arms in the air.

Colin slid his arm around Rosa. "Take it easy, love. Don't get yerself upset over this."

"And you call yourself a scientist!" Rosa shouted, pointing her finger at Sasha.

"And you are only woman. You, at your age, should be married, expecting fourth child by now. All women over 30 have many children. Why you not?"

Colin clutched onto Sasha's tie and pulled him in a stranglehold position. "That's enough, mate!"

Sasha pulled away from him and stepped toward Rosa. "I figure out how to fix vortex opening. You see, I have many scientific formulas. We will close it. You not worry."

"Sasha, it isn't an opening. It's a pathway that you must obstruct," Rosa said, while trying to compose herself.

"So, if it is pathway, what is difference? We still must block opening, da?"

"No, Sasha. You need to lead the pathway from its future, make it head back to the past, so not one prehistoric animal can leave its time. Please, Sasha, you must consider what I'm telling you."

"Why I must consider? You are only woman."

She sighed and glanced at Colin were he reciprocated with a wink and a refreshing smile.

"Sasha, sometimes I feel I don't even know who you are."

"Oh, you know me okay. You speak to me about prehistoric whale with this name you give it? This is not possible for you to know name of such marine beast."

"Colin showed me its tooth."

Sasha stared into space, while muttering to himself in Russian. The three of them gazed at each other in silence. A fly buzzed past them. Colin sat on one of the lab stools and focused on the wood planked floor. Rosa drifted to the window. Sasha remained standing. He ran his hands up and down through his blazer in search of cigarettes. There was relief on his face when he found them. He popped a cigarette in his mouth and fumbled for his matchbook.

31

Chapter Three

It was a crispy damp morning. There was a bold knock on the door. Amoli was in the kitchen making tea. She scurried to Colin who lay in bed asleep.

"Colin?" She fixed her housecoat to make sure she was covered. "Colin, my love, someone is knocking at the door." Colin rolled over to face her. He opened one eye. He took a deep breath and tried to shield the light from the window off his face.

"Feck it, lass, why can't ye just fetch the bleedin' door? Dressed, I'm not." He sat up and stumbled into the bathroom to reach for a towel. He wrapped it around his bottom half and went for the door. He opened the door and saw Rosa standing there. "Love, it's half past six. Much too early for ye to be callin', isn't it?"

Rosa entered the flat and removed her hat and scarf. "Colin, we need to chat."

"Chat? What's so urgent ye can't let a man sleep?"

Amoli entered the room and stood beside Colin. "Why is she here?"

"I haven't a clue, but it's not like she's breakin' the law. Come in Rosa, 'n sit yerself. Amoli was just makin' tea; would ye fancy a cup?"

Rosa removed her coat and hung it over Colin's arm, then sat down. "I'd love some."

"Grand. Amoli make another cup, would ye, sweet lass?"

"I will not! I don't her here!"

Colin sat across from Rosa and rubbed his face. "What's this crazy talk? Make another cup, please lass?"

"I am so very angry. I want her out of our home!"

Colin stood up and fixed Rosa a cup of tea and brought it to her. "What's all this, Amoli, actin' up again,

32

are ye?" He threw a few cubes of sugar in his cup. "Rosa, what brings ye here?"

"Colin, you and Sasha can't wait on this. You more than likely must time-travel again. That post dinosaur whale is terrorizing the sea. I'm surprised you haven't acted on this further. This isn't like you."

Colin sat back in his chair. "It's not like me? Feck, I'm not me-self these days."

"As I already said, there isn't a specific opening into the passage of time but rather a pathway. It's much bigger and more abstract than you thought. You have to do something, because Sasha seems to never be available these days."

"I know it."

"What's going on with Sasha?"

"I haven't the faintest. Ye know 'im. He's fecked up, so he is."

Amoli sat beside Colin. "Colin is not time-traveling again, Miss Emanuel. It's high time you accept that. He will never time-travel again."

"He may very well have to, Miss Sharma."

Colin glanced at both women. "I'm feelin' there's a need. We fecked up both prehistoric expeditions, 'n all has gone wrong. Keep feckin' up we do, over 'n over. Just wanted to prove how *Megaloceros giganteus* came to its demise. Aye, I'm a Darwinist, 'n so I am. I wanted the world to understand evolution. I never would've thought any mutations would've come out of this. A stupid arse I am sometimes. What a blunder this has all been."

"Please don't look at your time-travel expeditions as a blunder. You never created the gap in the first place. Sasha's time-travel device only indicated where the openings are. You didn't tamper with geologic history. What you need to do is follow the pathway and make sure that it shrinks to its minimum, so no more prehistoric life filters through."

Colin scratched his head. "How'd I do that?"

"You're a brilliant man; I'm sure you will come up with something."

"Perhaps we can sail the Irish Sea together 'n ye can see what I'm talkin' about. If we're goin' after yet another time-travel expedition surely we need to know if it's *Basilasuarus* floatin' about in the sea."

Amoli buried herself in his arm. "Is she ever going to leave?"

"Eh? What ye goin' on about? Yer bein' rude, ye is."

Rosa stood up. "Don't waste your breath. I was just leaving." Colin followed her to the door. "I know you will come up with something. If you ever get a chance to speak to Sasha, perhaps both of you could come up with something." Colin followed her into the hallway. She tossed her scarf around her delicate neck. "Things aren't going well between Sasha and me. I rarely see him, and when I do, it's rarely pleasant."

Colin nodded his head. "I see 'im, I do, but pleasant he usually isn't."

"Colin!" Amoli called from inside the flat. The front door was ajar. "Colin, aren't you coming in? Did she go yet?"

Colin smiled at Rosa. "Well, love, I bes' be gettin' in to me wench, eh?"

He took Rosa's hand and squeezed it tightly for a few seconds, and then stepped into his flat. Rosa remained in the hallway as the door shut in front of her.

34

Chapter Four

It was Thursday afternoon. Colin sat at the bar in the local pub and ordered whiskey in a glass. He sipped it slowly this time. Sasha appeared and sat beside him.

"Mr. Limmerick, I find you here, always."

"Where ye been, ye bleedin' shite?"

"Why so important to you where I am?"

"Number one, Rosa's been askin' about ye; number two, ye got to come with me to sea. I was just leavin' for the harbor. We need to find out if it's really *Basilasuarus* or somethin' prehistoric that's roamin' our waters. I want Rosa to come."

"We not need Rosa. We can detect this ourselves."

"Yer a physicist 'n I'm a naturalist, she's the archeologist. She has better knowledge of this than ye 'n me put together. Why aren't ye not gettin' on with her?

"Who say this? All is good with Rosa."

"Yer a liar, she's wonderin' where' yez at."

Sasha scanned the pub a few times, then he focused on Colin. "You say you have many problem, Mr. Limmerick. I have many more."

Colin drank up his whiskey. "Yer not half as knackered as me. I live in two worlds: half in London, 'n half at sea. I'm supposed to be gettin' married into an Indian family that I don't understand. Dr. Sharma, Amoli's overly protective father, hates me guts. Cushing is threatenin' to cut off me academic fundin'. Worst of all, some prehistoric beast is rippin' away at the sea. Top that if ye can, mate."

Sasha leaned forward toward Colin. "I top that. I have wife in Russia."

Colin's eyes widened. "Oh, shite."

"Da, I have wife six years. Natasha want to come here. She not so happy with me here. She not happy with

Russia. Too many problems for workers. Too hard life. I write letters to her and tell her about easy life in London."

Colin lifted one eyebrow. "Easy life? London?"

"Da, you may not think so, but I know life here so easy. Everybody have everything."

"Ye don't say? I never found anythin' to be a free ride."

"You are professional complainer, Mr.Limmerick. You make me laugh, to hear you make many complaints. Come to my Russia. Please."

"So, why haven't I met Natasha?"

"My wife? I not want her here."

"Mate, I can only conclude one thing from all that yer tellin' me. Yer an arsehole." Sasha fished his jacket for some cigarettes. He glared at Colin with a sign of disrespect. "Ye need to tell Rosa ye got yerself a wife."

"Why? What I say to Rosa?"

"The truth."

"She will kill me."

"Aye, that she will, no doubt."

"I not know how to say to her."

"Rosa's me friend, ye bes' tell her fast." Colin rubbed his tired eyes. "Ye put me through so much, ye knew it wouldn't last with her. Why? I was ready to marry Rosa on the spot. Why'd ye do this to her 'n me?"

"Rosa is very beautiful lady and she belong to you. I want to see if I could get what you have."

Colin leaned over the bar and placed some money down. "Another whiskey." He looked at Sasha. "Hate is a strong word, mate, but it's the only word I can use to describe how I feel about ye."

"She take me over you. You not so special man. You think you so special."

Colin chuckled. "Special? I don't think that of meself." He gulped his whiskey. "Fine, have it yer way, special is what I am." He focused on Sasha. "Deal with this, I won't, I damn well won't. Yer business this is. Ye

36

bes' fix it, 'n fix this problem with the time vortex as well."

"I have wife and that is all. Time vortex is good enough. This b-whale you say is not prehistoric. It is usual sea life."

"Whatever ye say, mate. Rosa will be on me ship this weekend 'n so will ye. Don't get into a scuffle upon me ship. We need to see if that creature will show itself."

Chapter Five

Sasha and Rosa met Colin at the train station. Rosa gave a nervous smile. The three of them boarded the train and sat facing each other. Colin gazed out the window with a look of concern on his face. Sasha pulled out a physics textbook and began to read with an unlit cigarette wedged between his fingers. Rosa looked through her large bag and found her knitting needles and ball of wool. She then stuffed it back and pulled out a needle and thread. She began to mend a pair of socks. She appeared fidgety.

They arrived at Fishguard Harbor. Colin led them to the dock where *The Atlantic Mermaid* waited as it did every Thursday afternoon to pick him up. Colin's first mate waved as he docked the sea vessel.

"Howye, Captain 'n friends!" Eddy called.

Colin smiled, as he motioned for Sasha and Rosa to enter the ship. Colin tilted his cap at his first mate as greeting gesture. Eddy returned the gesture to his captain. They sailed across the Irish Sea and docked at Rosslare Harbor, Ireland. Eddy sat on the deck with a bottle of beer.

"Ed, where's the crew just now?" Colin asked from the wheelhouse. "Thought I'd see me crew waitin' here so eagerly at the harbor."

"No point in havin' the whole crew go out tonight when there's been no catches this week at all." Colin paced around the deck a few times, while he cursed to himself. He lowered the gangway onto the pier. "Timmy is plannin' to meet a lass this weekend."

Colin stepped toward his first mate. His eyes widened. His lips were parted.

"Now?"

"I told 'im if he wants to court a lass tonight that it's dany with me."

Colin took a deep breath. "He can't go anywhere until I say he can. I'm needin' 'im in the wheelhouse tonight. I don't need the others. They can get pissed up tonight for all I care."

"Captain, what's all this about?"

Colin took Eddy's arm and pulled him a few steps away. "Look, Ed, there's no feckin' fish in the sea. Was there any catches this week? I'm damn concerned, so I am. I need to go the feck out there 'n see what the problem is, don't ye think?"

Eddy stared at the planked floor. "Nay, Captain, no catches this week. It's been grim, I must say."

"Don't know what's goin' on."

"Somethin' out there? What ya think it is?"

"Never ye mind about what it is, Ed. I would steer the vessel meself if I could, but I need to be vigilant tonight."

"What ye think is in our fishin' waters? Ye seemin' to know somethin'. It's got somethin' to do with that night when our vessel was shaken up good." Colin forced a smile with the look of concern on his face.

"Timmy should be arrivin' any minute now."

"He's navigatin' the ship tonight."

"He won't fancy the idea, I can tell ya that."

"The feck I care if he fancies the idea."

"Captain, he's but still a boy."

Timmy noticed his captain amongst others standing by the dock. He made his way passed his captain, and tipped his hat to Rosa; and walked toward the ship.

"Timmy, yaz best get yar arse here. The captain needs a word with yaz!" Eddy called out.

Timmy approached Captain Limmerick. "Captain, how ye?"

"I need ye to steer *the Mermaid* this weekend, that's all."

Timmy glanced at Eddy then back at the captain. "What's this, eh?"

"Ya heard yar captain's orders," Eddy said, with his eyes focused somewhere else.

"Well, I can't. I'm busy. Ya know I am."

"I need ye tonight," Colin said, standing tall with his arms folded in front of him.

Timmy stepped closer to his captain. "Captain, already asked Eddy, I did."

"Doesn't matter, I'm yer captain."

"I've waited far too long to get some time with this special lass, can't yaz do it yarself?"

"I'll be too busy. Ye can ask her along on the ship if ye may?"

Rosa glanced at Sasha.

"Not in yar life, Captain. Last time I had a lass upon the ship she ended up fallin' for yaz 'n forgot all about me. Ya lured her away from me, ya bloody shite!"

Colin closed his eyes and clenched his fists. "I didn't lure yer lass. I'm not interested in yer wenches. I need ye in the wheelhouse this weekend. I'll give ye next weekend off."

"I made arrangements with her for this weekend. Get Séamus to do it!"

"Reliable, sure he's not. Timmy, don't make me do somethin' stupid."

Timmy grinned without ease. "Somethin' stupid? Like what?"

"Captain, maybe we should consider Séamus," Eddy suggested.

"Seamus? Let the Lord help him." Colin stepped closer to Timmy. "I'm yer captain, 'n I give the bleedin' orders, eh? Bring yer wench on the ship."

"Then, she'll fall in love with yaz – then what? All be couped up in the wheelhouse 'n you'll have her to yerself."

Colin grimaced at Timmy's tone. "Yer talking nonsense. Stay far from her, I'll surely do. Bring her on the feckin' ship. Have her in the wheelhouse with yez. She won't even notice me."

Timmy snickered from the side of his mouth. "Yar not a hard one to miss."

Colin glanced at Sasha and Rosa. "Oh, shite," Colin blurted.

"Where she gonna sleep?" Timmy asked, with angst in his voice.

Colin looked up at the clouds. "Rosa will be in me quarters 'n yer lass can as well."

"I want to share a bed with her."

Colin clenched his fists. "Ya can share a bed with her any time, but not this time. For the sake of the good Lord, go fetch yer wench 'n we'll be off."

Timmy stared at his captain. "I won't."

Colin glanced at Eddy. "Don't go actin' the maggot, Timmy. Yer actin' as if you'll never see her again. Yer actin' like a stupid arse."

"Never would I ever bring another wench upon this stinkin' ship. I'm not spendin' this weekend on *The Atlantic Mermaid*. I'll be courtin' me belle lady instead."

Colin bit his upper lip. "Yer gonna feckin' work on this feckin' ship this feckin' weekend, 'n that's a feckin' order." Timmy pulled a switchblade from his jacket pocket and shook it at his captain. Rosa screamed as Sasha pulled her away. Colin stood straight and alert. "The moment yev been waitin' for has arrived. Go ahead, slash me throat."

Timmy twitched with fear. "Never again will I take another stinkin' order from ya, Captain Limmerick."

The captain stepped toward Timmy. Just as Timmy lunged forward to jab him, he grabbed Timmy's arm with tremendous grip, causing Timmy to drop the knife. Colin pulled Timmy against him and chin locked him until the pain was too much to take.

41

Chapter Six

Some hours passed. Timmy steered the ship with his lady friend, Deidre. Colin, Sasha, and Rosa remained on deck with telescopes pressed against their eyes. The afternoon turned into night and the ship remained between Wales and Ireland. The damp cold, pierced through their bodies, but they didn't flinch. Eventually, the snow turned into sleet. Later, Deidre entered the galley where Rosa was trying to warm up.

"It's too cold on deck. May I remain here for a spell?" Deidre asked in a timid voice.

Rosa smiled. "Of course. It's much too chilly. I can't really be of any help if I'm catching a cold, can I now?"

Deidre sat beside Rosa. She placed her tiny lace purse on the table and slowly removed a small delicate mirror. She primped her herself, while she had one eye on Rosa.

"Excuse me, may I ask you a question?"

Rosa smiled, and nodded.

"How long have you known Captain Limmerick?"

Rosa sat back in her chair and tried to keep the smile on her face. "Over a year, maybe two, perhaps even longer."

Deidre batted her eyelashes. "I find him to be absolutely breath-taking, don't you?"

Rosa's smile dissipated. "I don't think this conversation should continue."

"Oh, I'm sorry. Are you promised to him?"

Rosa stared at the wooden table. "No, no I'm not. I am definitely not promised to Captain Limmerick. That has a sour ring to it, doesn't it? But, someone else is."

"Oh, really?"

"Yes, your thoughts of him should end right now. He has someone in his life."

"Lucky lass, is she worthy of him?"

"Absolutely not."

"You know her?"

"Unfortunately, I mean, she and I don't really get on well. It has nothing to do with Captain Limmerick."

"But, she's not here."

"I don't know how Captain Limmerick managed that. She follows him everywhere he goes. Sickening."

"When will he marry?"

"Perhaps never."

Deidre fiddled with her bracelet. "Never?"

"Deidre, this conversation must end, as of now."

Colin and Sasha studied the icy waters, each with their telescopes in hand.

"Somethin' is out there, alright. Ye see that, don't ye, mate?" Colin nudged Sasha.

Sasha concentrated on examining the sea. "Mr. Limmerick, I see nothing."

"Ye don't know these waters as I do. Never have I seen such stillness. This sea used to be a lively place, surely it was."

"Water is water, Mr. Limmerick. It all looks same to me."

Colin lowered his telescope. "Freezin' ye must be. Just sit yerself in the galley with the wenches 'n I can stay here and watch. Don't mind if I do."

"I will do that. You will soon see this is waste of time. I should be in London now, not this cold wet place you desire."

"This is where ye need to be. I think once ye see it, ye'll be glad I brought ye here."

"If it so big as you say, will I even get chance to see it?"

"Ye'll know it's not from our time, but it's in fact prehistoric."

"If it is prehistoric, then what?"

"It means we would have to do somethin' about it, don't ye think?"

43

"I only create time-travel device, I have no control on anything else."

Colin chuckled as he pressed his telescope against his eyeglasses. Sasha stepped into the galley. He sat beside Rosa and smiled.

"Hello, Sasha. Why aren't you on deck with Colin?"

"He say I can come here. I say he wasting time. There is no prehistoric monster in sea."

Deidre's eyes widened. "Prehistoric monster? Is that why we're here?"

Rosa patted Deirdre on the shoulder. "Calm yourself. Dr. Dimitrikov can say silly things from time to time." Rosa stared at the wooden table. "Sasha, I really think you should be helping Colin."

"So cold out there. I stay here with you, beautiful Miss. Rosa."

"I see. I understand now. Why don't I let you two remain here and I will help the captain?" Deidre suggested, as she stood up from her chair.

"No!" shouted Rosa, tugging at Deidre's arm. "Sit down, Deidre. You can't help Captain Limmerick; only Dr. Dimitrikov and I can help him. You stay here and continue to make yourself pretty for Timmy."

"No, you two need to be alone. I'll just go see if Captain Limmerick needs me."

Sasha slid his arm around Rosa. "So, now my dear Rosa, we are finally alone."

"Sasha, we can't allow Deidre to join Colin. I don't want to see any trouble between him and his crewmembers."

"Who cares? Main purpose of escapade is to find fictitious whale. Soon Mr. Limmerick will discover it is his imagination. You must think positive. You no like Miss Amoli, so maybe now Mr. Limmerick will have young Irish girl in his bed tonight. Da?"

Rosa pushed Sasha aside. "I haven't heard from you in weeks. I don't really understand what you're trying to do here. Deidre is only 16 years old; please don't bring her into this equation."

"Sorry, I not speak to you in so long time because I must attend to family in Russia. So sorry."

"A quick note or something explaining that would have been helpful."

"Please accept apology from me."

Deidre crept onto the icy deck. She wrapped her wool scarf around her neck and shoulders several times. Colin lowered the telescope from his eyeglasses.

"Aye, lass. What ye doin' out here? Yer sure to catch cold."

"Did you find what you're lookin' for?"

"Not yet, but believe me, I will."

"Is it acceptable to you if I stay out here?"

Colin stared at the wheelhouse. "I suggest ye join Timmy. Gets lonely up there, I can tell ye."

"I'd rather stay here. Aren't ye cold out here?"

"Used to it, I suppose I am."

"I hear you spend most of your time in London at the university." The wind blew stronger, expressing a howling sound throughout the ship. "You are a scholar I hear."

"Winds are gettin' stronger. It's best ye join Timmy or go back to the galley. Out here is not suitable for a young damsel like yerself."

"Maybe you can keep me warm."

Colin sat town and held his telescope tightly. "I need to continue what I was doin', if ye don't mind me doin' so?" The boat rocked and swayed. Deidre yelped. Colin looked over the gunnel. "As I said, fair maiden, the sea is rough at this time of year."

"It felt as if something hit the ship, Captain."

"I hope so. Forgive me, Deidre, but I must tend to me work. Please join either Timmy or Rosa. She's in the galley."

A loud crashing sound came from the bottom of the hull.

"Awe! Captain Limmerick, what's wrong with this ship? Are we gonna be alright?" Timmy shouted from the wheelhouse.

Colin hung over the gunnel with his telescope against his eye. "Somethin's out there, alright."

The vessel rocked with a continuous crash. The waves grew to an uncontrollable size pouring icy water onto the deck. Colin took Deidre by the arm to lead her to the galley. She fell forward into Colin's arms. Timmy arrived at that moment.

"Captain! We hit somethin' or somethin' hit us. Hey, what the feck ya doin' with me wench? Bloody bastard is what yaz are!" Timmy expressed, drenched from the sea.

Colin hung over the gunnel with his telescope, while Rosa entered with Sasha trailing behind her.

"Colin! Did the boat hit something?" Rosa asked.

"Aye! Just tryin' to follow this through is all!"

Eddy came up just then. "I was gettin' meself some shut-eye in me bunk 'n I heard a loud thug, especially where I was at the bottom of the hull."

"Eddy, our bleedin' wanker of a captain was tryin' to take away me wench. Ya see, he's a man who can never be trusted," Timmy shouted until his throat cracked.

"That's where you're wrong, Timmy. Colin is the most trustworthy man I know!" shouted Rosa.

Sasha slid his arm around Rosa's shoulders. "And as for me, Miss Rosa?"

"Hush up! Shhh all of yaz! I think I do see somethin' beneath the Mermaid," Colin said.

Rosa nudged her way beside Colin. She pulled the telescope from him to take a look.

"Oh, my! There really is something down there."

Deidre ran back into Colin's arms. "What's in the water, Captain Limmerick? Are we gonna be alright? Save me, Captain!"

Sasha glanced at Deidre. "Are you good swimmer?"

Deidre screamed. "This water is frigid! Is the boat gonna sink? Save me, Captain Limmerick!"

Sasha grinned. "Whale must be hungry."

"Why is a whale hitting this boat? Captain Limmerick, please rescue us!" Deidre whined as she cuddled in Colin's arms.

Colin tried to detach Deidre from his body. "Sasha, are ye fecked in the head or somethin'? Why ye tryin' to bring about panic on this vessel?"

Sasha laughed as he threw his arms in the air. "Impossible. Rosa can examine this sea animal at a glance. You and Miss Rosa are not good researchers. This marine animal could be anything. Why you think this from prehistory?"

Colin lunged at Sasha and pulled him tightly beside him. He held onto Sasha's arm with force and used his other hand to position where Sasha should look.

"Look there, mate, just there, where I've positioned ye. Look as far to the horizon as ye can. Now take this telescope and place it against yer eye. What ye see?"

"I see water, what else?"

"Nay, ye see the end of its bleedin' tail splashin' about in the horizon. This is one huge early marine mammal. Our killer whales can't compare with these giant feckers."

"How you know this is mammal?"

"Because I know it's *Basilosaurus* 'n this prehistoric beast was a mammal. It's from the middle Eocene epoch. In the 1840s paleontologists first thought it a reptile, but too much work has been done on its teeth. It's a mammal, I know it."

"You do your homework, Mr. Limmerick."

Sasha lowered the telescope and handed it to Colin. He slowly walked into the galley. Colin glanced at Rosa.

"I think he's starting to understand," Rosa said, with a blank expression on her face.

"This calls for a shot of whiskey, 'cause lets face it, love, we got ourselves a problem. I need to get stinkin' pissed tonight, is all. How about yez?"

Chapter Seven

Colin sat in a London pub wearing his three-piece suit with a bottle of fine Irish whiskey in front of him. He pulled out several of his notes, placed his eyeglasses on, and began to read.

"Mr. Limmerick, I know to find you here drinking your favorite sludge," Sasha said.

Colin removed his glasses. "So, mate, what have ye concluded?"

"We must time-travel again. I already been working on device. It must be able to take us to prehistory without help of 1908 meteor strike in my Siberia."

"Can ye do that? Thought the meteor strike was the drivin' force that took us back in time before?"

"Da, it is. This not so easy. This b-whale you have in your Irish Sea comes from time many millions of years ago, unlike your *Megaloceros.*"

"Are ye goin' after sendin' us 35 million years ago?"

"I no think it works that way. However, we must be sent some time in prehistory."

Colin filled his glass with more whiskey. "Oh, grand that is, wouldn't want to venture to the post-dinosaur era. Just not equipped for it."

"But you so equipped for Pleistocene era? Because you strong like bull, you think you so equipped?"

"I almost was massacred by those bleedin' Neanderthals, if ye remember."

"You want so much to travel through time again, Mr. Limmerick?"

"I don't. Amoli would never agree to it."

"You like time-travel. It is like booze, only better. Like sex to you, only better."

"Nothin' is better than sex; go feck yerself, mate. Can we stay on track here?"

49

"Rosa say we must find path, not wormhole. I say this is the same. Wormhole make vortex so many prehistoric species slip through, maybe because too many wormholes make vortex...so many...too easy for prehistoric species to slip through. I still believe in dodecagon, twelve sides and twelve angels."

"Rosa thinks that idea was rubbish."

Sasha threw his hands in the air. "Rosa! Who is she? She not know! I not know why b-whale arrive here. I not know why you find bears in your Ireland. Not to do with my time-travel device."

"Everythin' is to do with it, 'cause yer device is leadin' us to forbidden fruit, is why."

"You speak like priest, you so far from that. If we time-travel again we must stop prehistoric species from entering. It not matter where in prehistory we travel, but we must stop entrance."

"Aye. Rosa suggests we bend the pathway."

"Shhh. I not want to hear you speak of Rosa!"

"Yer jealous of her?"

"She is woman."

"An' a damn nice lookin' one, as well, don't ya think?" Colin curled up with his drink. "I think ye bes' get yerself back in the lab 'n get yer nose to the grindstone."

"Not without payment. Where is it?"

"Cushing cut off me fundin'. I was just on me way to see the chancellor of the university. I've filed a complaint against him," Colin stood up.

"I hear chancellor is new."

"And a woman, no doubt."

"What is this? Woman cannot oversee university. Woman take over the world."

"It's 1909, perhaps she can oversea the university."

Colin gave Sasha a pat on the back and left the pub. Colin had to pass by several academic buildings until he reached the Chancellor's office. He removed his bowler hat before entering reception. A young woman stood up from her desk and smiled at Colin.

"Can I help you?"

"Aye, I've made an appointment to speak with the chancellor."

She sat down to check her appointment book. "Colin Limmerick? Oh, yes you're the doctorate student enrolled with Natural History. Please, sit for a bit and she will be right with you."

Colin sat down in the waiting area where his foot continuously tapped the floor. The receptionist noticed Colin's foot taping. She smiled at him. He caught her smiling at him. His eyes widened and he kept his foot still. The receptionist gestured for Colin to enter the chancellor's office. He stepped into a refreshing atmosphere: a rather large office filled with plants and opened windows. A petite, somewhat attractive, mature woman stood from her desk and smiled.

"Colin Limmerick I presume?"

"Aye, Chancellor Gordon." Colin partially bowed.

She sat at her desk. "I read over your written complaint. Your request for a different advisor could take some time."

Colin lifted his head. "Are ye sayin' me request could actually be granted?"

"Well, only if your current advisor agrees. He would have to sign off, you see."

"He's goin' after the severance of me academic fundin', Chancellor Gordon."

"Yes, yes, I understand that, and we can put a stop to that. You are one of our doctorate students. We can't expect you to get on well without funding, can we now?"

"Are ye sayin' I'll still have me fundin'?"

"Yes, that's much too important, and Dr. Cushing is showing an abuse of power by threatening such a thing."

Colin sat back in his chair and took a deep breath. "Oh, thank-ye. What a relief."

She smiled at him. Colin stood up as if he were about to exit her office.

"I was just about to have tea; would you like to join me, Mr. Limmerick? You just can't rush off."

Colin pulled his watch out of his pocket. "I suppose I can spend a wee bit of time here, but I bes' keep an eye on the time. I have to teach a lecture in a half hour."

"I'm expecting tea and crumpets. Please, remove your jacket and sit a while."

"Tea 'n crumpets, how grand. How generous of ye to ask," he said, as he removed his jacket. He noticed her eyes were fixed on every move he made.

"Chancellor Gordon, I'm beggin' yer pardon, but I must remind ye of someone 'cause ye keep starin' me down. Did I split opened me trousers?"

She laughed. "You are quite genuine, aren't you? I admire your candidness."

"How ye mean? Did I really split opened me trousers?"

He tried to look behind himself. The boxy looking gadget on her desk rang like a bell. She brought the cup-shaped instrument to her ear, where a long cord was attached to it, which led to the box.

"Yes, yes, bring it in. I hope the champagne is chilled," she said, to whoever she was talking to and hung up the gadget.

Colin gleamed at her. "So, I see ye have yer own telegraph."

"This is a telephone. The telegraph is passé" There was a faint knock on the door and a woman in a black and white uniform entered with a trolley of food. The chancellor gave the woman some money. "Oh, and could you pour the champagne? My companion here is in a rush? Thank you."

Colin's eyebrows lifted. "Champagne?"

"Yes, Mr. Limmerick, or would you prefer something else? I can call the caterers and make any change you want, if you wish?"

Colin's eyes widened. "Call the caterers? Not quite understandin' any of this."

"What's not to understand?" she said, while buttering her crumpet.

"I've never been in a chancellor's office before. Is this the regular routine of a chancellor? And, do all chancellor's have telephones?"

She laughed. "Please eat. Would you like to make your next appointment for tomorrow, perhaps when you don't have to teach a lecture?"

"Do I need another appointment?"

"Of course you do."

"I'll have to check me calendar."

"Why don't you just come in without a scheduled time, just enter. I'll let my receptionist know. I will definitely make time for you, Mr. Limmerick."

That evening Colin worked in the laboratory with Rosa.

"Have you seen Sasha lately?" she asked, brushing sediment off a small fossil.

"I was at a pub with him yesterday."

"Does he understand what problems lie a head due to the last prehistoric expedition?"

"Aye, he does."

"What's he going to do about it? It's all his fault."

"He wants his money."

"So, give it to him."

"I've got to get it from Cushing first, the bloody wanker."

"Can't you go above Cushing's head?"

"Saw the chancellor today."

"The Chancellor? Shouldn't you see the dean?"

"Did that. The dean is a bigger wanker than Cushing. The chancellor said she's goin' to make sure I get me money."

"The Chancellor is a *she?* What's she like?"

"She gave me tea, crumpets, 'n champagne, if ye can believe it?"

"Champagne?" Rosa stopped what she was doing and stepped closer to Colin. "You know what this means, don't you?"

"She seems like a very kind wench, so she does."

"You went to see her today to complain about how Dr. Cushing cut off your funding and she gave you tea, crumpets, and champagne?"

"I thought it was odd, as well."

"What's the matter with you? Don't you understand what's going on here?"

Colin gave a frozen smile.

"She's attracted to you."

He chuckled. "She's not. Maybe it's lonely bein' at the top."

"She shared a bottle of champagne with you; that's more than being a nice lady."

Colin chuckled. "Oh, love, yer always so wary of everyone. The champagne was quite good, I must say."

"You've been out to sea too long, you have absolutely no social skills."

"Social is what I am. How could ye say such a thin'?"

"You have no social intuition, Colin. She's attracted to you."

He packed up his lab utensils. "Look Rosa, the first two time-travel expeditions didn't go quite as planned. We left loads of loose ends. There's a gigantic prehistoric whale out in the sea. It's eatin' all the fish; it's put me crew out of work. I'm losin' loads of quid 'n I need that grant money, so I can pay Sasha 'n get this feckin' experiment to where it should be. I've been good to yez. Why the hell are ye pokin' fun at me for?"

"I'm not poking fun at you. You're a bit naïve sometimes. You've spent too many years on *The Atlantic Mermaid*. I'm just saying that you need to watch your step. Universities can be very political. You need to stay focused. You need that grant money, so you can close the path through time. Sasha needs to get paid; he's right."

"I promised Amoli that I would have dinner at her parents' house tonight. If I'm late, she'll kill me."

"Colin, have as little to do with that female chancellor as possible."

"I'm seein' her tomorrow, as well."

"Why? I thought you said that it's settled and you should be expecting your grant money? Why do you still need to see her?"

"Dunno, really. I'm supposin' there's somethin' else she needs to see me for."

Rosa smacked her hand over her forehead. "Oh, you're walking right into the fire. Don't see that woman anymore; this could cost you your reputation at this university."

"What's all this about me bleedin' reputation? I don't even have a feckin' reputation."

"Right now you are regarded as this heroic, dynamic time-traveler, who has taken research to a higher dimension. Don't destroy everything you worked for just because you can't stand Professor Cushing."

He put on his coat and hat. "Love, I really must leave now. I have an over-anxious lass awaitin me arrival."

***

That evening Colin sat a large table with several of Amoli's family members. Dr. Sharma stood beside Colin and watched him eat.

"Colin?" Amoli asked, with a tiny whisper.

"Aye, lass," he responded, with his mouth full.

"You appear so very nervous. Is something bothering you?"

"Well, since ye asked, I'm findin' it rather difficult to eat this fine cuisine with yer father hovering over me shoulder."

Amoli looked at her father. "Father, please allow Colin to eat. Shouldn't you be seated at the table, so you can eat this wonderful meal that I prepared?"

Dr. Sharma cleared his throat. "Pardon me, my future son-in law, I am waiting to hear more about wedding plans. You appear to be very silent. What is wrong with you?"

Colin placed his fork down. "Weddin' plans, sar?" The family members seated at the table stopped eating. "I haven't really thought of the weddin' just yet. I've been preoccupied with me research."

Amoli burst into tears. Her mother screamed and rose from her chair. The grandmother began to sing an old song from her childhood in India.

"I've discussed this with Amoli several times. I'm in the middle of some academic changes at the moment 'n I can't really give me fullest attention to plannin' a weddin'." Colin glanced at Amoli's mother. "I shall, but this just isn't the best of times for me."

"What is this I hear coming from my future son-in law? Your priority must and only must be my daughter, Amolia. Nothing is to surpass my Amolia."

Colin wiped his hands with his napkin and placed it over his plate. "I think I'm done eatin' now, thank-ye."

Amoi's mother was still standing. "You have not finished. Please, do not dishonor us by not completing this meal."

Colin took a deep breath and tried to smile. "Dr. Sharma, I don't think yer understandin' what I'm sayin' to yez. It looks like I may time-travel again."

Amoli stood up and screamed so loud that her mother tried to comfort her. Her sister held her hand. Amoli's younger brother laughed and continued to call Colin profane names. Colin remained in his chair. "Oh, shite, what did I just do?"

Amoli looked at Colin with tears running down her face. "Tell me, Colin, will that woman, Miss Emanuel, be traveling with you?"

Colin's eyes widened. "Dunno, really. Haven't discussed who should be goin'."

Amoli cried harder. "That means yes, doesn't it? She wants you back, I know it!"

Mrs. Sharma began to cry. "Oh, no, do not convey to me our Colin has another woman!"

Colin rubbed his face with his hands. "Oh, shite, this can't be happin'. Oh, shite, shite." Colin stood up. "Amoli, can I speak with ye in private, maybe?"

"I want my family to hear what you have to say to me!"

Colin glanced at each of her family members. "Alright, then. I told yez already there could be a slight possibility of me time-travelin' again. Well, that slight possibility has turned into a definite possibility."

"No! Tell me this isn't so. Why are you doing this to me? I love you!"

"I love ye, lass, but I have to do this."

Amoli cried so hard she ran to the lavatory to throw up.

Dr. Sharma paced around Colin. "You see what you have done, don't you?"

"An academic researcher is what I am, sar. Just like yerself. Surely, ye can understand that."

"Ah, yes, an academic researcher is what I am, but I don't go gallivanting through time trying to find the missing link? My research is done right here in 1910. You see, I am a good researcher and you are a bad researcher."

"But, sar, it was ye who raved over me time-travels. Ye put forth so much belief in them."

"But now that your time-travels are encroaching on your marriage to my Amolia, it changes everything."

"It does?"

"I never could understand what Amolia sees in you. You are a very bad man."

Colin bowed to the family. "I thank yez all. Lovely meal it was, really. I bes' be on my way. I need to catch last call at the nearest pub, so ye see."

Colin continued to bow as he walked backward toward the front door and made his quick exit.

Chapter Eight

The following morning Sasha stormed into Colin's office. Colin was still wearing the same suit as the previous day. His hair was disheveled and he had significant beard growth. He lifted his head to gaze at Sasha."

"Mr. Limmerick, you stink. What you do last night? You still drunk?"

"Likely so."

"Some big headline news in morning paper." Sasha placed his newspaper in front of Colin. Colin took the paper and placed his eyeglasses on his face. "Problem solved. Read."

"Over-sized whale, perhaps prehistoric, found beached on Welsh coast. Huh? There's a photograph here; it's *Basilosaurus*, oh, feck no!" Colin rubbed his tired eyes. "What ye mean problem solved? Nothin's solved."

"B-whale beached, your crew can now go back to work."

"Oh, feck, yer deranged. Not really knowin' how many other prehistoric species got through the passage of time."

"Passage? No passage; wormhole."

Colin took a deep breath. "I feel like a murderer. We took that poor animal's life because of our own ignorance. Scientific researchers we's surely not. "

"That animal was 35 million years old. It already dead."

"It needed to die where it came from. Time-travel is definitely in order here, but will we feck things up even more? Oh, Lord, I don't know."

"Even more? You so pessimistic."

59

"A realist is what I am, mate. Ye 'n I both are bloody wankers. Ye should've stayed in Russia 'n I should've stayed on me vessel."

"You talk like child. I discover route to past. I am genius."

Rosa walked in holding a copy of the daily newspaper. "I suppose you both have seen this morning's headline. Oh, Colin, I'm so sorry."

"Thanks, love."

"Is this why you look so unkept and disgusting?"

Colin chuckled. "More love, tell me more, more adjectives, please."

"He not know of b-whale until I show him newspaper," Sasha said.

"Oh, really? Is something else bothering you?" Rosa asked, as she sat down. "Didn't things go well at Amoli's little dinner last night?"

Colin scratched his bearded chin. "Did it all arseways, I did. If ye can believe it."

"What happened?"

Colin stood up. "Feel just awful about our prehistoric whale. This is gettin' out of control. Don't care to speak about last night's dinner with the future in-laws. I bes' get to me lecture, despite me manly appearance."

Rosa and Sasha looked at each other. They watched Colin stumble out of his office. It was late afternoon the following day, when Colin sat in his academic office grading his students' papers. One of the secretaries of his department knocked on his door.

"Instructor Limmerick, are you in?" a young woman asked.

"Aye, can I help ye?"

"This is a letter from Chancellor Gordon," the secretary said, as she handed it to him and made her exit.

"Ah, forgot I was supposed to meet her today."

Attention Mr. Limmerick,

This letter is to inform you that you either forgot about our meeting today, or that you still expect to keep it. Please see me in my office as soon as possible.
Chancellor Evelyn Gordon

Colin sprung from his desk. He placed his hat on his head and swung his coat over his shoulder. Amoli gingerly poked her head through his doorway.

"Ah, lass, so good of ye to show up."

"Colin, we have matters to discuss. I have been very distraught over your last visit with my family."

"I've been distraught, as well, lass. A scene is what it surely was."

"A scene? You purposely made me cry in front of my family, now I am so ashamed. I cannot even look at them." Colin slid his coat on. Amoli watched him grab his umbrella. "Are you leaving?"

"Aye. Would ye like me to come see ye tonight so we can chat about this further?"

"You cannot come to see my family; they are very upset with you."

"Can I meet ye somewhere, then?"

"I must help my mother and my aunt tonight. I cannot leave the house. Why can you not speak to me now?"

"Gotta run, I do. I'm expected at the chancellor's office."

Amoli's eyes filled with tears. "Am I losing you? What has become of us?"

Colin held her tightly in his arms. "We've got some matters to discuss, is all."

"Why do you not set a date for us to marry?"

"'Cause need to venture through time, so I do."

Tears ran down her cheeks causing her make-up to drip off her chin. "I do not wish you to venture through time. Please allow Dr. Dimitrikov to take this serious trip."

"What would Dr. Dimitrikov do once he got there?"

61

"I don't know. He is a scientist, therefore he would know what to do."

"He's a physicist, not a natural historian. A mistake that would be."

She held onto his arm. "Please don't leave now; we must discuss our wedding."

"After me meetin' with the chancellor I'll rush off to see ye, I will. Surely, yer mother 'n aunt would let ye spend a few minutes with me."

Amoli began to shake. "You can try it, but it will not be pleasant. Come at 7:00."

"How about half past?"

"Too late."

"I'll try make it by seven," He said, and kissed her several times on the lips.

Colin noticed the chancellor's office door was ajar. The secretary had already left for the day. He stepped in to see if Evelyn was present.

"Oh, Mr. Limmerick, how good of you to come so promptly," the chancellor called out, as she watered her plants.

"Forgive me, Chancellor Gordon. I completely forgot our meetin'," Colin said, as he removed his soaked hat and coat.

She gleamed at him. "Did you get yourself caught in the rain?"

"Aye, sure did."

"Come sit down. I have fresh tea."

Colin smiled. "It's grand that yer not ravin' mad at me."

"We really didn't set a specific time, but it's 6:00 now; much later than expected."

"Six already, is it? Me time is limited once again. I haven't the time for too much chat, if ye don't mind me sayin'."

"Yes, alright, I will make it quick. I wanted to tell you that I have read your work." She smiled while she stirred her tea. "You're a brilliant man, Mr. Limmerick. I didn't realize that you were the chap who actually ventured through time in order to prove his research question. Your work is extraordinary."

Colin smiled, "How brilliant it is that ye fancy me work, Chancellor."

"Please address me as Evelyn." She paused while she gazed at him. "I looked up your file and learned that you run and own a fishing trade. That explains it."

Colin's smile dissipated. "Excuse me?"

"Your rugged appearance, of course."

"I've heard this song before. I don't quite fit the look of a doctorate student. Me academic advisor always held that one against me."

"Well, actually...no you don't resemble whatever a doctorate student is supposed to look like. I would never hold something like that against you. One's appearance should have nothing to do with one's work."

"Glad ye feel that way."

"By the way, tomorrow you will have your grant money. It will be in your mailbox in the Natural History office."

"So soon? Impressed, so I am."

"It's not all of it, but this is the first installment. If you need an advance, let me know."

Colin drank up his tea. "Yer too kind."

She stared at him. "Tell me, getting off topic, what are some of your hobbies?"

"Hobbies? Don't know if I have the time for hobbies, Chancellor."

"Evelyn, call me Evelyn. There must be some recreation that you partake in."

Colin smiled. "I dance a mean jig 'n reel, so I do. Ye should see me. I may be big, but I can be light on me feet when I'm feelin' me Irish blood rush through me."

63

She snickered at him. "Maybe sometime you can take me to an Irish pub with live entertainment. I'd love to see you dance. What else do you do for fun?"

"When I'm not hammered, I sing. Me crew, they play some instruments 'n such. I play the bodhrán sometimes, ye know it, the Irish drum. Some have said me voice holds up, but I dunno."

"Can you sing for me, Mr. Limmerick?"

Colin chuckled. "Here? Now?" Colin blushed. "Can't really say if I can. What if someone passes by? Surely, me reputation 'n such will be affected, don't ye think?"

"Please, I would absolutely love to hear you sing."

He tried to get comfortable in the chair. "Oh, shite, dunno, if I can, really...rather embarrassed I am. What if ye just hate me singin', then what?"

"Well, tell you what, if I deplore your singing we will never mention this again to each other and we will just simply move on."

"Alright, let me think of a dany tune for yez." He stood up and smiled at her. "I have a tune ye may fancy. *The Meetin' of the Waters* should be suitable for ye, I think."

There is not in the wide world a valley so sweet
As that vale in whose bosom the bright waters meet
Oh! The last rays of feelin' and life must depart
Ere the bloom of that valley shall fade from me heart
Ere the bloom of that valley shall fade from me heart.
Yet it was not that nature had shed o'er the scene
Her purest of crystal and brightest of green
'Twas not her soft magic of streamlet or hill
Oh, no! It was something more exquisite still
Oh, no! It was something more exquisite still.
'Twas that friends, the belov'd of me bosom were near
Who made every dear scene of enchantment more dear

And who felt how the best charms of nature improve
When we see them reflected from looks that we love
When we see them reflected from looks that we love
Sweet vale of Avoca! How calm could I rest
In thy bosom of shade, with the friends I love best
*   the storms that we feel in this cold world should*
cease
And our hearts, like thy waters, be mingled in peace
And our hearts, like thy waters, be mingled in peace.

"Oh, my word, what an enchanting voice you have. I too am a lover of music."

"Grand to know it, Chancellor Gordon." Colin smiled as he moved toward her and kissed her hand. "I can see the clock on yer wall. It's already seven. There's somewhere I've gotta be in a short while. If I don't get there, I'll be drinkin' meself to me death tonight. Late is what I already am, I'm afraid."

"I understand. When you receive your grant money, come here and we will dine out at noon as a sort of celebration."

He put on his coat and hat. "Dine out tomorrow? Oh, I see."

She gleamed at him. "You're very original. You appear to be a very serious man."

He laughed. "I fancy good *craic* every now 'n again, so I do. Serious? I wouldn't say that, nay I wouldn't."

She gazed at him with a penetrating stare. "I greatly enjoy every meeting I have with you, Mr. Limmerick."

"Very kind, so ye are. I bes' be on me way 'n such. I want to thank-ye for all that yev done," he said, and took her hand and kissed it with a slight bow.

"Don't forget tomorrow at noon. We'll dine out."

"Time may be a factor, I'm afraid."

"When you receive your grant money, you will want to celebrate, most definitely."

"Surely, some time I can spare," Colin said, with a smile and exited her office.

Colin arrived at Amoli's family home at 9:30. He knocked on the door. Dr. Sharma answered.

"Colin? You were not invited to our home tonight."

"Can I see Amoli, sar?"

"No," Dr. Sharma said, and shut the door in Colin's face.

"Father? Was that Colin?" Amoli asked, with her mother and sister trailing behind her. Oh, father, please open the door."

Dr. Sharma opened the door. "Colin, please enter. Amolia insists you enter."

Colin stepped in. "Thank-ye," he said, removing his hat.

"Colin, you're late. I told you to come at 7:00. It is now too late."

"Too late for what?"

"My family would like to pray."

"Can't ye do that at church on Sundays?"

"Why are you being so rude? You and I do not share the same faith. Oh, my, I hope you are not drunk again," she whispered.

"Haven't had a drink since noon, I haven't. Drunk I'm not."

"What kept you?" She continued to whisper.

"Had to see the chancellor about an urgent matter." He glanced at her family members. "Can I take ye outta here, so we can talk?"

"I don't think so."

"Alright, then." Colin noticed her mother standing behind her. Her young brother sat on the floor beside Amoli. Dr. Sharma paced the room, while her grandmother and sister paced about behind her mother. "Amoli," Colin said, in a whisper. "I'm findin' this is givin' me loads of pressure 'n anxiety."

Dr. Sharma glared at Colin. "When is the date? I want to know the exact date."

"Can't tell ye that just as yet. Havin' to deal with some obstacles with me research. To assure ye, as soon as the loose ends are tied you'll be the first to know."

"Not good enough, Colin!"

Colin got hold of Amoli's hand and pulled her out the door with him.

"What are you doing? My father will be outraged at this." He pulled her behind a large tree. "Colin, this is not the way to deal with my family. You must get used to this if you marry into an Indian family."

Colin chuckled, as his eyes scanned her body. "Yer lookin' so good tonight." He kissed her neck several times.

"Colin, please, what if my father finds us?"

"Won't be the first time, sure it won't."

Tears ran down her face. "Please, I am very sad about something else."

His kisses ran from her neck to her breasts. "Sad? Ye can't be sad."

"Remember when I told you," she looked around, "when I said I was missing my monthlies?"

"Aye. We's havin' babies, are we?"

"No, we're not. My monthlies returned."

Colin stopped kissing her. "Shite. How long have ye known this?"

"Three months now. I didn't want to tell you, because I wanted to wait and see, but my monthlies are continuing as regular now."

"Oh, yer not expectin'?"

"No, I'm not," she cried.

He tightened his arms around her. "Yer just a young lass of twenty, so much opportunity for later."

"You are not angry with me? Then when can we marry?"

"Next year, I suppose."

"Too far in the future, but it will give us time to prepare, won't it?"

"But I need to time-travel immediately. Please don't start plannin' anythin' yet."

"Why not?"

"'Cause, lass, there's always the chance I won't return."

She stared at him.

"I was nearly killed on the last expedition 'n it's a great possibility."

"So, then, don't go."

"I haven't a choice. I fecked up too much prehistory, so I did."

"Then I'll have to come with you."

He chuckled. "Don't think so. It's too dangerous."

She wept in his arms.

68

Chapter Nine

"Alright Miss Rosa, we now put block in path. We stop prehistoric species from leaking through worm hole," Sasha said, while in the university laboratory.

"Stop calling it a wormhole; it's a path," she said, with a curt tone.

Sasha chuckled at her. "You think you so smart lady? It not matter what it is. It is opening and it make Mr. Limmerick drink more whiskey."

Rosa laughed. "Fine, how are you going to block this path?"

"I have created magnetic barrier. I design it when magnetic barrier stops prehistoric life from leaking into twentieth century; it will also draw back prehistoric life that is already here. We must time-travel and place it in precise spot."

"Oh. This sounds as if it could be tricky."

"All is tricky, Rosa, when scientist travels through time. So sad about b-whale."

"*Basilosaurus* was a remarkable early mammal. Colin is very upset about it not surviving here in our time. He's blaming himself for all of this."

"He is right. This is all his fault."

"You're so hard on him."

"You love him like no other. You always do."

She tightened the ribbon in her hair. "Can we just get back to work?"

"We should time-travel by summer."

"What's the delay?"

"I have problem with precise time we enter. There is always chance we will not end up in time of prehistoric mammals. I always see on indicator device that we have good chance to go in not so distant past."

"To what time period? Fifty years ago, perhaps?"

"Nyet. More. Indicator saying 500 to 1,000 years ago."

"That's no good."

"Da, I understand. Not good. I need time to find out why indicator do this."

Colin entered the lab. "Howye." He glanced at his two colleagues. "Yer both lookin' rather serious, I must say."

"Colin, pull up a stool and sit with us. Sasha has come up with a fabulous idea."

Colin smiled. "Grand of ye to come up with somethin' so soon, mate."

"We will use magnetic barrier on path of time. But it is important we put barrier in specific place on path. We miss right spot, nothing will change and all prehistoric life come to our time. Da?"

"Fine, how will we know what this specific place is?"

"I try to find out by working with time-travel indicator, which say me this."

"Worth a try it is, don't ye think?"

Rosa placed her hand on Colin's chest. "Not so fast, big boy, there is a catch. Sasha is finding that his indicator is only looking at a more recent time frame."

Colin's eyebrows lifted. "How recent? Like last week, or King Arthur and the Round Table?"

Rosa glanced at Sasha. "Your second guess could be a closer match. What do you think, Sasha?"

"Da, maybe King Arthur's time."

"Yer bloody well kiddin' me aren't ye?" Colin sighed. "Not much good that'll be."

"I do so much so far, Mr. Limmerick. If you only know how much; you go off with your Miss Amoli here and there when I stay in lab and work so hard."

"Not accusin' of shite all, ye feckin' arse. I have yer money."

70

"Dr. Cushing gave in and he gave you your funding? How wonderful," Rosa said, and jumped into Colin's arms.

Colin smiled at Rosa. "Ye can thank the chancellor."

Rosa removed her arms from Colin and stepped back. "She pulled through just as she said she would, and gave me the first installment of me grant money, so now Sasha can get paid. She moves fast, she does."

"Good, give me money. I am poor scholar," Sasha grunted.

"I've got it here all prepared in this envelope for ye. So get the feck off me back 'n do what I'm payin' ye to do."

Rosa crossed her arms. "I don't like the sound of this. Was this university money or was it her money? Sounds like she's buying you because she's attracted to you."

"Ah, she's a fine wench, not bad to look at either."

Rosa tugged on Colin's arm. "Are you mad? Aren't you in the process of planning a big wedding to Amoli, the little princess of India?"

"Aye, so I am."

"Then, do not see this woman. This is not university money, Colin."

Colin looked at Rosa and smiled. "Yer gettin' yerself in a stir, love. She's a fine woman. Ye'd fancy her if ye met her."

"I doubt that very much. Don't get yourself into a mess you will never be able to undo. Sasha, give Colin back the money. Colin return this to her and never deal with her again."

"What's gone on with yez? Need to take some time off or something,'?"

"This is not about me, you big lug, this is about you, who is about to destroy everything you have worked for in this university. Don't be so naïve, Colin. Your social skills never really developed."

Sasha laughed. "This is true. Who is this chancellor? She pretty lady, da?"

"Older, but nice lookin' so she is."

"I want to meet her," Sasha cackled.

Rosa threw her arms in the air. "Oh, my God! No wonder I'm still not married. Men can be so gullible sometimes." Rosa grabbed the envelope from Sasha and gave it to Colin. "Give this back to her."

"That, I won't do, love. Here Sasha, take this."

Sasha give it back to Colin!"

"Nyet. I will never. I am poor man."

"Colin, you should know by now when a woman is attracted to you. Aren't you over forty?"

"Aye, that I am. Ye don't have to rub it in, love."

Rosa grabbed Colin's blazer lapel. "Look me in the eye. Did you sleep with her?"

Colin chuckled at Sasha who was bent over with laughter. "Sleep with her? I'm soon to be a married man."

"And when is your wedding date?"

Colin's expression changed. "Don't know as of yet. Dealin' with another prehistoric journey, just now."

Rosa paced the lab. "Do you think I enjoy this?"

Sasha looked at Colin. "Sit down, Rosa. This is not for lady like you. Too excited about so much all the time."

Colin took Rosa's hand and kissed it. "Enough of me personal life, love. What ye come up with regardin' Sasha's experiment?"

Sasha smiled. "I now see this path. I create magnetic barrier. It must be placed in precise spot along prehistoric pathway, because it powered by *tachion-flux* between two time periods. It must also be placed at precise time, because *tachion-flux* must be sufficient."

Colin scratched his head.

"Not worry, my time indicator will say us if it is," Sasha assured.

Rosa tugged at Colin's tie. "I hope you know that I'm coming with you."

72

"On our next prehistoric journey, yer tellin' me? So, ye are definite about this?"

Sasha laughed. "You hate time-travel. Why you say us this, now?"

"Because I'm the only one who knows anything around here. You two blokes will make a mess of things like you did when you scuffled with Neanderthal."

"Wasn't me fault, the prehistoric wanker couldn't handle any competition," Colin expressed, like a guilty child.

"What you say, Mr. Limmerick? Neanderthal almost kill you. You no match for him. He almost crush you."

Enough of this rubbish. It's best I come on this third expedition," Rosa blurted out.

"Amoli wants to be included as well, so she says," mentioned Colin.

"Absolutely not. She'll make matters worse," Rosa instilled.

"Just don't think it'll be the place for the lass, 'is all," Colin added.

Sasha grinned and wiggled his eyebrows to Rosa.

Chapter Ten

Late spring 1909:

Colin stepped into Dr. Cushing's office. "Sar, could ye spare some time?"

What is it? Can't you see I'm in the middle of my morning tea?"

"Ah, so I do." Colin sat on Dr. Cushing's rusty stool. "Sar, just wanted to inform ye that I got meself some fundin' for me time-travel research."

Dr. Cushing spewed out his tea. "Pardon me? What did you just say?" Dr. Cushing laughed. "Of course you did. How much did you sell your boat for?"

"The Atlantic Mermaid is still very much with me."

Dr. Cushing tried to sit up straight. "Alright then, how did you manage to get the money?"

Colin smiled. "Ah, a secret, so it is."

Dr. Cushing fiddled with some of the papers on his desk. "So, what's next? Are you going back in time to bother that Irish elk again?"

"Deer, sar. It was a deer. Aye, I'll be venturin' back in time once again. Some unfinished business I must tend to."

"And when will you be entrenching yourself in this next escapade?"

"Soon, sar. Aye, very soon."

"And who will take over your classes, Colin?"

"Sure, Timothy Duncan or even ye, sar, would do the honors."

"Timothy has far too much work to take on your load, and I can't possibly…"

"Ye have no choice in the matter. I'm allowed to pursue me field research. That clause is written in the graduate student expectations. It's at the foot of the page. Do ye have that student agreement form on yez, sar?"

"I'm not going to waste my precious time looking for such a form. I'll just ask my friend, the dean for a copy."

"Aye, do seek it from yer good ol' boy." Colin stood up and placed his hat on his head. "Enjoy yer tea."

Colin grinned and left his academic advisor's office. That afternoon, he met Amoli at a restaurant.

"Lass, I'm afraid I can't spare loads of time with ye."

Amoli buried her head in his bicep. "You can spare some time for me. Soon I will be your wife."

Colin pulled Amoli's chair out for her to sit. He slowly sat down.

"Lass, ye need to know I'll be time-travelin' soon. How does that suit ye?"

Amoli grimaced. "It doesn't."

"Thought that'd be yer response."

"I forbid you to go."

He chuckled at her. "So, yer forbiddin' me to go, are ye? Lass, gotta go, so I do."

"I love you! You're me one and only. It is very dangerous."

The waiter approached their table. Colin ordered a whiskey. He paused and then took Amoli's hand. He brought her hand to his lips.

"I need to do this."

Amoli pulled her hand away from him. "Is she going with you?"

"Ah, Rosa, yer speakin' of? Aye, she's comin' with us. A scientist is what she is. Understand this will ye?"

"No, I will never understand when that woman is concerned."

Colin got his glass of whiskey. He put his glass to his lips and stared at Amoli.

"What's this all about? Yer jealousy of Rosa is startin' to turn me belly sour."

He guzzled his whiskey. Amoli began to shake and cry.

75

"Colin, don't you love me anymore? She can't come with you."

"Oh, shite, don't start that now." He pulled out a kerchief and tried to wipe her soggy eyes. Colin sat back on his chair and crossed his arms. He took a few heavy sighs. "Another whiskey is what I need."

"No, you drink far too much."

"Gettin' langered is me only means of survival."

She smiled at him. He sat forward in his chair and took her hand. "Is there somewhere we can go later?"

"Your flat is all I can think of," she said, with a girlish giggle.

"I really want ye now. I suppose it'll be me place." He pulled his watch from his vest pocket. "Around four? How late is that for me to wait on ye? I want ye now." He pulled her onto his lap. "Skip the food we should. Come to me flat now, will ye?"

He left some money on the table. He held Amoli and threw her over his shoulder. The restaurant patrons and staff wore mortified expressions on their faces.

He carried Amoli over his shoulder until he unlocked the door to his flat. He pulled her into his flat and yanked at her sari. She leaned against his door with a continuous giggle. He tore off his tie and unbuttoned his vest. Her sari fell off her shoulders where her ample breasts were exposed. He kicked off his shoes with the laces still tied. He stripped off his trousers and she helped him pull down his boxers.

He protruded and aimed at her vagina. He placed his large hands under her full buttock and pressed her against the door. She could feel herself being lifted by his strong hands. His enormous penis aimed in the right direction and penetrated her with a surge of power that had her moan and scream. Her long black hair hung in front of her face as she cried and screamed with a pleasure-pain.

When he finished his job, they both descended to the floor. He stayed on top of her and fondled her breasts. She delicately sighed. Her big dark eyes pierced through him. He slowly rolled off her.

"Sorry, lass. Too rough am I? Or, am I simply too big?"

She smiled. "Both."

"I apologize. Work on it some more, I will. I promise. The size of me pipe is somethin' that I can't change. I'm sorry for that."

She sat up and pushed her hair from her face. "Please, stop apologizing. What are you very sorry for?"

"Keep forgettin' ye was a virgin when I met ye."

"Of course I was." Her facial expression changed. "I wish you were a virgin as well."

He held his head down. Then he stood up and lifted her from the ground.

"Yer father has a fine young gent awaitin' ye in India. Surely, he's a virgin."

"I don't want him. I want you."

"I love ye. Ye take me for who I am. Hard to find in a lass, that is."

"That woman most likely never accepted you for who you are, am I right?"

"That woman? Ah, Rosa. She's a good friend, but yer right. She never accepted me for me."

Amoli smiled at him and pressed her naked body against his. He rubbed his large rough hands up and down the sides of her body. She could feel the sweat on his skin. He tightened his arms around her and kissed the top of her head. There was a knock at the door.

Amoli blurted a faint gasp. "Were you expecting somebody?"

"I wasn't. We's both standin' here naked. Feck! A man can't even bang his wench in private anymore."

She scooped up her clothes and scurried to his bathroom.

"Who's there?" Colin asked, with his ear to the door.

77

"Sasha is here. Why you make me wait so long in hallway?"

Colin opened his door. "Mate? How'd ye guess I was here?"

Sasha pushed in. "You not in your lab, office, or pub. I know you not teach lecture at this time. Where would you be?"

Colin hopped on one leg as he put on his trousers. "What's so urgent?"

Sasha glanced at him. "Why you not have clothes on?"

Colin buttoned his trousers. "Why ye think?"

Sasha grinned. "Oh, Miss Amoli is here?"

"Aye, so she is. What brings ye here, anyways?"

"I say we ready to travel through time."

"So, ye don't say? Ye sure yer device 'n magnetic barrier are ready?"

Sasha stepped back. "Wait, you first must understand that anything go wrong with time-travel and nothing is hundred percent to block barrier."

"What's the probability we can block the path through time 'n not let anymore prehistoric life through the openin'?"

"Maybe thirty percent, if we lucky."

Colin sat down and reached for an opened bottle of whiskey on the table. He placed it to his lips. Sasha watched him drink down the entire bottle. Then, Colin stood up and walked to his liquor cabinet. He found a smaller bottle of whiskey and brought it to the table with him. Sasha pulled out a half smoked cigarette from his jacket and smoked it. Amoli entered the room.

"Well, hello Dr. Dimitrikov. How are you today?"

Sasha smiled at her. "Hello Miss Amoli, I was just leaving. Please look after Mr. Limmerick. He not look too good."

Colin placed the larger empty bottle on the table. He finished the smaller bottle and stared at the floor. He stood up and staggered to his liquor cabinet, searching for another bottle of whiskey. Amoli remained still.

"Colin? What's bothering you?" He continued to search his liquor cabinet. She focused on him. "Please. I think you have had enough."

"What's all this shite I got here? I've got me stash of Irish liqueurs, but where's me feckin' whiskey?"

"You must have drank it all."

He halted his search, but kept his back to her. "Aye, lass, so yer right." He pressed himself against his liquor cabinet. "Can I hail ye a carriage to take ye home?

"Why? Are you going back to the university?"

"I was goin' after workin' in the lab; don't think I will after all."

"What did Dr. Dimitrikov say to you? You seem so very upset."

Colin staggered to her. "Nothin' of any interest to yez." He took her hands and kissed them both. "I thank ye for a luscious afternoon."

"You're drunk."

He smiled and placed his hands on her shoulders. "Lass. Can ye believe it? He says maybe thirty percent? What's that shite, eh? Ye need to get home, lass."

"I'm sorry I distracted you from your workday again."

"Lass, thirty percent, maybe? Feck! What's wrong with a hundred?"

Amoli began to tremble and cry. "What is thirty percent? I am so very afraid that I don't understand you."

He took her shawl and placed it over her shoulders. He awkwardly put on his coat and hat and they exited his flat. Colin kept his arm around her.

"Colin? What happened to your automobile?"

"Sold it. Needed the quid."

"Are you having financial trouble?"

"Not different than other years, but I must admit the lack of fish in our waters lately has brought forth some financial discomfort."

"London is a difficult city to live in, isn't it?"

"Costly is what it is. Don't know if I'd be makin' London me permanent home."

"Perhaps, after we marry, we can live in India?"

He smiled and tightened his arm around her shoulders. "Aye, lass."

Chapter Eleven

Early Fall 1909:

Sasha shut the door in the laboratory. He faced Rosa and Colin.

"Alright colleagues, I have re-shaped time-travel device with magnetic barrier. I call you both here this day so I can say how all has changed with experiment, da?"

Colin glanced at Rosa. "Aye, just get on with it. Gotta teach a lecture in 30 minutes."

Rosa gave a faint grunt. "Colleagues? Now, I'm just your colleague?"

Sasha removed his blazer, then lit a cigarette. "Good news! I have good percentage for stopping prehistoric animals from crossing into twentieth century. Much greater chance for success."

Colin and Rosa smiled at him, Sasha did not return the smile. "We will travel in some months, maybe. Time-travel device will help indicate where magnetic barrier must be placed along pathway. Percentage of no more prehistoric animals leak-through is now very good."

Colin smiled. "What's the odds of any leakin' through, mate?"

"Fifty percent," Sasha said, while he applauded himself with heavy clapping.

Rosa stood up from her stool. "Sasha. Fifty-percent isn't very promising."

"I knew it!" shouted Colin. "Not worth riskin' our lives if we only have half a chance. Not good enough, mate."

"What you say? This so good. It is worth all."

Rosa crossed her arms. "We need more of a guarantee. Don't you see this?"

Sasha loosened his tie. "I am not God here. You try find other scientist who develop this kind of experiment.

Do it! Nobody in our year, 1909 has sent anybody back in time. You find someone! Go!"

Colin sat on the lab stool. "Oh, shite! Don't start cryin'."

"You, Mr. Limmerick! I can take you no more!" Sasha said, pointing his finger at him.

"If I had it me own way I wish we's never stepped foot in the prehistoric past. We now opened a feckin' Pandora's Box. We got to fix this mess, so we's do."

"Oh, but you so wanted to travel to prehistoric past to prove to your Professor Cushing that your big deer had so big horns for sex."

Colin lifted his eyebrows and glanced at Rosa. "What's he sayin'?"

Rosa snickered. "You should understand Sasha's broken English by now. In fact, I think Sasha's English is very good. I applaud you, Sasha."

Colin almost fell off his stool with laughter. "Oh, sweet Christ, help me. I'm supposin' a fifty-percent chance of closin' the pathway through time is as good as it's gonna get?"

"It is very good. This is a time of great mechanization and technology. This is not when your parents were born, Mr. Limmerick. You are potato famine people."

"Aye, it amazes me how me parents 'n grandparents survived it; stamina is what they had back then."

"Alright, Sasha, you need a bit more time you said? Why is that?" Rosa asked, as she gently paced the lab.

"Want to make sure all is well and no mistakes."

"Very good, Sasha, you're a fine scientist," Rosa said, with a smile.

Sasha gave a slight bow. Colin remained sitting on his stool as he pulled his watch from his vest pocket.

"Can we cut the shite here? Time is runnin' short for me just now."

"Oh, yes, Colin. I just wanted to confirm who will be venturing on this prehistoric journey," Rosa asked.

"Sasha, meself 'n ye, love?" Colin said.

"Yes, I will be traveling with both of you on this third expedition through time. Nobody is to know of this. We must keep it confidential, yes, Colin?"

"Amoli won't be comin', sure of that I am."

"Good. When will we depart, Sasha?"

"November, maybe early December. Not sure yet. We may return in new year."

"That long?" Colin commented.

"Da, this will not be easy operation. You must inform your Miss Amoli."

Colin rubbed his face. "She's gonna hit the feckin' roof. It's too long of a time to be away. She's anxious to marry."

"Aren't you, Colin?" asked Rosa.

"Me head won't clear 'till this prehistoric time-travel is over with. Just afraid I won't be comin' back is all." He looked at Rosa with a fake smile. "Was almost killed on the last prehistoric journey."

"No more fights with Neanderthals," said Rosa. "Don't get yourself upset over what may have happened on the last expedition. The important thing is that you're alright and that you're more than willing to time-travel again." Rosa pursed her lips.

"I've got to confront Amoli with this. She'll cry, she will."

"Don't worry about your little sweet Amoli; she's made of steel. She makes you think she's so brittle. It's all hogwash, if you ask me."

"Aye, she can be a strong wench, so she can. This, however, is a time where she wants to get started with weddin' plans 'n all."

"So, bring her along. What so hard?" Sasha asked, with a snicker.

Rosa hit Sasha's arm. "Are you mad?"

"She comes with Mr. Limmerick and all is happy."

83

"Absolutely not. If she comes, then I'm staying behind."

Colin rubbed his hand over his face.

***

An hour later, Colin was in the middle of a lecture with his class. He paced around the lecture hall.

"What is survival of the fittest, 'n what is natural selection? Some species just died off, whilst so many branched off to a more developed species." He watched his students jot down notes. He leaned against the podium and removed his round specs. "Darwin has coined the 'term survival of the fittest'. To be naturally selected means a species adapts or doesn't adapt. In the case of Megaloceros giganteus, this creature was sexually selected due to its over-sized antlers, which attracted the females. Unfortunately, it led to its demise, where it could no longer rummage about in the forest in search of food." He rubbed his tired eyes and loosened his tie. Two female students sat in the corner, passing notes to each other, while they kept their eyes on their handsome instructor. "Any questions?" Colin asked his diligent class of first year students. Everyone continued to write. He unbuttoned his vest and continued to loosen his tie. He felt someone poking at his back. He turned to see the chancellor. "Chancellor Gordon?"

"Hello, Colin," she said, with a whisper. "I wanted to catch you before your lecture ended to ask if you received your funding."

Colin took her hand. "Forgive me. I've been so rude. Aye, I did receive it, yet I neglected to inform ye about it. I can be so rude sometimes."

"Rude? Not at all."

He chuckled. "Ye don't know me well enough, then do yez?"

The students stood up for the chancellor. Colin grinned as she gestured for them to be seated.

"Well, I'm glad you received it." She stepped closer to him and continued to speak in a whisper. "I was on my way to get something to eat and I wouldn't mind some company, if you're interested." He smiled as he tried to button his vest and straighten his tie. "You can name the restaurant. I'll leave this one to you."

"Can ye give me a few? Just got to get me students underway for their homework assignment, is all."

"You're a very structured professor-in-the-making. I must say that I'm very impressed with your dedication to your students and research. I'm sure the faculty could use a great scholar like you."

Colin kept one eye on his students as he semi-focused on Evelyn. "How would ye know me ways with me students 'n me research?"

"From what I've been gathering on you. You're highly regarded at this institution."

"Yer very kind, but I'm not sure I'm ready to leave me fishin' business. Done it all me life. Started doin' it on me uncle's trawler when I was just a lad. Don't know if I even want the life of a lecturin' professor. It's the research I thirst for 'n that's all, I suppose."

"I've been learning a lot about you. You would be an asset to this academic institution. You've done so much and you have such a diverse past. If you were to join the faculty you would not just be performing lectures, you would also have your share of research."

Colin walked in front of the podium and stared at the students who were finishing the last note. "Don't forget to have your comparison ready for next day. That is all." The class packed up their books and left the lecture hall. Colin watched his class trickle out of the room, as he turned to Evelyn. "I don't think I can join ye for lunch. I'm sorry."

Her eyebrows lifted. "Oh, I'm sorry, I'm sure you must be too busy. You live a double life, so I've gathered." She took his hand. "Such big strong hands. You're a fisherman, as well as a brilliant scholar."

"Too many compliments in one day," he said, as he cleared his throat. "Can't really stay here, another class will enter soon enough."

"Of course. But what must I do to hear your enchanting singing once again?"

He smiled and placed his other hand on top of hers. "Yer too kind about me singin'. Ye know, I could use a wee bit of grub right about now. Some ale could wash it down nicely, don't ye think? In fact, whiskey would suit me better."

She took his arm and he led her out of the lecture hall as the next class entered. It was midday. Colin took Evelyn to one of his favorite pubs in the heart of London. She winced at the unkempt ambiance, but wore a smile at all times.

"Fancy this place I do, 'cause it usually has musicians who sometimes play Celtic tunes. Reminds me of home, it does. Also, I'm not lookin' me best today. At this place it's acceptable to not always have yer best clothes on, if ye know what I'm sayin'?" They sat and examined the menus. Colin lowered his menu to the table. "Chancellor?"

"Please, call me Evelyn. I hope you don't mind that I call you by your Christian name?"

"I don't, Evelyn. How ye know so much about me?"

"I looked up your file. That's easy to do when one is the chancellor of the university. Do you live permanently in London?"

"I don't know where I permanently live."

She smiled at him. "Shall we order some drinks?"

Colin bowed his head to her. "Please."

"How do you feel about Champagne?"

Colin chuckled. "Ale 'n whiskey would do me fine. Don't think a place like this would even carry anythin' like Champagne."

"Of course not." She smiled. "What do you like best?"

86

"What ye like best?"

She took his hand in hers. "I know what I like best." She smiled and glanced down at her menu. "Are you teaching any more lectures today?"

"Done for the day, so I am."

"Then, you can come to my house after we eat."

"Sorry, but I can't do that. You're the chancellor of the university. Shouldn't even be here with ye now, should I?"

"Is that the reason? Or is it because you find me attractive?" She squeezed his hands as they rested over the table. "It's warm in here. Why don't you remove your jacket?"

"Why don't ye order, whilst I go fetch us some drinks, eh?" He fumbled as he stood up and he prodded to the bar. Colin returned with a bottle of whiskey and a bottle of wine. He removed his jacket and flopped into his chair. "Thought ye'd like some wine. Got ye Italian red."

Evelyn laughed. "Do you expect me to drink an entire bottle of wine in one sitting?"

"Whatever ye don't finish won't go to waste." He uncorked the wine and poured her a full glass. He opened his whiskey and filled his glass as well. "Bottoms up, Chancellor, I mean Evelyn."

"Better yet, lets toast to your brilliance."

"Brilliance? Too many compliments for an undeservin' sailor like me."

"Nonsense. They're well deserved. How enchanting it is that I'm having drinks with a professional time-traveler."

Colin laughed so hard he spewed whiskey out of his mouth. "Professional? I stink at it, so I do."

"There's no written instructions to be found on how to time-travel, is there?"

Colin sat back and scratched the reddish bristles on his chin. "Nay, there's not; just loads of trial 'n error, is all, but more error than trial."

"Why do you say that? You're here to tell your story, aren't you?"

"Just by the mere scrapin' on me arse, I am."

She sipped her wine. "You make me laugh. You can be quite amusing."

"Don't try to be," he said, as he drank up his whiskey. A three-piece band set up their stage in the corner of the tiny pub. One man had a fiddle, the other had a bodhrán, and the other had a tin whistle in his hands. "Ye see, the music will soon start. Love this pub, so I do."

The music began. Evelyn caressed Colin's hand. He slowly pulled his hand toward himself.

"Colin? You're not married, are you?"

The music was melodic, filled with old Irish folklore. Colin turned to the chancellor.

"Married? I'm not. Are ye?"

"No, I never married."

"But I've got a lass, whom will soon be me wife. Don't mind spendin' some time with ye, but this shan't continue. Ye takin' me hand 'n spendin' time together like this."

"Oh? Where is she, then? How come I never see you with her?"

"'Cause I'm always here 'n there, that's why. She stays with her aunt."

"Oh, I see." Evelyn crossed her arms in front of her. "When's the wedding?"

"Don't know as of yet. Just not ready to set a date, not with me time-travelin' schedule 'n such."

"I see." Colin had one ear perked, as he listened the instrumental music play. He poured his last bit of whiskey into his glass. "Do you always drink this much?" she asked, with her eyes widened with amazement.

He grinned. "A man of me size can take large quantities, don't ye think?"

"Of course. It's just the afternoon, but I suppose you know what you're doing."

"Surely, I do. A sailor is what I am. A man of the sea knows how to finish a fine bottle of Irish whiskey, don't ye think?"

"Oh, yes, you are a man of the sea, aren't you? Forgive me. I hope I didn't offend you in any way."

He chuckled. "How's that? Offend me, ye didn't. Ye should watch me academic advisor take his potshots at me. Then, surely, ye'd catch me grow rather offended, I must say, so I should."

"That bad?"

"Ah, 'n so he is." He scanned the patrons sitting in the pub. "Thanks again for rustlin' the fundin' for me research, which can continue 'n all is well. I'm supposin' a woman of yer great stature can surely get the fundin' when needed, eh?"

She beamed at him. "I'm quite enjoying this place. The musicians are worth listening to."

"I'll drink to that one, I will, 'n so should ye," he said, holding the wine bottle above her glass.

Her hand covered the top of her glass. "Not for me. I've only had one glass and that's my limit. Would you like to finish the rest?"

"One glass? Surely, ye can down yerself another glass? I wouldn't mind seein' the chancellor of the university get herself blitzed, so I wouldn't."

"Oh, I think one is all for me at this time. Please, a man of your size and of the sea at that, can definitely finish this lovely bottle. Please."

"I've already drank me quota today. I have a history of gettin' stupid if I go beyond it."

"What are you alluding to?" she asked, with a snicker. "You? Stupid? I couldn't imagine. You wouldn't take advantage of me now would you?"

He glared at her with a puzzled expression. "Now, what ye meanin' by that?

"I'm just a helpless woman and you're such a big, strong man."

89

"Nay, I wouldn't." He poured the wine into his empty whiskey glass. "Cheers."

She listened to the music, while she watched Colin drink. When the band completed their set, they stepped away from their musical corner. Evelyn noticed Colin's eyes looked heavy.

"Are you alright?"

He smiled. "I am. Just shouldn't be mixin' red wine with whiskey, is all. Mixin' can make me even stupider." He guzzled the whiskey glass full of wine.

"Can you stand up?"

"Of course." He fumbled as he stood, almost knocking his chair to the floor.

"Colin, can you walk?" She took his arm.

He tried to put one foot in front of the other, but staggered each time.

"Shall I call for a carriage?"

"No need. Me flat is near. How about ye?" He tripped several times.

"Oh, my?" She said. "I'll get a carriage and we'll go to my home."

A carriage taxi was stopped at the side of the road. The driver had to help Colin in. Colin climbed in with difficulty. They traveled to her house. She had the driver help Colin in. Colin staggered in and slumped on her satin loveseat. She helped him remove his hat and coat. Colin tried to smile at her.

"Y-ye know ye not need to do all this for me, Chancellor. Why ye doin' all this? Not used to this, I'm not."

His words slurred so much so that he tried to speak as little as possible from embarrassment.

"Colin, you poor dear, you really are quite intoxicated, aren't you?"

He chuckled. "Drunk? Aye, maybe just a wee tad. Oh, Lord knows I've been worse."

He sat with his strong legs spread wide apart. He kept flicking his long forelock back; but then would fiddle with the buttons on his vest. Slender hands rested on his chest. Each button on his vest became undone, one by one. He took her hands and clenched them in his.

"What ye doin' that for? Me vest can stay on, don't ye think?"

"I think you need to relax, instructor," she whispered, in his ear and continued on his shirt.

"So, ye remove me shirt?"

She completed the job. His vest and shirt were unbuttoned. Her hands traveled beneath his undershirt. She boldly rubbed his pectoral muscles. He spewed out a drunken laugh as she delicately pulled off his undershirt. His eyes were half shut, almost as if he were in a dream state.

"Y-ye got me bare chest here! Don't know why yer doin' all this? Yer the chancellor."

"Yes, I am the chancellor."

"Well, ye can't be goin' after this like ye is. Ye just can't."

She laughed. "You're so funny when you're drunk. What am I going after?"

"I-I'm knowin' what yer up to. Yer after me tanker, aren't ye?"

She lowered her eyebrows. "Tanker?"

He pointed at her. "Yez knowin' about me tanker. Not for sale, it isn't."

"Now, I don't know how I'm going to get you to my bed. You're much too big to carry. You'll have to allow me to lead you."

"Yer bed? Shite! I-I've got to be gettin' me way home, I do."

He struggled to stand up. She took his hand and led him to her bedroom.

"I find the tattoos on your arm to be very intriguing."

He giggled. "So, ye noticed me tattoo?"

91

"What is it a picture of?" She asked pressing herself against him, while he tried not to topple over.

"It's me ship, of course. It ye follow it carefully, its gotta fisherman's rope attached to it, windin' all the way up me shoulder 'n to me chest. Surely, it's not that easy to see, 'cause of me reddish fuzz on me chest, that covers it up."

"How extraordinary."

He saw the bed. He closed his eyes and opened them again. The room was a blur. He tried to focus, but couldn't. He stepped toward the bed, but didn't make it. He crashed to the floor with a heavy thump. He lay flat on his belly with his head pressed against the floor. "O-oh, feck! Have mercy on me."

He sighed with every breath. She stood beside him and watched him try to move to a different position. He struggled to get off his face.

"Shall I help you up?"

With him on the floor, beside the bed, she removed the pins from her salt and pepper colored-hair and threw it behind her shoulders. He rolled over onto his back with his eyes half closed. She worked on getting at least one of his heavy boots off.

"Just dream and all will be well."

She hesitantly brought her lips to his. He slowly reciprocated. They kissed. She huffed and screeched while she lusted over him. His kisses were reluctant with partial drool, dripping from his lips. She rubbed his hard pectoral muscles in a circular motion. He found himself breathing heavily at moments, but then he would pause. She rubbed her hands over his crotch, where she felt an astonishing hardened mass. She yelped with excitement and unbuttoned each button of his trousers. She cupped her hands over it and rubbed with vigor. She could feel it almost exploding inside his trousers. She worked and worked on getting his trousers off, but it was too late. His eyes were half closed. He lay on her floor, bare-chested with one arm resting over his face. His trousers were still on, and saturated. She sat beside him and sighed.

"Now, what I'm I going to do with you, half asleep and drunk on my floor? You drenched your trousers and made a dreadful mess." He didn't respond, except for his vibrating snore. She stood up and watched him. "My, my you are handsome, but what a drunken state you're in."

He snored and snorted at times. She took his shirt, vest, and blazer and gently hung them in her closet. She wrapped a silk robe around her body and pulled the blanket from the bed to throw over him. She looked out the window to notice dusk setting in.

Chapter Twelve

A fortnight had passed where Colin walked along the campus grounds with Sasha.

"Mr. Limmerick, you act strange. You have problems with Miss Amoli? You not with her any more?"

"Been avoidin' her, so I have."

"You do so bad thing. She find me so many times in lab, always looking for you. You must go to her."

"Aye. I just don't know anymore. Am I worth it all for her, I don't know?"

"She say she go on time-travel expedition."

"Rosa don't want her there, that's for sure." Colin stopped walking. "Are we ready to go, or what, mate?"

"Da, we ready. You decide if Miss Amoli come. I cannot listen you and your love life."

"Yer the feckin' wanker who's married 'n leadin' Rosa on. Did ye tell her yer married yet?"

"I do it when time is right."

"Ye tell her, or I'll tell her."

"I kill you. Remember, I so good with sword you not so good. I cut your throat."

"By the time ye draw yer bleedin' sword I'd already have me hands wrapped 'round yer neck."

"You would have no hands, because I would chop them off."

Colin stepped closer to him and brought his face to Sasha's. "Try it." He took a deep sigh. "What's happened to us? We can't even control our personal lives 'n here we are playin' God with all this time-travel shite."

"My personal life is under control. It is you who cannot control so many things."

"How long has it been since ye last saw yer wife?"

"Not long enough."

94

"I would never feel that way about the woman I married. Yer a bleedin' shite."

"You not get married. You over forty and not married."

"Amoli would have us married already if it was solely up to her. I just want this final time-travel expedition out of the bleedin' way, is all."

"You run from her. You run like child. Face her and tell her wedding is off."

"It's not off, ye fecker! Runnin', surely I'm not."

"She wants to come on time-travel."

"It's no place for her. I'm avoidin' her, 'n the chancellor."

"Chancellor? Why?"

"Ah, long story. Rosa was right. I'm avoidin' her, too."

"You avoid Miss Amoli, chancellor, and Rosa? You stay away from all women? Who you screw now?"

"Me trusty hand does the job most of the time. It works quite well, actually."

"I not do that, I have real thing."

"Where yez goin' these nights?"

"Miss Rosa is still good. She almost thirty years, she better be good."

"Feckin' arsehole is what yez are. Yer gonna live to one hundred, no doubt, 'cause ye have no soul. The more I get to know ye, the less I like ye."

"You should have died years ago. Why you still here? If you not drink yourself to death, you die of syphilis like your uncle. You stick your pole in too many places."

Colin's expression changed. "Problem is I'm always langered, so I don't know where I'm puttin' it." He stood closer to Sasha. "Listen to me, mate. Don't breathe a bleedin' word to Rosa about this. Might of plowed the chancellor. Don't know for sure."

"Where you do this?"

"Her place."

"You not know if you give it to her? Why you not ask her?"

"Avoidin' her like the plague, so I am."

"Mr. Limmerick, you always in such big mess. Miss Amoli will cry."

"Wait just a minute, mate! What if I didn't plow her?"

"You at her home and you not know this? You do it. I know you do it."

"I found meself on her floor by her bed. I was dressed. She was in her bathrobe."

Sasha grinned. "Strange behavior from you, always. Why you on her floor?"

"Can't remember, really. She didn't say much to me when I awoke, so I left."

"You must tell Miss. Amoli this, nyet?"

"Lets just go on our prehistoric journey 'n get on with shuttin' the pathway through time 'n forget all this shite. When we leavin' here?"

"We can leave tomorrow, do you want?"

Colin stepped back while he scanned the campus building's façade. "Tomorrow ye say? Aye, I rather fantasy the sound of that, so I do."

"Tomorrow we leave, you me, and Miss Rosa."

"Me ship, how about me ship? I've got to send a telegraph message to Ed." Colin sighed. "Tomorrow's too soon."

"You so anxious, always bothering me. Always asking when we go, now I say you we go tomorrow and you not want. You are crazy man."

"Just don't know how to tell Amoli. Don't really know if I can bear to be apart from her. Don't know what to do, really."

"She say she will come. I not care if she does, only Rosa cares."

"Travelin' through a passage of time, or via a vortex, is not for Amoli. Don't want Amoli to go through it, surely, I don't. But can't imagine bein' away from her 'n all."

"So she come. Settled."

"What to do, I don't feckin' know!" Colin held his hands over his head as he raised his voice. Sasha focused on a dog defecating on the sidewalk. He then pulled a package of cigarettes from his blazer pocket. "I'm gonna see Amoli just now 'n I'll get the answer from her, how's that? Then she'll bloody well come."

"Miss Rosa say no. Then what?"

Colin rubbed his hands over his face. "What for? Why she so against Amoli?"

Sasha lit a match and lit the tip of the cigarette that hung from his lips. "Why you think? Rosa and Miss Amoli not like each other. They hate each other. Not good situation. You caused all trouble, Mr. Limmerick."

"Enough of this rubbish. I'll be off now to see Amoli 'n I'll lay everythin' in front of her 'n the chips will fall as they will, don't ye think, mate?"

"This all take so long. Stand up to ladies and you will see. You never do."

"I'm not standin' up to these two lasses. They's both too headstrong for me to deal with. I'm gettin' too old for this, so I am."

Sasha laughed in Colin's face. "You so funny man."

"I've got to get someone to teach the first year course. Cushing surely won't. Timothy Duncan, perhaps he may, or may not. He 'n I, never got on well."

"You say Timothy Duncan hate you?"

"So he does. Don't know what I bloody well done to him. He's one of Cushing's protégés."

Both men stared at the ground.

"Just go to Miss Amoli and say her." Sasha noticed someone approach them from the corner of this eye. "Speak of devil, your Miss Amoli has arrived."

Colin turned to find Amoli standing behind him. "Ah, lass 'n there ye are standin' before me."

"Where have you been for so many days, even weeks? You are very much avoiding me. I don't like this. No, I don't like this at all."

Colin stepped close to her and rubbed her shoulders. "We need to chat 'n now is as good as any." He noticed a tear trickle down her cheek. "Please, don't think ye need to forgive me for anythin' 'cause yev only been too good." He pulled her toward him and held her tightly in his arms. "I'm so sorry."

"Why have you been avoiding me?"

He glanced at Sasha. "Could ye leave us for a bit, mate?"

Sasha smiled as he smoked his cigarette. He walked away. Colin led Amoli to a bench and motioned for her to sit beside him. "I know that yer anxious for the weddin' arrangements to begin. A time-travelin' expedition is near 'n ye won't be seein' me for I don't know how long."

She tried to suck back her tears. "How long?"

"Don't know."

"I don't even think you will be missing me. I think you no longer love me," she said with a few sniffles.

"I'd be thinkin' about ye every second. But me question here is why me? Why such a lovely young wench as yerself fancies a drunken ol' sailor like me?"

"Colin, why do you speak this way?"

He ran his finger along her lips. "Don't think I'm worthy of ye. Don't think ye'd be happy with a shite like me."

Her head hung down. "I love you, Colin. What are you saying to me?"

"You deserve so much better, lass. Our two religions will continue to clash 'n we're just not a brilliant match."

"Are you leaving me?"

"It's best if I do. Really, I'm doin' ye such a grand favor, so I am." He held her tightly in his arms. He pulled a handkerchief from his blazer pocket to wipe her eyes. "Yer father would surely fancy the idea, don't ye think?"

98

"My father is very fond of you, Colin." She buried herself in his arms. "I'm never going to let you go, so now you will have to marry me."

"It's not as if I don't wish to marry ye. I want to, but I'm not a good man for yez. Haven't even been to confession lately, can ye imagine that? It's somethin' Catholics do when they've sinned."

"Sinned?" She wiped her eyes and stepped back. "What did you do?"

"Ye need to marry a good man, not someone like me." He took her hand and held it to his lips. "If I don't leave now, I'll start to slobber like a child. Ye can't have me doin' that, now can ye?" He turned away from her and walked a few steps. He stopped and turned to her. "Don't know if I can live without ye. Don't know if I can. I'll be time-travelin' in a day or so. I'm supposin' I'll have to, won't I?"

"What did you do? Were you with Miss Emanuel?"

"I wasn't. Ye can ask her about that, aye, ye can." He bowed to her and lifted his bowler hat from his head. "I must be goin' now." She stood and gazed at him in silence. Her tears continued to roll off her face and onto her bright colored sari. "I want to look at ye. I can see some of yer tears are ceasin' 'n maybe some anger is comin' across yer face. Ah, but I need to look at ye a wee bit more."

"I hate you, Colin Limmerick! I hate you so much that I could kill you."

He bit his bottom lip and looked at her as if in a trance. "Yer beautiful when yer mad, so ye are."

"Just be off, then! Go! Leave me be, you awful man!"

"You'll surely make a fine gent happy. I'll be off, but just a long last look at ye, is all I ask. Yer in me heart, always."

99

Chapter Thirteen

That weekend, Colin worked with his crew to make the final catch into the early morning. He glanced at Eddy as he wiped the sweat from his face. He took a half-empty bottle of whiskey and placed it on his lips.

"Lad? Yer actin' the maggot, aren't yez?" asked Eddy.

"Ye won't be seein' me for a bit. Don't know when you'll be seein' me again, Ed."

"Where ye goin' about now?"

Colin grinned. "Ah, ye know it's a secret, don't yez?"

Eddy rolled his eyes back. "How's the weddin' plans with your little foreign lass?"

"Don't ask."

"Oh, for shite's sake, Captain. When ya gonna hold onto a wench?"

"Feck it. I'm not the marryin' type, so I'm not."

A disheveled looking Lorelei staggered by Colin. "Too early in the bleedin' mornin' for yaz all to be talkin' so sober, I'd say."

"Blyme! So sorry, yer majesty." Colin blurted.

"What ya doin' up so early?" Eddy asked Lorelei. She tried to fix her undersized corset. "Yaz lookin' like yar bubblin' over as usual, ya slut."

She pretended to slap Eddy across the face.

"We gotta finish the job, don't ya think? The fish returned to our waters. Can't waste a good thing, eh, Lorelei?" Colin said with one eye on the nets.

She nudged her knee into Colin's groin. "It was nice bein' in your bed again, Limmerick."

Eddy's face was still stern. "Oh, sakes, Captain! Go back to your little foreign wench 'n marry her."

Colin worked on winding the net. "Can't do that, Ed."

"Eddy, shut yar feckin' face," Lorelei grunted.

"It don't matter, really. What's done is done," Colin said, with a stone-like expression.

Lorelei nestled herself to Colin. "How about a little later? Some afternoon fun?"

Colin continued to work. "Sure, some afternoon fun, it is. Don't forget the whiskey, though. I don't mean rum. If ye bring me rum, I swear I'll toss it overboard." She grinned and stepped into the galley.

"Ed, I've been on me feet all night. Goin' to get some sleep. Wake me when we reach the Quays. I'm meanin' to see me parents 'n such. Been so long since I've seen them," Colin said.

"Don't start up with Lorelei again. Makin' a big mistake," Eddy said, nodding his head.

"Finally, I saw meself in the mirror 'n what I saw wasn't pretty. Amoli deserves better than I, so she does."

When the *Atlantic Mermaid* docked at the Dublin Quays, Colin stepped off and hustled to his parents' house. There was a heavy knock at his parents' door. Both Grace and Brian answered it. When they saw their son standing before them, Grace began to cry.

"Oh, dear Lord, what a fine surprise to see ya, son," Brian said, taking Colin by the hand and pulling him into the house.

Colin took a deep breath and smiled. He hugged and kissed both his parents.

"Don't have long, but just wanted to see yez both."

"Yar lookin' well, Colin, I must say," Brian said.

"No, he isn't," Grace expressed. "Ya look tired 'n run down."

"Aye, so I am."

His father took his coat and hung it in the closet. "Can ya stay for a meal? Your mother is makin' your favorite."

"Aye, but then I must get back to the vessel. There's too much to do."

"Ethan 'n Mary will be joinin' us for dinner. Their little lads are with Mary's parents today, so they won't be here, I'm afraid," Grace said, while she tugged on Colin's arm to bring him to the table.

Colin sat and watched his mother place a plate of biscuits before him. "Mum, thank-ye. I've got somethin' I must confess to both of yez."

The door opened wide and Ethan and Mary stepped in. "Oh, look Ethan, Colin is here! What a surprise it is!" Mary shouted.

Brian gestured for his younger son and daughter-in law to sit at the table. "Please, sit. Colin says he wants to tell us something."

Colin stood up and walked to the server in the parlor, which contained an ample liquor stash. He poured a full glass of whiskey and walked back to the table. Grace forced a smile.

"Let me guess. Are ya gettin' married to that young foreign lass from India?"

"I wish it was that."

Ethan glanced at his father. "I don't think anything you tell us will shock us anymore. You've made our parents go gray before they were ready. What is it?"

"I'm goin' on a prehistoric journey. It'll be me third expedition. Me research at the university has been based on it."

Brian glanced at his wife. "Prehistoric journey? What do ya mean?"

Colin took a few large gulps of whiskey. "I mean that this will be me third expedition comin' up. Need to go again, so I do, 'cause I made a bleedin' mess out of prehistory, so I did."

Ethan stood up and walked to his brother. "Are ya referrin' to time-travel? Or are ya just stinkin' drunk?"

"Drunk? I wish I was."

Ethan's facial expression froze. "Yar talkin' nonsense."

102

Colin stood up to face his brother. "Nonsense? I'm tellin' yez all that I have become a time-traveler, a rather dreadful one at that."

Colin's family members glanced at each other. Grace raced into the kitchen and brought out a pot of stew. The plates were already set on the table. Brian hurried to get a place setting for Colin. Brian stood beside Colin.

"Time-travel? How?"

"Ya met Sasha, Dr. Dimitrikov. He invented a time-travel device. It doesn't always work precisely, but it does help teleport people from our time, 1909 A.D. to travel through a vortex or passage through time. I know it does, 'cause I've done it meself already, twice."

"Sasha does that?" Brian asked, with a confused expression on his face.

Mary smiled. "So, Colin, you've done this already twice'n you're going to do this again?"

Colin peered at his empty glass of whiskey. "Aye."

"When?" Mary asked.

"As soon as I make it back to London."

Mary sat back in her chair. "Oh, my word, Colin, you are so courageous. With your good looks and wits about ya, you'll be in all the newspapers. You'll be a celebrity."

Ethan placed his hand on his wife's shoulder. "Mary, your days with Colin are long done. Don't wanna hear another thing about it. Time-travel, huh? How stupid."

Colin glanced at his younger brother. "Stupid? Perhaps."

"Time-travel, hmm…what time period did you go to?" Ethan asked, while he broke a bread roll.

"Firstly, I went 10,000 years into the past. Secondly, I went 40,000 years. The first time went smoother than the second, to say the least."

"Why'd ya do that for?" Brian asked.

"Me academic research is on *Megaloceros giganteus*, yez all know it. I wanted to prove to me academic advisor that *Megaloceros giganteus* came to its demise by bein'

103

sexually selected against. Darwin wrote chapters on natural selection 'n I wanted to prove me point."

"And did ye?" Brian asked.

"I did."

Mary helped Grace place helpings of stew on everyone's plate.

"Let's eat, shall we?" Grace said, with an encouraging voice. She took Mary's hand and held it in hers as they sat at the table. Everyone bowed their heads to pray. Colin found himself praying aloud.

"Thank-ye, God, for allowin' me to survive the first two attempts of the initial prehistoric expeditions. I'm hopin' ye will allow me to survive the third."

Grace lifted her head and looked at Colin. "Son, are ya expectin' danger?"

He paused, before he answered. "Aye."

Ethan blurted a cracking laugh. "Oh, please, stop this rubbish. You've finally lost yar mind. Time-travel? How absurd."

Colin glared at his brother. "I don't care if ye believe me. The university asked for proof, 'n so I gave them proof. Take it up with them, if ye wish. I'm too tired to deal with yer bullshite, Ethan. Go feck yerself."

Ethan sprung up from his chair. "There ya have it! This is so typical of ya to speak to me like that. Yar really terrible, aren't ya? Ya think because ya moved to London to become a great scholar that ya have the right to speak to me like that."

"Ethan, please," Grace pleaded.

"Ya banged me wife before she married me. Who wasn't in yar bed in this town?"

Mary sank into her chair and turned a shade of red. "Ethan, maybe we should go now, hmm?"

"I'm tired of everyone around here making it look like Colin is some kinda God. He can never do any wrong, because he bought our parents their house. How nice of him. So, now this wonderful sweet brother of mine time-travels as well. How nice."

Colin turned to Ethan. "Don't ye ever think how much I wanted what ye have? I'd love to be married to someone like Mary with a couple of kids to boot. Yer just too much of an arse to realize how good you've got it. Arsehole!"

"Like hell! Ya always wanted to bag as many wenches as possible because ya got the biggest cock on this side of the Atlantic. Yar playboy lifestyle suits ya pretty well, I'd say."

Colin sighed and rolled his eyes back. "Yer a stupid feck, so ye is."

"Academic, so what? Yar still a lush and always a lush and yar cock is still in every whore's mouth."

Colin stood up and made a fist. "I hate yer bleedin' guts. It's like I don't even know yez."

"Ye never had much to do with me. I'd say all I know about ya is yar reputation."

"Reputation? What's all this I keep hearin' about me reputation? I left Dublin years ago as a young fisherman."

Brian stood up with an alarmed expression on his face. "That's enough! Don't go about another scuffle in me house. Yaz two brothers never got along. Never!"

Colin lifted one eyebrow. "Ah, feck. Thought I'd come here to explain this double life I've been livin'."

"Don't care," grunted Ethan.

Brian walked to where Colin was sitting. "I believe what yar sayin', son."

Grace stood in the corner and cried. "Colin, can't ya just move back to Dublin? And, why aren't yaz gettin' married?"

Colin placed his face in his hands. "'Cause I'm a feckin' arse, that's why. I also won't be movin' back to Dublin any time soon, Mum, at least not yet."

"Time-travel, how absurd. Nobody can ever believe what comes out of yar mouth," Ethan said, while standing up from the table.

Colin stood up to face Ethan. "Call it what ye wish, don't care, really."

Brian smiled. "Son, I believe ya. Surely, I do."

"Believe it, Dad, if ye will. I came here today to make Mum cry, to get Ethan in another one of his huffs, 'n yet I can always count on ye."

Brian went to Colin to pat him on the back. "Ya can always depend on me."

Colin smiled. "Well, I've wasted enough of all of yez time. I bes' be headin' back to the ship. Got loads to do still before the weekend's end." He walked to the closet for his coat. "Oh, 'n Ethan, I'll tell yez why I'm not gettin' married."

Colin put on his coat and placed his tweed cap upon his head. He wrapped his wool scarf around his neck. Ethan sighed with frustration.

"What now?"

"I slept with the chancellor of the university, so I think. A lovely wench."

Ethan looked at Mary. "She?"

"Aye, a *she*, so *she* is." Colin chuckled, hugged both his parents and left.

Ethan paced the room. "Yer son is a shite," he said, waving his finger at his parents.

Chapter Fourteen

Colin returned to London, late Sunday night. He walked down the street, exhausted and made his way to the entrance of his flat.

"Colin," a tiny female voice blurted, while he fumbled through his coat pocket in search of his key. He turned his head several times to see whom it was who called his name.

"Colin, I'm cold. I'm very saddened from our last chat," Amoli said, standing behind a lamppost. "I haven't slept the weekend."

He removed his coat and threw it over her shoulders. "Lass, it's late. Why ye out here? It's even snowin', so it is. Ye need to be with yer family now, don't ye think?"

"We need to discuss. I know you love me. I know that is for certain. I also know Miss Emanuel loves you, but I think you love me more than her. Tell me."

"Tell ye? I won't lie to ye, I love her, but in a different way. I love ye in a way that I would spend me life with ye."

Her face gleamed. "I knew it."

He took her cold hands and rubbed them in his. "Lass, ye 'n me can't marry."

"Why are ye doin' this to me?" she shouted, with tears.

"'Cause I'm no good for ye, is why. Did ye tell yer father?"

"Of course not. We need to set our date and plan our wedding."

"Nay, me love, we can't be doin' that. If we were to marry," he said, and took a deep breath. "I would, surely, destroy yer life. Ye mean far too much to me. Don't wanna be hurtin' ye, so I don't."

"But, you're hurting me right now. I want to stay with you tonight, Colin."

"Think it's best, so I do, take ye home meself. Yer father already wants to kill me."

"Don't say that. He is very fond of you."

"I need to be up very early. I'm meetin' Sasha 'n Rosa in the lab at half six."

"I'm coming with you."

"Yer not. Rosa won't have it, 'n that's where she's right. Remember that episode with the cave lion? That was a mild situation. Travelin' through time is life threatenin'. Prehistoric beasts are just that; they's beasts."

"I'm staying with you tonight. I don't understand why you're running from me."

"Runnin'? Ye think I'm runnin'?"

"That's exactly what you are doing. I don't like it, no I don't." He took her hand and led her to his flat. She kept his coat wrapped around her body and sat down. He sat beside her. She fell into his arms and cried. "Will you share your bed with me tonight?"

He removed his tweed cap and rubbed his face. "Shite, I don't know what to do."

She nestled her head in his arms. "Just love me; that's what you should do."

"Amoli, do you realize who I am? I drink. Most of the time, I'm drunk. I'm a sailor. I've slept with other types of women."

"Bad women?"

He looked at her. "Aye. But, I'm no better than them. And the worst of it is I'm a time-traveler. Ye can't get worse than that, so ye can't."

"I think that is very exciting."

"It's deadly stupid is what it is."

He took his coat off of her and brought her inside his building to his flat. "Yer sleepin' in here tonight, not with me beside ye." He led her to his bedroom. "I'll sleep in the other room, if ye can fancy that."

"I need you beside me."

He took her in his arms. "I can't anymore with yez. It's not possible, so it's not."

"I'm going to time-travel with you, Colin."

He sighed. "Why ye doin' this, lass?"

"I can never love anyone as much as I love you. I will not let you out of my sight, Colin Limmerick."

"So, ye should. There's better out there for ye, lass."

"Stop it! I should write to your mother and tell her what you are saying to me."

He chuckled. "Ye want her address?"

"Yes, in fact, I do. She'll be very upset with you."

"Me mother, has seen 'n heard much worse from me. Nothin' ye say in a letter will even phase me mum, surely, that's the truth."

"Did you tell your parents about me yet?"

"Aye."

"And what did they say?"

"I don't remember, really. They was happy when I told 'im."

"Well, I'm going to write to your mother and tell her how you think so little of yourself."

"Go ahead."

He noticed that she was removing her sari. He quickly turned from her and shut the door. It was 6:30 in the morning. Colin opened one eye and watched the sun peek through the clouds. He had tried to position himself into a comfortable position, but one could only get so comfortable on a hardwood floor. He sat up and rubbed his face, while he flicked back his long hair. The door of his bedroom opened and Amoli stood before him undressed. He quickly dropped his eyes to the floor.

"Haven't ye found yer clothes yet, lass?"

"Oh, I'm so very sorry."

"Yer not, I'm sure of it."

He hoisted himself from the floor. She glanced at his bare chest. He was only wearing boxer shorts.

"You look very inviting to me, Colin."

He focused on the floor. "I can't say the same for ye, 'cause there's no chance I'm castin' me eyes upon yer beauty. I have to get dressed 'n get to the lab. Already I'm runnin' late, so I am. Please, get dressed." He ran to the lavatory to wash up. She got dressed and sat down to wait. When he was washed and dressed he noticed her sitting quietly. "Lass, yer not comin' with me. Please go home. It's no place for ye."

"I'm coming. You love me and you desire me, so why are you going with Miss. Emanuel?"

"She's an archeologist, that's why."

"I'm coming with you."

He grabbed her arm. "Have it yer way. Ye should tell yer parents first, don't ye think?"

"I don't trust that you will wait for me.

"Oh, mother of God! I'll wait for ye."

"Since when you care about my parents?"

"I told me parents. I figured, this time I'm sure to die. They needed to know."

"Is that what you really think?" She began to cry.

"I almost died last time. I'm meanin' what I'm sayin' to yez. It's easy to die if one time-travels. We shouldn't be playin' God, nay, we shouldn't. I made a bleedin' mess out of things, now I must lie in me bed 'n take what God has in store for me."

"Is this what Dr. Dimitrikov thinks?"

"Dr. Dimitrikov, surely will live to be one hundred."

"Is this what Miss Emanuel thinks?"

"She deplores time-travel with a bloody vengeance. She's a clever wench 'n, she'll survive, no doubt."

"Oh, well, I should tell my parents, or they will worry very much."

"And so they'll have good reason to. Just tell them you'll be with me. I'm sure they'll be relieved," he said, with sarcasm in his voice.

"Do you promise to wait for me?"

"Promise." He placed his coat around her again and firmed up his bowler hat on his head. They made their way to the street level. He bent down to her and kissed her on the cheek. "Go to yer family 'n tell them you'll be away. I'll be awaitin' ye, but don't take too long."

Her face gleamed with joy and she ran to her aunt's house. He pulled the collar of his blazer toward his neck and wrapped his tartan scarf around. Light flurries scattered the streets as he entered the university building of Natural History. He entered the laboratory to find Sasha and Rosa.

"Finally, Colin. We have a busy morning a head of us and it's already after seven. We have to catch a train, remember?" Rosa said, pointing to the clock on the wall.

"Aye, aye. Just waitin' for Amoli, 'n we'll be off."

There was silence in the room. Sasha glanced at Rosa and pretended to be interested in his physics notes. Rosa's facial expression changed.

"We're running out of time, because we're waiting for who?"

Colin crossed his arms in front of him. "We's waitin' for Amoli. We's no longer a couple 'n such, 'cause I don't think it's right we marry 'n she's hurtin' a wee bit now. She's insistin' on comin' along with us."

Rosa took a few heavy steps toward Colin. "Are you mad?"

He focused on the floor. "Likely, so likely I may be."

Sasha tried to resist his laughter. "We will wait for Miss Amoli and we will go, da?"

"No, Sasha, this can't be. We are going on a dangerous expedition. We're not going to the fair. This is ridiculous. She can't come."

Colin paced around the room. "She needs to come, 'cause she's feelin' kinda down just now, ye know."

"So, you ended it with her, finally. What made you do this?"

"I'm just not the best man for her, ye know."

111

Sasha snorted a few laughs. "Mr. Limmerick, you are fool."

"If she's no longer in your life, why are we wasting valuable time waiting for her?" Rosa asked, collecting papers of data.

"She insists on comin'. I can't stop her, really."

"Yes, you can!" Rosa shouted.

"I can't do that. She's made up her stubborn mind, 'n that's it."

"Mr. Limmerick, you fool for leaving her."

"Since when ye give a bloody shite who I'm with?"

Sasha continued to laugh. "You make big mistake, you know this. She is only woman in world who can put up with such awful man like you."

Rosa shoved Sasha. "Speak for yourself, Sasha."

"Don't really give a feck what Sasha thinks. We's gotta wait for Amoli's return 'n then we'll be off via Sasha's time-travel device that always fecks up."

Sasha's smirk transformed into a frown. "You show me who else in your London has device to take you back in time?" Sasha demanded, raising his voice, pointing his finger.

Rosa put her hand on Colin and Sasha's shoulders. "Gentlemen, please. Fine, we'll wait for Amoli. She is coming on this time-travel expedition. It's obvious there's nothing we can do about that. We can't afford to be in a constant scuffle over such silly matters."

The laboratory door swung opened and Amoli tore into the lab. "Hello!" she called out. "Hello everyone! Thank-you for waiting!" She had a large cloth bag stuffed with her belongings. She sat it on the floor beside Colin. "Are you glad I am coming with you?"

His eyes focused on the floor. "I'm glad to see ye, if that's what yer askin'? Not thinkin' this is the smartest thing yev ever thought of, I don't."

"Someone has to watch over you," she said, with a serious smile.

112

"Oh, good Lord, help me," Colin said, rubbing his rough hands over his face. Rosa glared at Amoli in silence.

"Shall we go, then?" Colin said to his colleagues.

Sasha gathered his things. "We must take train to harbor. Since we have much luck before, we must go to your Ireland."

Rosa rolled her eyes back and crossed her arms. "This is stupid. Why can't we just go through time here in England? It's such a bother to take a train and then a boat."

"We must close what you say is pathway, da? Then we must go same way we got there in first place. Who is so stupid? You are just woman, that is all."

"Perhaps, Rosa, changin' our departure place could feck things a tad, wouldn't ye think?"

Rosa glared at Colin and Sasha. "No, I don't think so at all. If Sasha's time-travel device can take us through time, then I don't think where we depart from is an issue."

Sasha sighed. "It is best we depart from same place as last time. We have much success then."

Rosa snickered. "Do you really think fighting Neanderthals head on is much success, Dr. Dimitrikov?"

Sasha threw his arms in the air. "Alright! We depart from England, but I cannot say all will be well."

Amoli leaned toward Colin. "Colin? Is Dr. Dimitrikov angry with Miss Emanuel?"

"Aye."

Amoli smiled. "Good."

Chapter Fifteen

Late that morning the four time-travelers sat on a train enroute to the harbor. Rosa and Sasha sat on the train in silence. Amoli continued to chat about marriage customs of India. Colin sat back and sipped on a glass of whiskey. He took a few deep breaths as he undid a button or two on his trousers. He gleamed at Amoli, while he felt the whiskey in his veins. He noticed Rosa in the corner of his eye.

"Rosa, ye got somethin' botherin' yez?" Colin asked, while he finished his drink.

"At least you could kindly cover up your display."

Amoli noticed Colin's eyes were fixed on her. "I'm so excited about traveling through time. Imagine me a time-traveler."

Rosa noticed Colin brought his hand to rest over his expanding crotch. She rolled her eyes back at him with disgust. "We're on a train, Colin. This is not your bed chamber in your ship."

Sasha sipped tea with a cigarette wedged between his fingers.

"You better not get us all into deep trouble, Amoli. I don't think you realize how serious your decision to come along really is," Rosa said, tightening her lips.

Sasha read some academic papers on time-travel. He pretended not to hear any voices. Colin straightened himself in his chair.

"Ah, Lord love ye, Rosa. Can ye just relax a bit? Amoli will thoroughly be in me supervision. No worries."

"Perhaps this is what you think. But Amoli Sharma is known to be a trouble-maker."

Amoli sprang from her chair. "Colin, did you hear what she called me?"

"Aye, lass, she called ye a trouble maker. Maybe that's what ye is, so be it. Just stay with me on this expedition, eh?"

Sasha lit a match. "Miss Amoli, you will have to be careful. Time-travel is not so good. Listen to Miss Rosa; she is right."

The train jigged and Amoli fell into Colin's arms. Rosa stared out the window. Amoli giggled and amerced herself in Colin's arms with her plunging cleavage in his face. Colin smiled as he forced himself not to kiss her.

They arrived at the harbor and boarded a small ferry. Colin sat by the window with a drink in his hand. Amoli sat beside him. Rosa paced down the aisle while Sasha smoked a cigarette.

Sasha sat across from Colin. "Mr. Limmerick, I just notice there are animals in water with so big teeth."

"Ye not referrin' to sharks now are ye?"

"Nyet."

Colin removed his hat. "Of course there's all kinds of strange marine life in our waters. Isn't that the reason for us to be venturin' through time? We've tainted our earth by misplacin' these prehistoric beasts." Colin took a deep breath and glanced out the window at a glimpse of marine life he had never seen. "Amazin' how these prehistoric species seem to keep themselves afloat. Interestin', that is."

Sasha put his cigarette out on his tea saucer. "I see primitive marine life in water. I do see it. I see all."

The ferry cut through some difficult conditions, but finally docked at Dublin. Colin stood up and stared out the window.

"Ah, me home sweet home."

Amoli clung to him. He took her bag as well as his own. Sasha took his bags as well as Rosa's. The four of them stepped off the ship and stared at each other.

115

"Well, Sasha, I suppose we should travel to Wicklow if you are being so precise?" Rosa said, wrapping a scarf around her delicate neck.

"Da, we must be precise."

Colin placed his tweed cap on his head. "I'll get us a carriage 'n we'll be off."

"We're in the middle of nowhere," Rosa commented.

"Where's there a dock, there should be a carriage, don't ye think?" Colin responded.

They arrived in Wicklow. Sasha scanned the rustic terrain.

"It is best we find exact spot of our previous departure, da?"

They walked around, but Colin felt the most comfortable in pinning the exact location. Amoli sat on her bag and watched them search. Colin stopped.

"Here, maybe, what ya think?"

Rosa looked at him. "Wasn't it over there somewhere?"

"Nyet, it was that way."

"I know it was here, surely I do," Colin said.

Amoli stood up and pranced around the tall grasses. She sang a few Indian love songs and giggled like a child. Sasha knelt to the ground to flip the dial of his time-travel device. He noticed Amoli in the background.

"Miss Amoli, stay close to group. We will be leaving soon."

"Colin!" she called. "Do I not look so very enchanting to you?"

Colin turned to notice her tumble onto her backside. "Lass? We's about to travel through time. I need ye near us."

She lay on her back and giggled. "Oh, my, Colin. What is that terrible smell?"

Sasha perked his head up. Rosa stopped looking, and Colin ran to Amoli. Sasha walked to Amoli.

"So, you find exact spot? Good girl."

116

The four of them banded together. An array of different colored smoke filled the air. Sasha pressed the final button of his device and they fell through the vortex of time.

Chapter Sixteen

Sasha opened his eyes and stared at the sky. He concentrated on moving his fingers and toes. He sighed with relief when he realized that he could. Then he moved his arms and legs, which put a smile on his face. He turned his head and saw Rosa lying next to him. He shoved her several times.

"Rosa!" he called. She twitched a few times. "Thanks so much you are okay."

She turned to him. "Sasha, yes, I feel fine and how are you?"

He slowly sat up. "No problem."

Amoli sat up a few meters away from them. "Oh! I feel terrible! Oh!"

Sasha noticed her. "Please, Miss Amoli, do not panic! We just go through time vortex. It is big ordeal!" Sasha helped Rosa up and they both ran to Amoli.

"I feel so terrible. My hair is so messy," Amoli said, as Sasha helped her up. "Where's Colin?'

Rosa had already found Colin. She jiggled his arms a bit.

"Sasha, Colin's not coming to." Rosa continued to tap his face. "I'm worried."

Sasha knelt beside Colin. "He will come out of this. He does this with time vortex. Give him some more minutes and he will soon wake and then throw up."

Amoli watched them tend to Colin. "I'm very worried."

Rosa looked at Amoli. "So am I."

"Stop all this fuss. Mr. Limmerick is very big boy. The bigger they are, the harder they fall."

Sasha amused himself. He cackled with laughter. Colin's eyes opened. Amoli ran to his side. He turned to his side to vomit. Rosa took Amoli's arm.

"Just let him be sick."

He fell onto his back. "Feel awful, so I do," Colin grunted.

Rosa looked at Sasha. "Fetch him some water. He could be dehydrated."

"Why you not ask Miss Amoli? I not even know where we pack water."

"It's in my brown bag over there by that tree stump. Stop wasting time and just get it!"

Sasha stomped over to her bag and found their supply of water. He looked up and noticed two men in the distance. He ignored them and continued to collect the jug of water. He carried it to where Colin lay with Rosa and Amoli at his side. Rosa took the jug of water and gave it to Colin, who was already sitting up.

Sasha looked at Colin. "So glad you are feeling better. If you were not, we could ask people over there for some help."

Colin's eyes widened. "What people? *Neanderthals? Paleolithics*? Who?"

"They not look like any of what you mention. I think I must check indicator. We could be in different time."

Rosa squealed. "Different time?" She stood up to face Sasha. "Did they look prehistoric at least?"

Sasha scratched his head. "I would say not."

"What were they wearing?" Rosa asked, in a panic.

"I did not examine clothes on these people. I am sorry. I must check indicator. It should say us what time we in."

Amoli helped Colin up with some difficulty. "Why is Miss Emanuel so very upset? She can't possibly be half as upset as I am right now."

Colin tried to stand straight. He kept one hand on Amoli's shoulder.

"I don't see any bloody people."

Sasha laughed. "Okay, they gone now. No more worries. We now carry on."

119

"No worries? Ye really must be outta yer bleedin' mind, man! If there's modern people here, we just went through a vortex of time that could of killed us all, for feck's sake."

Sasha stepped closer to him. "They not modern. I could see they use primitive tools."

Rosa and Colin looked at each other with their lips parted. Rosa took Sasha's hand and squeezed it.

"Sasha, we set out on this prehistoric journey so we could block the passage through time. There are too many prehistoric mammals slipping into the twentieth century. We need to do something about this. Can't you see on your indicator what century we're in? It doesn't look as if we are in prehistory."

Sasha knelt to the ground where his time indicator lay. "It give me strange reading. Not familiar with this reading. I see letter 'A'. Maybe beside it is letter 'D'."

Colin's eyes widened. "A.D. feck! We won't get our answer here, that's for sure. Just do what ye do 'n send us back. This won't work, surely it won't."

"Not so easy to do, when we just arrive."

Rosa smacked her lips in a huff. "Why, Sasha? Why?"

"You find me scientist with time-travel device and I will shake his hand," Sasha said, squinting his eyes.

Amoli nestled up to Colin. Just then, a differently dressed man sneaked up behind Colin and tapped him on the shoulder.

"Cén t ainm atá ort?" the man inquired.

Colin turned to him, and responded. *"Colin, Colin is ainm dom."*

The man smiled.

Rosa's eyes widened. "Gaelic? You're speaking Gaelic?"

Colin looked at Rosa. "Aye."

The man stepped closer to Colin. *"Dia duit."*

Colin tilted his head forward to the man. *"Dia duit."*

The man bowed at Colin and walked backwards with his eyes fixed on Colin's towering and broad structure. Colin stared at the man until he couldn't see him anymore. Colin took Rosa's hand.

"Did ye notice the man's clothes?"

"Definitely. This man is an ancient Celt. If he speaks Gaelic he has to be a Celt," Rosa said, appearing nervous.

"Aye, I'm in agreement with yez. He looked at me as if I was God, did ye see that? Why so much respect for someone he doesn't know?"

"If this is the time of the ancient Celts, then they were having a terrible time with Viking invasions. He may have thought you were a Viking."

"Viking? Why would he think that? I'm as true an Irishman in me appearance."

Rosa took a deep breath. "No, you're not, Colin. You are the spitting image of a Viking."

"Nar, the Celts looked like me as well."

Rosa gripped Colin's arm. "Where do you think you got that ginger hair of yours? Even your eyelashes are crimson."

It's a great Irish trait, is what it is. Loads of us Irish carry the crimson hair that I have."

"A true Irishman would have black hair. Your hair is definite ginger. That's a Viking trait. The Vikings gave their traits to the Celts when they invaded Ireland for so many years. They took over Dublin, your fair city, completely."

Colin stepped back. "Yer sayin' I have some Vikin' blood?"

"Not some, but perhaps loads of Viking blood. You don't even resemble your parents or your brother. You look like your uncle. Your brother Ethan looks more Irish than you with his black hair."

Colin began to pace. "Well, if that isn't a slap in me face."

Rosa took his hand. "The Vikings plundered their way through Europe. They invaded Ireland and settled for a very long time."

Colin looked at her with a puzzled expression.

"I'm intrigued with what was here before us. I am an archeologist."

A deep galloping noise penetrated the ground. Amoli squealed and ran to Colin. A band of men on horses approached them. They wore chain mail tunics with helmets. They held their swords above their heads and blurted to Colin in Gaelic. Rosa remained still and whispered.

"Colin, what are they saying to us?"

"They want to know if we's Vikings or Celts. I just told 'im, we's Celts."

The man that resembled a chieftain slid off his horse with his sword in hand. He walked toward Colin. He commented on Colin's size and muscular bulk. The chieftain ran the tip of his blade along Colin's throat. Rosa and Sasha were quiet. Amoli panted with terror.

"Lass, hush up!" Colin said to her. The chieftain told Colin what village he resided at. "He wants me to join his band of men and be a soldier," Colin informed the others. The chieftain continued to converse with Colin in Gaelic. "He says they's havin' loads of trouble with Viking invasions. He wants me to help him with it."

"Colin, no!" Rosa blurted.

The chieftain stared at Amoli and got back on his horse. The band of men rode off. Colin smiled.

"I'm not completely understandin' the ancient gents, ye know it."

"Thought you speak fluent Gaelic," Sasha said.

"I do. But not Gaelic from such an ancient time, if ye follow me?"

Rosa noticed Amoli nestling up to Colin. "Amoli, I'm sure you and I will bunk in the same tent tonight."

Amoli gazed up at Colin. "My love, will you not protect me?"

"I'll be in the next tent with Dr. Dimitrikov. Yer not to worry. Rosa's a fine wench, so she is. Yez two should get on whilst on this journey, don't ye think?"

Amoli backed off. Her head hung low with disappointment. Sasha barged in.

"Tomorrow I find way to return us to our time," Sasha said, bending down to gather his belongings.

"Return to our time, yer sayin'? Can't do that. We's gone through a passage of time for a bleedin' reason. Couldn't bare to think of us returnin' with nothin' accomplished."

"You wish to be in other time, Mr. Limmerick?"

"Aye. We need to be in a prehistoric time, so we should."

Rosa glanced at Sasha. "Yes, Sasha we risked a lot to venture back in time. We really need to solve the problem of prehistoric life slipping through the time vortex."

"Da, da, so tomorrow I find way."

Colin placed his arm around Sasha. "Ah, good man."

They set up two canvas tents, ate some canned food, and went to bed. The following morning was crisp and chilly. Colin was the first to leave the tent. He gathered some bark and branches to build a fire. Amoli exited her tent.

"I thought I heard someone out here," she said to Colin.

"Aye, so ye did, lass," Colin said, while trying to make fire.

"I don't like it here. Why can't Dr. Dimitrikov get us out of here?"

"He'll try today I suppose, lass. No worries."

"I don't like the way that chieftain man looked at me. Did you notice him looking at me?"

"Aye, so I did. Every man can't help but look at ye."

"You are still so very attracted to me, Colin."

123

Colin smiled. He tried to focus on something else. She took a few steps toward him, and sat on the other end of the fire he built.

"Why can't we be together?"

"Because I'm no good for ye. Ye deserve a fine gent. Yer father was right."

A tear trickled down her face. "Why do you keep saying this?"

He stood up. "Sayin' what? Speakin' the truth, so I am. Don't waste yer life with me. Ye need a good man 'n I'm not him."

She stood up and faced him. "My father has always said I am a strong-willed girl. I will never give up. You and I will someday marry. I know this. I can't imagine marrying anyone but you."

Rosa approached them. "I hate to interrupt, but Sasha needs to concentrate on changing his device to another time in history. In the meantime, maybe we could gather something to eat like berries, anything that doesn't appear poisonous."

"Got a better idea, so I do. We can look for the chieftain's settlement. We could perhaps get ourselves cleaned up 'n fed properly. What ye think?"

Rosa stared at the ground. "Sasha's indicator says we're in the year 840 A.D. I really don't expect a hotel service in any of the neighboring villages."

Colin crossed his arms in front of him. "So, we's plenty far from prehistoric life."

Rosa nodded. "One could say that."

Colin smiled at Amoli and Rosa. "Lets let Sasha work on the device 'n we can gather berries 'n whatever else looks edible, shall we?"

Amoli took Colin's arm and Rosa took Colin's other arm and off they went with a large basket for gathering. Sasha sat on the ground by his tent. He didn't even realize his colleagues were gone.

"We in time period 840 A.D. Mr. Limmerick no like this. If I set clock backwards, will it take us to prehistoric time?

The ground vibrated with the sound of horse hoofs. Sasha looked up to notice three warriors in leather battle vests and helmets on horses. They stopped in front of Sasha and stared at him. He continued to work. The man in the middle lifted his sword and shouted at Sasha. Sasha continued to work. The warrior slid off his horse. He repositioned his helmet and threw a sword at Sasha. The man pulled out another sword and held it in position. Sasha placed his device down and gingerly took the sword.

"You want battle with me? Why you want?"

Sasha stood up and held the sword in *guard of the long tail (posta di coda longa)*. He indicated his guard was good against his opponent's attack. The warrior thrust his sword at Sasha, but Sasha was quick in dodging the blade.

"You look like Viking warrior to me. You come here to kill me!" Sasha said, knowing the warrior wouldn't understand him.

The warrior snarled at Sasha. Sasha held his sword in *women's guard*, where the sword was held over his shoulder with the point high and back at a 45° angle. Sasha stepped forward and lunged at the warrior. The blade cut through the man's leg. Sasha stood still with his sword ready for the next attack from the other two warriors. The wounded opponent lay on the ground moaning in pain. His two cohorts tended to him, while Sasha watched. Colin, Rosa, and Amoli approached their campsite with a bushel filled with berries. They heard the sound of a wounded man.

"Colin? Someone is hurt!" Rosa blurted.

Colin stood tall to focus. "Aye. Sasha has somebody with him. I bes' be with him, if he may need any help." Colin tore himself from the two women and made his way to Sasha. He stopped in his tracks to see a man in agony

125

with blood pouring from his leg. "Sasha? What happened here? Who are these men?"

"Viking warriors, maybe. I not really know. They come here to kill me. I almost kill him."

One of the other Viking cohorts stood tall to face Colin. He snorted and grunted at him as he shook his sword. Colin looked at Sasha.

"They's not a cheery bunch, are they now?"

Sasha looked at Colin. "Nyet." The two other men shook their swords at Colin. One of the men spoke a few sentences. "You understand their kind of talk?"

Colin shook his head. "Not a single word. If they're Vikings they would be speakin' Norse. How's yer Norse, mate?"

"Not like my Russian."

Colin stepped closer to Sasha. "Just by the way they're actin' I'd swear they want to fight. Why me? Yer the one they had the scuffle with."

"But you are built like mountain and you have long red hair. You look like Viking."

"Me freckles aren't a Viking trait, now are they?"

"Mr. Limmerick, you want to stand here with two hot-headed Vikings armed with swords and debate your freckles?"

The two men stepped closer to Sasha and Colin with their swords extended in front of them.

"Mate, yer lucky they gave ye a sword. I'm supposin' I'm the unlucky one here."

"I think they want to impale us, Mr. Limmerick."

Rosa pulled Amoli away from the two-armed men. One of the men stepped closer and swung his sword over Sasha's head. Sasha was quick enough to slice the man's arm. The man yelped and backed away. Colin stood behind Sasha. The two men had their swords ready to thrust. One of the men stepped forward and tried to thrust his sword into Sasha. Sasha swung his sword in the air to stop the blade from coming his way. The two swords clashed. Colin stepped away from Sasha and managed to grapple the man to the ground.

"What did we ever do to them, mate?"

"They are Vikings. They not need reason."

"Yer pretty grand with a sword, aren't ye, mate?"

"Spasiba. I learn when I was boy."

"Did, ye find us a way outta here?"

"Not yet, but close."

Rosa and Amoli approached the men. "Sasha, here-here, I didn't realize you were so handy with a sword," Rosa said.

"This man try to kill me. He give me sword, so I use it. That is all."

"Rosa, take Amoli outta here!" Colin shouted. The wounded Viking opponent tossed Colin a sword. Colin picked it up. "Nay, man. I can fight ye with me bare hands, but not with a sword. Haven't a clue how to use it."

The Viking shook his sword at Colin and lifted it above his head. He yelled and chanted. Colin and Sasha glanced at each other, but remained still.

"Mr. Limmerick, just try to thrust sword at opponent. If they try to do it to you, you must parry their sword, da?" Sasha held his sword in position. "You good?"

"Not at all."

"We in 840 A.D. You better get used to sword or you be dead man."

Colin nervously held the sword in front of him. The Viking charged Sasha with his sword; Sasha parried the sword and knocked it out of the opponent's hand. The Viking scrambled to obtain his sword again, but Colin kicked and punched him. The three wounded Vikings stumbled to their horses and rode off. Colin took a deep breath.

"As long as we's here, we best find that Celtic village. Celts surely can be trusted, don't ye think?"

"How you know these three men not Celts?"

127

"I'm a Celt meself. Why would they want to brawl with me for?"

"Because you look like Viking."

"I've got me Irish features."

"Red hair makes you more like Viking." Colin gave a stern nod that Sasha was mistaking. Sasha laughed. "Mr. Limmerick, we do good here."

"What ye mean? I'm not feelin' too comfortable knowin' there could be danger."

"We got two good swords from this."

"Never handled a sword in me life, so I haven't."

"Some day you may have to again."

Colin glared at Sasha as he watched Rosa and Amoli approach them. Amoli scampered to Colin and buried herself in his arm. Rosa tried not to look.

"Well, Sasha, you frightened off our visitors. I hope this is the last of these goons. I wouldn't want to be in a position where we have to live by the sword. As long as we're in this dreadful time period, we may need your expertise."

"Mr. Limmerick say they spoke Norse, but how would he even know they were speaking Norse?"

Rosa stood beside Colin and nudged him in the side. "You wouldn't know Norse if you heard it. How do you know they weren't Celtic?"

"Because if they was Celtic, they'd be speakin' Gaelic. I speak Gaelic."

Sasha smiled at Rosa. "Mr. Limmerick speak Gaelic. He know everything."

Rosa laughed.

Colin crossed his arms in front of him. "Not nearly everythin', especially how to duel with a sword, feck. Well, Sasha, just get us out of this time period 'n get us to our time of prehistoric mammals."

"Da, Mr. Limmerick, you operate so much better with hand ax in hand."

Chapter Seventeen

The four time-travelers made their way through the dense brush. They followed the direction of the three warriors. They could hear drumming and chanting. They poked their heads through dense bushes and spotted a settlement at the bottom of a valley.

"Ah, there it is, folks; a mighty grand lookin' Celtic settlement. They have shelter 'n they're cookin' their food. Grand to see, so it is." Colin glanced at Sasha. "A step up from *Neanderthal* with his primitive ways, eh?"

Sasha scratched his head. "How you know they are Celts? They could be Vikings. Don't they all look the same?"

"Blyme, that's where yez bloody wrong, mate. They are certainly Celts. Just think, these Celts are me ancestors. I'm almost feelin' like it's home."

Rosa rolled her eyes back. "Oh, rubbish, Colin. You're such a silly romantic at times. If these people are ancient Celts they could be just as dangerous as Vikings. We need to be vigilant. We're from the twentieth century. They will detect there is something very different about us. Our style of dress, the way we speak, is a dead give away."

"Give away? They wouldn't have even a slight impression that we's from their future time?"

"Of course not. They'll just know we don't belong here. That's enough to cause loads of trouble."

Colin wore a serious expression on his face. "Perhaps we's makin' a bloody mistake then."

"All these time-travel expeditions are a mistake!" Rosa blurted with uneasiness in her voice.

They made their way down the rugged slope, where Sasha and Colin helped their two female companions. They tried to act relaxed as they walked to where most of the people gathered at the fire. The drumming stopped. Colin smiled and bowed as low as he could. He gestured for his cohorts to do the same.

"T Dia duit," greeted Colin.

The chieftain they had met previously sat in the middle. He slowly stood up.

"Gurab amhlaidh duit," the chieftain reciprocated.

The chieftain walked toward Colin. He placed a spear in Colin's abdomen. He slapped him on his shoulder and tilted his head to him. He looked to his people and they cheered. Colin glanced at Rosa.

"I don't know why they's so happy to see me."

"I think you better keep quiet. Just speak Gaelic when you can," Rosa cautioned.

Several of the chieftain's men stood behind Colin and poked him lightly with their spears. They escorted Colin to their main round house. Rosa, Sasha and Amoli remained standing by the fire. The chieftain stared at Amoli. He stood very close to her and grinned. Amoli tried not to look at him.

"Oh! Oh! Dr. Dimitrikov, please protect me! I'm very scared! Where did they take Colin?" Amoli spewed, with fear.

"Don't worry, Miss Amoli. I think boss likes you."

"Sasha!" shouted Rosa. "Don't speak! These people are barbarians!"

Sasha chuckled. "These barbarians make Mr. Limmerick feel at home."

"Shut-up!"

The lead chieftain took Amoli by the hand and sat her down beside him. He had Rosa and Sasha sit with them. The flutes and the drumming began. They kindled the burning fire and chanted to the sound of the instruments.

Colin stood in the round house while several female slaves tried to dress him. They fitted several plates of armor over his shoulders and chest. They sighed with frustration regarding his size. His frame was too large for

130

the plates of armor. They flustered and tried to place more armored plates over him, but nothing fit. Colin took one of the young slave's hands and held it.

"I'm not gonna fit yer armor, wench, no matter how hard ye try." She gazed at him with her lips parted. He held both her hands and rubbed them. "What ye chieftain have planned for me, eh?"

She looked at him with wide eyes, but remained silent. They left him alone in the round house. He paced around feeling nervous. The lead chieftain entered with the same slaves trailing behind. Colin looked at the chieftain and bowed his head to him. The chieftain reciprocated the gesture. He grunted at the slave women. He asked them why the armor didn't fit Colin's body. The nervous slaves tried to fit the armor over Colin with no success. The chieftain paced around the room and muttered. Colin stood still in silence. The chieftain told the slaves to get more armor made to fit Colin's size. The slaves ran off to get to work. The chieftain faced Colin and spoke to him in Gaelic.

"Again, please. Didn't quite catch your last sentence," Colin requested, in English.

The head chieftain sighed. *"Several Viking invasions have been occurring,"* he said, much slower.

Colin tried to appear empathetic. Then he asked, "Where's me friends at?"

The chieftain left the round house. The female slaves re-entered. They brought cooked pork, rye bread, an assortment of cheeses, and wine. They laid the spread on the floor. Colin smiled.

"Le do thoil " Colin said, with thanks. He knelt to the floor and gestured for the slaves to join him. They smiled and giggled as they faced away from him. *"Le do thoil.* Yez gotta join me. Yez can't let me eat alone, now can yez?" he said, in English." They filled his flask. He tasted it. "Too sweet for me likin,' but I'll guzzle it down the hatch anyways."

131

The young women stood up and left the round house. Colin sighed and decided to eat the feast that sat before him. In a few minutes the slaves returned with wool blankets and placed them on the floor. They added kindles to the small fire. They smiled at Colin, where one of the young women stepped closer to him so she could touch his face. She frightened herself and they made their exit. As the evening ripened Amoli sat beside the chieftain, where he offered her food and wine. Rosa and Sasha sat at the other end of the feasting Celts. Rosa winced at the sight of some of the food.

"Sasha," she whispered. "I'm not partial to eating an entire pig in one sitting."

"I eat it. It's good. Just do as these people do and all will be well."

"I think the head chieftain is expecting something from Amoli tonight. She looks jittery. We don't know where they took Colin. I hate it here. I want to leave. You have to get us out of here."

"I explain to Mr. Limmerick months ago we could have big chance of landing in time period that is not prehistoric. Now, we are here and I cannot get us out yet."

"Big help you are, and you call yourself a scientist?"

"Biggest problem here is we not speak Gaelic. Mr. Limmerick has advantage."

"Definitely. We have no idea what they're saying about us." Rosa stared at her plate for a few seconds. "It was never in the cards for us to learn how to speak Gaelic, because we shouldn't be in the year 840 A.D."

"You complain again about me? I say you before departure that all may not go well. You were warned. I no want to hear anymore. I am human like you. I am not magic."

"I thought your silly time-travel device was magic. All it does is trip us into other time periods."

"We must find Mr. Limmerick. What intensions would these people have for him? Maybe they want to eat him?"

"Oh, who knows? If they wanted to eat him they would have done it already."

"Maybe it is Mr. Limmerick on our plate, da?"

Rosa shoved Sasha. "Stop it! Enough of this. That head chieftain, who is attracted to Amoli, also seems to have some kind of attraction to Colin. I wonder what his intensions are?"

"I don't know why anyone would like Mr. Limmerick."

"This is no time for jokes. You can't let that chieftain have his way with Amoli."

"Why you care? You hate her."

"She's still a girl. I don't think I could stand it if that disgusting chieftain had his way with her."

"You so good friend to Mr. Limmerick, aren't you?" Rosa tried to smile. "Vikings, earlier, give me sword. I will confront head chieftain to a dual and fight for Miss Amoli."

Rosa took a sip of wine. "How sweet and chivalrous of you, Sasha."

"I am good man. You not ever give me credit for anything, only to Mr. Limmerick. Look, head chieftain is moving closer to Miss Amoli. He will soon kiss her."

"What a horrid thought."

Sasha stood up from the feasting and walked to the head chieftain. The chieftain appeared bothered that he had to take his eyes off Amoli. He glared at Sasha and grunted something in Gaelic. Sasha extended his hand to Amoli.

"She is mine. Give her to me."

He grabbed Amoli, pulling her away from the chieftain. The Celts at the gathering stopped eating and stared at him. Sasha roughly took Amoli by her waist and stomped off. Rosa kept her eyes on the crowd as she stood up and tried to blend in. She followed Sasha and Amoli to the round house they were appointed to.

"Oh, thank-you, Dr. Dimitrikov," Amoli said, trying to catch her breath.

"Do not say yet. I am getting sword ready for fight."

"I'm scared, and where is Colin?" Rosa said, pacing the room. We must find him. We need his muscle to get us out of mess."

Some time elapsed. Sasha sat by the door with sword in hand.

"Maybe Chieftain get tired."

"I hope he decided not to bother with us," Rosa said, pacing the room.

Amoli gathered some wool blankets and wrapped herself in them. "I'm getting so tired. I really must sleep. I'm going to try not to think of Colin tonight. He doesn't want me anyway."

"Go ahead, Miss Amoli, sleep. I will find way to find your prince," Sasha said, trying to smile.

Rosa scratched her head. "At least we ate something."

"Rosa, try to sleep. Miss Amoli is right. I will think of something."

"I can't relax until Colin is back with us."

Sasha's smile dissipated.

Colin was gathering his woolen blankets and getting comfortable on the hard floor. The mead had gone to his head. His exhaustion overwhelmed him and he fell asleep. When light beamed through the tiny windows of the round house, he rolled over a few times and opened his eyes. He glanced at the ceiling and took a breath. He turned his head to one side, only to realize one of the slave women was lying beside him. He turned to his other side to notice another slave women beside him. He sat up.

"What the feck is this? Yez two are me whores now?" They smiled and stroked his chest. "Did anythin' happen last night? Didn't even know yez were beside me."

The head chieftain stormed in and grinned at Colin. He shouted at the two slave women with demands. He clapped his hands. *"Tapadh leat! Tapadh leat!"* he commanded.

They quickly got up from Colin and made their exit.

"What's this, eh?" Colin stood up, while trying to wrap a piece of cloth around his lower half. "The feast last night, the wenches? Do I remind ye of some long lost friend?"

The chieftain continued to grin at Colin. A few minutes later, the same two slave women returned with hose for Colin. They pulled the cloth from him, where he stood naked. They held the fitted trousers in front of him, where they tried to eyeball if they were Colin's size. Colin slipped them on.

The chieftain smiled and nodded at Colin, appearing as if he was satisfied with Colin's attire. The women fit the breast armor over Colin's chest as well as the shoulder armor. The chieftain's body language showed that he was satisfied enough. *"Keep our newcomer happy until our enemies arrive,"* the chieftain said to the women. Colin could understand only pieces of what the chieftain was saying. *"Some of my men have been appointed to the round tower in the front of the village with the monks. They are vigilantly trying to spot out the Viking attackers."*

He glanced at the women and then at Colin and left. The two women sat down on the piled wool blankets. They began to take their long tunics off. Colin stood and stared at them with his armor still on.

"N-no. I can't with yez now. I need to know why I'm standin' here wearin' armor that ye so conveniently manufactured to fit me." The two slaves ignored his gibberish and smiled. He tried to remove the armor. The women jumped up to help him. The heavy armor was off. He knelt down on the wool blankets. "I'm yer lord's soldier, aren't I?" The two women encouraged him to

135

mount them. Colin took a deep breath and lay down beside them. "I'm gonna die, so I will. A soldier, so I'm not."

Colin took a large gulp of the mead that sat in a flask on the floor. He rolled on top of one of the women while the other woman waited patiently for her turn. Late that morning, a woman stepped into Colin's roundhouse. He had the two slave women lying on top of him asleep. Colin woke to the other woman's footsteps.

"Another slave for me? I think two's enough, don't ye think?"

"Shhh, Colin, it's me."

"Rosa? Good God, yer dressed like a slave? How'd ye manage that?"

She pretended to clean his floor. "Shhh. That head chieftain has intensions for Amoli. Sasha is getting nowhere with his time-travel device. None of this is working at all. He can only look at it at night, when everyone is asleep. If that chieftain ever saw it, things could get even worse."

Colin sat up, trying not to wake the slave women. "He's got intensions for Amoli? Has he touched her, do ye know?"

"Not yet. She's with us now. Sasha has been acting as if Amoli belongs to him. He's also been swinging that sword around."

"Good man. We've got to keep her safe."

"What are you doing with these prostitutes?" Rosa asked, making a grimace.

"Prostitutes? They're slaves. That head chieftain has been keepin' me fed 'n drunk, 'n I'm gettin' all the sex a man could want. There's just one catch."

"What?"

"I'm now his head warrior. He wants me to fight the Viking's. The Celts are expectin' a Viking attack. Don't know when. He's given me swords 'n spears. Don't know

136

how to use that shite, so I don't. I fight with me bare hands."

"Oh, Colin, no! Maybe Sasha can teach you how to handle a sword."

"How can I learn in such short time? Surely, I'll die 'n Amoli will fall into the hands of that fecker."

"You're never one to give up. Sasha can teach you what you need to know. I can't really stay here. I had to reach you somehow. Maybe we can meet tonight."

"If I'm not dead by then."

"Don't talk like that. You're big and strong; these Vikings are no match for you."

"Never was I one to fancy war, never did. Ye know it. I evaded The Boers."

"You said you were rejected because of your age."

"I lied. I was only in me early thirties. Wasn't too old. Just didn't believe in that war, is all. Hate war, so I do. Now, it's caught up with me."

Rosa knelt down on the floor. "Don't give up," she said, caressing his face.

Colin chuckled. "They's Vikings. A twentieth-century man is what I am. Can't see a light shinin' on me for this one, nay I can't."

"You can't lose this battle. We're depending on you."

"These time-travels are beatin' me down, so they are. Guilt 'n regret are me feelings. I've been tryin' to play God for too long. It's time I get what I bloody well deserve, don't ye think?"

"I'm not going to listen to your silliness."

"Amoli needs to look toward her future. I'm not the man for her, never was. I'm not gonna win. I'll lose this battle, surely I will."

Tears ran down Rosa's face. "I can't believe I'm hearing you talk like this. You got Sasha and me into this mess, and you're going to get us out. You're going to face those Vikings, and you are going to be a true Celtic warrior."

"Love, can't ye see? No good with a sword is what I am. I don't have a hope in hell with these professionals. They live 'n die by the sword. All I can do is brawl in a pub every now 'n again."

"These men don't have your size or strength. Utilize your assets, and win this war for the Celts. These people are your ancestors."

"Ye was right the first time in sayin' me ancestors are Vikings. I'm the spittin' image of a Viking."

"To me, Vikings and Celts look the same. Oh, who cares?" He stood up.

The two slave women opened their eyes.

"These wenches need to fit the armor they made on me body. Never wore armor before. Not a comfortable material, I must say."

"They made it for you?"

"Aye, I'm too damn big, it was made specially for me."

"I better leave before that chieftain character walks in."

Rosa and Colin embraced. "Colin, you mean too much to me. Let's meet tonight and Sasha can show you a few moves with that sword."

"I'll tell the chieftain that I need to see yez tonight. He's been workin' hard at tryin' to keep me happy, I suppose."

Rosa stood on her tip-toes to reach Colin's face. "I love you. Please do this for all three of us."

Colin kissed her several times on the lips. "Ah, that felt good. Be watchful of Amoli, please."

"I will. I must go now."

She wrapped her cloak around herself and ran off. The two slaves got dressed and mentioned that they needed to fit the armor on Colin.

"The battle with the Vikings could be at any time soon," one of the slaves said.

138

Colin winced while they fit Celtic battle gear on him. He wore a short-sleeve tunic with a wide bronze belt around his waist with tight-fitting hose. His boots were just below his knees. They were made heavy with armor. His knees and shoulders were fitted with armored plates as well as his chest and shoulders. His arms were exposed. He knelt toward the women, so they could place the armored helmet upon his head.

"Shouldn't I have chain mail over me arms?"

The two slaves left stared at Colin with no response.

"I need to make sure Amoli is safe."

Colin gingerly left the round house. There was several Celts going about their business fetching jugs of water, skinning fish, and mending garments. He walked behind a group of people hoping he wasn't noticed. Two of the chieftain's guards appeared out of nowhere and ran the blades of their swords along Colin's back. Colin stood still.

"It doesn't pay to be built big."

They escorted him back to the round house. They made several comments in Gaelic and left. He found it difficult to move around with such heavy armor attached to his body. He tried to sit on the floor. He supported himself by using the rounded wall. Then Sasha appeared.

"Mr. Limmerick, Rosa say me you prepare for battle. You so not look happy to see me."

"Aye, I'm happy to see ye. Just feelin' frustrated 'n scared."

"You are now soldier, so you must know how to use weapon, da?"

"Wait, first, tell me how Amoli is 'n where she's at? I want to see her."

"Your engagement to her is off, remember? She is with Rosa in roundhouse on other side of village. I make it clear to head chieftain that she is my woman."

"How ye make it clear to 'im when he speaks Gaelic 'n ye surely don't?"

139

"I use sword as threat."

"He backed off is what yer sayin'?"

"For now, maybe, maybe not."

"I feel like shite 'bout everythin'. Can't move too well with this armor, either."

"Da, you afraid to be soldier?"

"Too big 'n clumsy is what I am. Never thought I'd be goin' on a time-travel expedition to be an ancient warrior."

Sasha tried to help Colin up. "Do not remove armor. Wear it as much as you can. Get used to it. Here is your sword. I bring my sword. When he swings at you, you stop sword with yours. Watch every move he make. Only thrust sword when you have chance, da? Keep sword above shoulder to give strong swing. Hold sword up to your eyes when over your shoulder."

Colin tried to swing it the way Sasha suggested. "It doesn't seem so hard."

"Because you are strong, you will not have problem. Only problem is your size. You are too much target. Try to stay back. Let sword work for you."

"I can't die, 'cause I need to protect Amoli 'n Rosa."

"Da, da. If all goes bad I have back up plan."

"Back up plan? What's that?"

"I won't say now, but you will find out soon enough."

Sasha slapped Colin on the shoulder and left. Colin practiced his swordsmanship.

Chapter Eighteen

It was early morning. The head chieftain and his band of men were on guard for the attack. Colin was placed in the middle of the village with his spear, sword, and shield in hand. The village was silent with as little activity as possible. The chieftain's right-hand man rallied the troops. *"Erin Go Bragh!"* he shouted.

The Viking warriors raided the village, some on horses, some on foot. They swung their swords and jabbed with their spears. The Celtic warriors retaliated. Two angry Vikings charged at Colin yelling and screaming in Norse.

Colin used the weight of his body to knock their swords and spears from their hands with his shield. He looked at them struggling on the ground. He held his sword in front of him. He waved his sword, but then lowered it. Another Celtic warrior noticed Colin's reluctance to impale them, so he did it for him. The two Viking warriors lay on the ground impaled with the other Celtic warrior's sword. Blood oozed, where Colin's armored boots were drenched in their blood. The other Celtic warrior grimaced at Colin.

An angry Viking hurtled himself onto Colin from behind. Colin flipped him over his head and sliced his arm. The Viking lay on the ground with a bleeding arm. He yelled at Colin. Colin watched him bleed. The wounded Viking stood up. He lost blood, but continued to thrust his sword. Colin managed to knock his sword from his hand with his sword. The Viking opponent remained standing, so Colin charged him with his sword and thrust it into him.

Colin quickly turned his head, for he could not bear to look. He managed to dodge another Viking who approached from behind. The Viking turned to Colin and swung his sword. Colin managed to parry the sword with his, putting forth enough force to plunge the opponent to the ground, using Colin's strength and mass. Colin shut his eyes and thrust his sword into the Viking who was squirming o n the ground.

Colin shouted. *"Erin Go Bragh!"*

He waved his sword above his head so he could convince the Celtic warriors that he was one of them. Another Viking charged Colin. He swung his sword a few times where Colin dodged it with his shield. Colin managed to jam his sword against the man plummeting him to the ground. He sliced Colin's leg, but Colin swung his sword and sliced one side of the man's face.

"Ireland forever!" Colin shouted, at the ancient warrior.

A Viking charged at Colin with his horse and swung his sword. Colin threw his spear and it pierced the warrior's shoulder, causing the opponent to fall off his horse. The Celtic warriors cheered. Colin didn't know why. They stood around him and cheered, lifting their swords and spears above their heads. Colin scanned the village with his eyes. He noticed the dead warriors scattered about, drenched in their own blood. Colin removed his helmet and took a deep breath. The other Celtic warriors smiled and bowed their heads to him. The head chieftain approached Colin. He smiled and bowed to him.

"You are from another village, and yet you have proven yourself to us today." The Celtic warriors raised their spears and swords above their heads and cheered several times. The head chieftain grinned. *"We don't know much about you, but you will fight the head Norse warrior later this day. If you defeat him, there will be a celebration in your honor and you will be presented a golden sword."*

Colin forced a smile as he tried to catch his breath. He bowed to the head chieftain and the Celtic warriors and the villagers cheered.

A few hours passed, Colin sat on the damp straw floor of the round house with Sasha. Several plates of cooked meat, fruit, cheese and wine sat before them. Colin sipped on his wine.

"In a few hours I'm supposed to sword fight with the head Viking. Not lookin' forward to it, sure I'm not."

"Mr. Limmerik, how it feel to be great warrior?"

"Great warrior? Oh, feck off! I just want to get back to our time. I wouldn't mind even if I had to listen to Cushing go on about his stupid horseshoe crab."

"I cannot believe you say this. You are now worshiped in this time, you have wine, women and fame."

Colin finished his last drop of wine. "I've got nothin' of the sort. Whoever this hot-headed Viking is, I'll be his opponent. I know nothin' about bein' a warrior. I'm just not a product of this time. Can't you get us out of here, for feck's sake?"

"I still have to turn clock back on time-travel device. It is not so easy to do in dark."

"We wasn't supposed to be sent to this time. What the feck is goin' on, man?"

"I explain you before we leave, that something like this could happen, and it did."

Colin lay back on the piles of woolen blankets on the floor. "Now I've got to prove me bravery with some ancient Viking warrior who'll probably slice me balls off."

"You do so well in this morning's battle."

"I was lucky 'n I wasn't alone; there was other Celtic warriors there to help pick up the pieces I left."

"You must win this battle because Miss Amoli loves you. She will fall in hands of head chieftain."

Colin sat up. "Where's she at now?"

"She is with head chieftain, I think."

143

"I thought you had him believe she was yer property?"

"Da, but he approach me with double-handed sword. Too big for me to conquer."

Colin gasped for air. "What the feck ye tellin' me this so late in our conversation? She's in trouble, unless she fancies the bloke."

"She hate him."

Colin dropped his wine glass, as he stood up. "I've got to save her from that shite."

"The only way you can do this is to win duel with head Viking."

"How'ye know that'll do it?"

"Because head chieftain will forever honor you. He will do whatever you ask, even if it means you get girl."

"Ye make this shite up as ye go along, ye bleedin' wanker."

Sasha stood up to face Colin. "I am tired of your bad language and rude behavior. I do not care anymore. Do not shoot messenger. I tell you as I see it. I am never wrong."

"Wrong is yer middle name. Ye got us in this bleedin' mess in the first place."

Sasha remained still. "You dare blame this mess on me? Prehistoric journey is all your fault. You want it, so you get it. You are unrealistic man. I won't even help you when Viking cuts your balls off."

Colin took a few deep breaths. "Okay, okay, for the sake of our two wenches that have come along with us, we must contain ourselves and act like men."

"Da, Mr. Limmerick. I must take break from you. I will find Miss Amoli and bring her back to round house Rosa is in now."

"I've got to rescue her. It is no longer yer place."

"Enough! It is my place, because you must prepare for next battle, which will be very soon."

144

Sasha left the round house in a huff of frustration. The Celtic guards stood outside the round tower and the monks kept watch for their enemies' arrival. The monk sounded the horn. The Vikings were spotted. The Celtic village was surrounded with Celtic warriors.

Colin sat in the round house with several female slaves to help him with his armor. He pulled his rosary beads from his jacket. He held each bead between his fingers and prayed. The slave women watched him stand on his knees with his beads clutched tightly.

The Vikings marched in on foot and on horseback. Large numbers of spectators gathered around the center of the village. Villagers scattered about and searched for refuge. The head Viking appeared. He walked toward the crowd with his spear, sword, and shield in hand.

Colin approached the large group. The Celts of the village cheered. He towered over everyone as he walked toward his Viking opponent. The two men stopped and stared at each other. Colin spotted Rosa in the crowd dressed in slave girl rags. Sasha stood a ways from Rosa further back in the crowd. The head chieftain appeared with Amoli at his side. Colin flinched as he gripped his sword in *boar's tooth stance.*

His opponent drew his sword ready to duel. Colin stepped back with his sword in front of him. The Viking took the first thrust. Colin pulled back to dodge the cut. Colin continued to hear Sasha's words on how to use a sword in combat. He held the sword beside his eye with the tip jutting outward toward his opponent. He jabbed the Viking, wounding his arm.

The Viking was quick with his retaliation and sliced Colin's thigh. The wound was deep and bloody. Colin stepped back a few steps. The Viking charged at him, hoping to thrust his sword into Colin's belly, but Colin slashed his sword and knocked it from the Viking's hand. The crowd of Celts cheered.

The Viking took back his sword and slashed Colin's arm. Colin tried to ignore the penetrating pain and stepped back from his opponent. The Viking charged at Colin again. Colin defended his position by trying to flick the sword from the Viking's hand again. The Viking's grip was solid and relentless; he managed to get Colin off balance and drop his sword.

Colin tried to grab his weapon, but the Viking sliced his hand. Colin stood back and held his spear in front of him. The Viking raged and sliced the spear in half. Rosa screamed. Amoli covered her eyes with her hands while she screamed and cried. Rosa looked through the crowd and found Sasha.

"Sasha! We can't stand here and watch Colin die!"

"He not doing well."

"No, he's not! Didn't you have a *plan B?*"

"Da, da. I must get closer. I must get in front of crowd. Not worry, I will fix all!"

Sasha pushed through the spectators. Colin was on the ground drenched in his own blood. The Viking had one foot on Colin's back and waved his sword with aggression and pride.

"As you can see, this giant warrior has lost this battle. I don't know who he is, but he must die now!" The Viking opponent shouted, in Norse.

A deafening gunshot went off. The crowd screamed. Sasha got lost in the crowd. The head chieftain stood up and ordered his men to find out what the noise was. The Viking opponent fell to the ground with a bullet wound to his chest. Colin stood before the dying Viking and peered through the crowd for Rosa. The spectators ran in different directions in a fit of wild frenzy.

"Rosa!" Colin called. He pushed through the crowd calling her name.

She suddenly appeared and took his arm. "Let's get out of here."

146

Colin pulled her back to slow down her pace. "What happened? Did I hear a gunshot or am I losin' me bloody mind?"

Rosa tugged on his arm. "Let's go, Colin. Now!"

"Did Sasha fire his gun?"

"No time to chat. We've got to find Sasha and get him out of sight. Were they using gun powder in 840 A.D?" Rosa asked.

"Don't know. Perhaps a wee tad of it was in sight every now 'n again. Don't know for sure, can't say," Colin answered, as they ran through the crowd. "Don't think gun powder was in the cards for this battle, I can tell ye that."

"I didn't think so, move. Lets go!"

"Did ye know Sasha was goin' to do this?" Colin asked, as they made it back to the round house.

"Of course I didn't know. What choice did he have? Sasha saved your life his way."

"Did yez think I was goin' to die or somethin'?"

"Yes, Colin, you were definitely going to die."

Amoli burst through the crowd, running frantically. "Colin, my love! I can't tell you how glad I am you are alright!" Amoli ran into his arms in tears. Colin held her tightly against him. "Oh, Colin you're wounded. I'm so very sorry."

Rosa tugged at Colin's arm. "We really need to find Sasha and find a way out of this horrible century."

The head chieftain followed Amoli from behind and grabbed her by the arm. He grunted at Colin and pulled her away. The head chieftain showed a slight bow to Colin. *"Forgive me. You are a warrior of magic. What happened to your opponent?"*

Colin glanced at Rosa. "Aye, I'm a warrior of magic, that I am," Colin responded in English to the chieftain.

"This girl keeps slipping away from me. Tell her she is to be with me for now on."

147

Colin's eyes widened. Rosa stepped closer to Colin and he took Amoli's hand.

"She belongs to me," Colin said in Gaelic.

The chieftain stepped closer to Colin. *"She may have once belonged to you, but she is now mine and that is all, warrior."*

Colin licked his dry lips. Amoli gazed at Colin with her large dark eyes.

"Colin?" Amoli said, with her tiny voice. Colin glanced down at Amoli by his side. "What is he saying to you? You look very worried."

Colin forced a smile, while staring at the head chieftain. *"I have a request."*

The head chieftain stood straight. *"A request? You request something of me?"*

Colin nodded, and took a step closer. *"Give me the girl and I will always be yer warrior. Ye have me word."*

Amoli stood beside Colin sweating with uncontrolled nerves. "Colin, I want you, not him. Please, don't let him take me."

The chieftain stepped closer to Colin. *"Enough of this! The girl is mine!"*

Colin's lips parted.

"You will receive a gold sword and spear, but the girl belongs to me."

Colin watched the head chieftain take Amoli away. "I can't let 'im do this. What if he tries somethin' on her?"

"I could tell by your conversation that things didn't go well. I'm so sorry. We've got to leave this century, or we'll die here," Rosa said, stroking Colin's hand. "I don't want that ugly chieftain to lay a hand on Amoli, either.

"All we can do is try our best to make sure he doesn't have his way with her," Rosa said with worry in her eyes.

"He's gonna spend the night with her? I can't let that happen."

"And how many slaves have you slept with since we've been on this horrible expedition?"

"Rosa, this isn't the time or the place."

"He really wants her. You might have to fight him for her."

"Shite, I'm tired of all these battles. No good with a sword, so I am. I'd rather use me bare hands 'n grapple the bastard to the ground."

"We really need to leave. Sasha shot a Viking warrior."

"Rosa? Stay with me tonight. I can't be alone, or I'll likely drink meself to death."

"We've got to find Sasha. I'm worried about him."

"We'll find Sasha, but don't leave me side, please don't."

He took her hand and held it. She gazed at him.

"Alright, then, I won't leave your side. Colin, are you going to be alright?"

He clutched her hand tightly. "Aye, I will. Lets go after Sasha's whereabouts."

He pressed his body against hers. She pulled away. "Colin, what are you doing?"

He stopped and smiled at her. They wandered through the crowds of people. Cattle and sheep sat on the dirt paths, while struggling families went about their business. They entered the round house Colin was staying in. The slave women appeared startled when they saw Colin and Rosa enter. Colin approached them and smiled with a slight bow. He asked them in Gaelic if they had seen the fair-haired man who was his friend. They smiled, but shook their heads. Rosa tugged on Colin's arm.

"Maybe he's in the roundhouse. He was initially placed in with me."

"Aye, we'll try there."

They entered to find Sasha sitting on the floor cross-legged, fiddling with the time-travel device.

"Sasha!" Rosa blurted loudly.

"Shhh. I almost find way to fast-forward clock to take us to future."

149

"Mate, ye used yer bloody gun on me opponent. Ye don't trust me capability as a Celtic warrior, so ye don't?"

Sasha looked up at him. "Celtic warrior? Mr. Limmerick you are far cry from Celtic warrior. You are fisherman and that is closest you are to warrior. You say yourself you not comfortable with sword."

"Ye shot the bloody Vikin' dead, so I think ye did."

Sasha stood up. "Da, it was either you or him. Take your pick, Mr. Limmerick. I already tell you I have *plan B*."

"Gentlemen! Please! Do you think anyone saw Sasha do this?" Rosa said, with her hands on each man's shoulder.

"Even if they did, they not know about gun powder. They only know catapults, slings, arrows, spears and swords. They would not understand, but I must stay out of sight, because some Celtic guards and chieftain see me with time-travel device. I know they want it."

Rosa's eyes widened. "How do you know this? You don't speak Gaelic?"

"They stare at it always. They watch me with it. This is no good place to be with device. They want it, I know."

"I thought you weren't going to let anyone see you with it?"

"How can I work with it at night, no light for me? At night, I can see nothing. I must work with it in day."

Colin rubbed his tired eyes. "Feck, feck this. If they take it, we's stuck in this God for saken time period forever. Feck!"

"Oh, my God! Colin, we can't allow that to happen. We need to leave this Celtic village. It was a bad idea coming here in the first place."

"I thought this village would be a help. They gave me slaves, 'n feasts, 'n wine."

She yanked on his arm. "Yes, for a price."

"The bleedin' wanker has Amoli. I've got to get her back. That's a big price." Sasha continued to work on the

150

time-travel device, while Colin and Rosa lay down on woolen blankets. "Amoli isn't here. What's he doin' to her right now? So I wonder," Colin said lying down face to face with Rosa.

"It's a scary thought. If you try to get her back now, he might kill us all. Sasha has to get that device ready to go."

Colin sighed with frustration. His hand reached for Rosa's. She smiled at him.

"Colin, close your eyes and rest."

"I'm goin' to hold yer hand all night, so I will."

She smiled back at him and they both fell asleep. Sasha continued to work on positioning the clock on the device to go forward. Two Celtic guards before the chieftain entered the round house. They commented that they got word that another battle was to take place the next day. Sasha continued to work. They stepped closer to Sasha with their eyes on his device. They asked to see the device. Sasha ignored them. They raised their voices and demanded to see the device. Sasha stood up and faced them. They pointed to the device. Rosa woke up.

"Sasha? What's going on?"

"I think you must wake up Mr. Limmerick. I will draw my sword."

"What do they want?"

"They want time-travel device, what else?"

Rosa gasped. "Sasha get your sword ready for a fight. Colin, wake up! Wake up, now!" She ran to Sasha and grabbed the time-travel device from his hands. "Sasha, you and Colin keep these two blokes busy. I'm going to run out of sight!"

She fled from the round house with the device in hand. She wrapped it in a woolen blanket and ran through the darkened village. She stayed low and crept behind baskets of fruits and vegetables. She figured her way out of the village and into the countryside. She ran through the dense brush without taking the time to catch her breath or look back. Colin sprang up and grabbed his spear. He told the chieftain's guards that they had nothing that would interest them.

"Mr. Limmerick, keep them busy and I will get gun and blow their heads off!"

Colin drew his sword and realized he was no match for the two Celtic guards who appeared to be expert swordsmen. They shouted at Colin and warned him to move out of the way, because they were going to go after the girl. Colin realized all he could do was defend himself with his sword, because a thrust would cost him his life with two experts who were ready to kill. Sasha pulled his gun from his bag and shot them both.

"Sasha! What's with ye, man?"

"You want to die instead of them? We must find Rosa."

Rosa sat behind a huge tree to catch her breath. She was so exhausted she fell asleep. Two Celtic hunters were walking in the woods carrying fur pelts on their backs. They noticed an attractive woman asleep beside a large tree. They knelt to her to see if she was all right.

Rosa opened her eyes and screamed. They laughed and covered her mouth to muffle her screams. One of the men took her arm. She pulled her arm away from him. The other man sneaked behind her and picked her up by the waist. She kicked and screamed and the device fell to the ground. She had wrapped it in a blanket, but the wind blew the blanket off. The two men noticed the device.

Rosa swooped down to snatch the device away from them. They grabbed her and threw her on the ground. She struggled, but they pinned her down. She elbowed them both in the eyes, kicked, and bit them. One of them sat on top of her and smacked her across the face causing her nose to bleed. She screamed. They took the device and ran off.

She sat up. Her bloody nose stained the peasant garment she was wearing. She ran after them and jumped

152

on one of the hunter's backs. He dropped the device, the other hunter swooped down to snatch it. She bit his leg; he yelped and dropped the device again. One hunter was so frustrated, that he pinned her to the ground while the other hunter smacked her several times in the face. They took the device and left. She lay there drenched in her own blood. She sat up and cried.

"Now, what are we going to do? We're doomed," She said, sniffIng.

Colin and Sasha ran through the crowded village. They tried to blend in, but it was impossible with Colin's towering height and bulky physique. Everywhere they went, someone noticed them.

"Mr. Limmerick, what we do now? Rosa is nowhere to be found and Miss Amoli is with chieftain. Our women are in trouble, da?"

"That they are. I'm terrified that Amoli could get raped by that wanker, 'n where is our Rosa?"

"You attract so much attention wherever you go, Mr. Limmerick."

They stopped walking. "This isn't workin', is it?"

"Red-haired giant!" the villagers blurted in Gaelic.

"Who?" Colin replied. "Are they meanin' me?"

"You? the people say, because they point at you."

Colin glanced at Sasha. "Aye, mate, I'm attractin' too much attention. I think I'll tie me hair back."

"Big deal! That does nothing; you are size of mountain."

"Gotta do somethin', don't I?"

"Where would Rosa go? We not finding Rosa here. Where would she go with time-travel device?" Sasha wondered.

Colin scratched his beard. "Would she have remained in the Celtic village or would she have gone to the forest instead?"

"She clever lady. She would stay far from Celtic people. She would go to forest."

153

"Aye, so she would. Which direction?"

"We begin in roundhouse. She would go from there, maybe?"

"Shite, I don't know. She could be anywhere."

The male time-travelers walked back to the roundhouse where the slave women were. There was a feast of food waiting for them. The slave women were glad to see Colin had returned. Colin told them he wouldn't need them until the morning. The women informed him another battle with the Vikings was looming for the following day. Colin offered them some food. They took it and ate it. Colin smiled at them.

"They're always here waiting for me."

"That is good."

"Sometimes. There's another battle tomorrow with the Vikings."

"Not good. Can you postpone it?"

"Who the feck postpones battles? I haven't the choice, I'm sure of it."

"The slave girls will do *what* with you now?"

"They'll wash me back, give me a rub down. They give me sex, as much as I want. They keep me fed. They give me wine, lots of it."

"You not need twentieth century; your life is better here."

"I can do without the on-goin' battles with the Vikings. I'd take the twentieth century back in a heartbeat. Besides I'm missin' me mother 'n father."

"You not see them that often, do you?"

"About once a month I see them. They's happy I make some effort to spend time with 'im, ye know."

"You so nice boy, Mr. Limmerick."

Colin grinned. "Try to be."

"Where is our Rosa? Where is Miss Amoli?"

"I want our wenches back 'n I want them now. It's seems like it's gettin' so late 'n Rosa could be anywhere.

Also, I can't stand the thought of that grubby shite with his claws all over Amoli."

"We must go in forest to find Rosa first, then we must think of plan to save Miss Amoli from brute."

Chapter Nineteen

Rosa stubbed her toe a few times on the gnarly roots below her feet. It was too dark to see where to step. She whimpered and cried as her nose slowly clotted. She tried to find her way back to the village, but she was confused because of her anguish. She felt the cold wind chill her bones as she tried to talk to herself into calming down. She was afraid to call for Colin and Sasha, because the wrong people might answer her. She continued to rustle through the brush. She heard a hard sound. Branches were cracking loudly. The leaves crackled. Someone was behind her.

She stopped to look around. It was too dark. She could hear heavy breathing. She was terrified it was those two hunters who stole the time-travel device. The heavy breathing sounded almost inhuman. She remained still.

"Is anyone there?"

Rosa could only see the moonlight, which shone down behind her. A large shadow of mass appeared behind her. She shivered from horror as urine dribbled down her legs. She heard a harsh snorting sound. What was behind her, she thought to herself? Something was closer to her than she imagined.

She put her hands out in front of her to feel what was in front of her. It was an animal, a bull of some sort. She had trouble breathing. Then she felt large horns above its head. She tried to catch her breath, but she couldn't. She looked up as the moonlight. She heard a snort or two. She had heard that sound before. She tried to control her trembling, but she couldn't. She looked at the silhouette before it. It was *Megaloceros giganteus*. She fainted to the ground.

Chapter Twenty

Colin and Sasha tore through the forest with torches in their hands.

"Mr. Limmerick, we out here for hours and still no Rosa. I'm so tired. We not sleep in so long. I must rest or I will fall over." Sasha leaned against a tree.

"Sit a bit. I'll continue lookin'."

"Too dark. We can wait for daylight, da?"

"Never. We can't afford to wait that long, 'cause I've got to fetch Amoli, 'n yer gonna get us out of this bleedin' century, so ye are."

Sasha sunk to the ground with his weight against the tree trunk. He held the torch in his hand, while his eyes shut. Colin continued to hike through the dense brush. Sasha's torch fell from his hand and onto the damp grass.

"Ouch!" a female voice blurted.

Sasha abruptly woke up. "Who?"

"Sasha?" cried Rosa.

"Mr. Limmerick! We find Rosa! Come!" Shouted Sasha.

"You burned part of my ugly dress with your torch," she said with a serious smile.

Sasha held her in his arms. "So good to see so beautiful face again. I love you."

Rosa squealed out of his arms. "Can you stop with this rubbish? You don't love me and you never did. We really don't have time to waste. Where's Colin?"

Sasha pointed. "He come now. Look."

Sasha helped her up as Colin approached them.

"Oh, how lucky we are that yer standin' before us, love." Colin swooped her into his arms. "So, glad, love. Scared is what I was."

"I'm alright. I don't know how I'm surviving all this," she said with a sigh.

157

"Ye look like ye got yerself a bloody nose, so you have. Did ye get yerself into a scuffle with someone?"

She tried to look at her dress. "I was attacked. I think the blood stains are an improvement for the dress, though."

Colin gently placed her back on the ground, but kept his arm tightly around her.

"Attacked? By who?" asked Sasha, wiping the blood from her face with a handkerchief.

"Two hunters wanted their way with me. I put up a fight, so they smacked me in the face." She whimpered. "They took the time-travel device. Oh, God! What are we going to do?"

Sasha and Colin looked at each other. "Did ye get a good look at those shites? Could ye sight 'im in a crowd?"

Rosa started to cry. "Maybe. I don't know. I'm just so tired. I want to sleep in my own bed. I want a hot bath."

Sasha put his arms around Rosa. "No crying here. If worse is worse, I will make new device. It will not be easy; we are in so primitive time. It can be done."

Colin smiled. "Ye sure, mate? There's no modern labs 'round here."

"We will create what we can from earth. We can do this. We are intelligent."

"First, in the mornin', we gotta find these hunters, so we must," Colin insured.

"Colin," Rosa said, wiping her wet eyes. "Don't you have another battle?"

Colin sighed. "So, I do. Terrifed, so I am. Surely, I'm bound to lose soon enough. Why is the chieftain so head-strong on me bein' his top warrior? Why doesn't he choose one of his expert men, so I don't know."

"Again, it's your appearance. You're bigger and stronger than any man in this village. You're the chieftain's Hercules," Rosa said.

"Appearance, it's always me appearance. I'm cursed, so I am. Always been judged on me appearance. Tired of it. Professor Cushing hates me bleedin' guts, simply 'cause of me appearance. Not fair, so it isn't."

Rosa took Sasha and Colin's hands. "Maybe we can get back to the round house and get a few hours of rest."

Colin stopped Rosa from walking. "Don't think we can do that, love."

"Because I shoot two of chieftain's guards. They wanted fight, so I shoot them."

"Did you kill them?"

"Da."

"Sasha, so far, you've shot three men since we've been in this century."

"They want to kill Mr. Limmerick, so I defend him. I am good man."

"You can't be doing this anymore, because you could be shooting Sir Isaac Newton's great, great grandfathers," Rosa said, in curt tone.

Colin glanced at her. "Newton? It would never be Newton's great grandfathers, don't ye think? Try Jonathan Swift, maybe."

"Oh, alright, some famous Irishman, perhaps."

"Aye, thought of that one meself as well. Can't just be shootin' at the gene pool, so he can't. Sasha, yer a scientist, ye should know this."

"I have no choice sometimes. You terrible with sword. Next time, fight with bare hands."

"I'll ask if I can do that tomorrow. Doubt they'd adhere to me request, what ye think? Just don't think any form of democracy was formed durin' these times."

When the sun finally rose, the three time-travelers had slept in the cold damp grass. Rosa lifted her head.

"Colin, Sasha, wake up. We've got things to do."

"Aye, the first task on me agenda is to get Amoli back," Colin said, in the middle of a yawn. "I slept like shite."

Sasha stood up. "Second task is to get time-travel device."

"Third task is to get some food. I'm starved," Rosa said.

Colin smiled. "How am I goin' to battle when I'm feelin' this awful?"

"We need to get back to the roundhouse so you can rest and eat," said Rosa.

"Maybe our tent on our arrival still there. I will go there."

"Think the Celts would've destroyed it by now, don't ye think, mate?"

"Rosa rubbed her tired eyes. "Look, let's keep Sasha out of sight from the Celtic village. Maybe we should go look for our tent, but I've got to tell you both about this odd dream I had last night."

"You could dream with so much discomfort? How is that?" Sasha asked.

Colin chuckled. "Hopin' Prince Charmin' rode on by with his white horse 'n swooped ye into his arms."

"Better than that. I dreamt I was face to face with *Megaloceros giganteus*."

Colin chuckled again. "Where was that?"

"Right here in this ninth-century leper pit that we're in right now."

Sasha laughed. "Mr. Limmerick's Irish deer was here in this time of Celtic and Viking people?"

"Can you believe it? It seemed so real. I was touching its antlers. It even snorted at me. I could even smell its vile stench."

"How depressin'. We're supposed to have time-traveled on a prehistoric expedition 'n yet here we are in this sorry time of warlords, where Vikings raped 'n pillaged the lands. We're just lucky I guess."

"I explain before we go that time-travel device could take us to wrong time period. You know all this, but you ignore it," Sasha said, raising his voice.

160

"Feck, man, what bleedin' choice did I have? Prehistoric life was filterin' into the twentieth century. How wrong was that, mate?"

Rosa put her hand on Colin and Sasha's shoulders. "Look, you two, we don't have time to argue. We've got to get the device back, or we're going to die here."

"More so, I've got to fetch Amoli. I've been such a cad since we got here. I've allowed her to fall in the hands of that monster."

"Don't be silly. You've been a battling warrior since we got here."

"Got to fetch the lass now. I can't wait any longer. Ye 'n Sasha can get to the round house. I'll go with ye 'n I can tell the slaves to pamper yez a wee bit."

"Rosa, you must find men who took time-travel device," Sasha instilled.

"Alright, I'll see if I can find those two hunters. We'll go see if our tent is still standing later. I just hope I can recognize them; it was very dark."

They arrived at the round house. The female slaves were cleaning it and laying another spread of food. Colin smiled at them. The slaves reciprocated the gesture. *"Bain sult as do chuid,"* one of the slaves said as she offered the food.

Colin reluctantly sat down and encouraged Rosa and Sasha to join him. He took a few bights of roasted pork. He kept his eyes on the slaves as he chewed the meat.

"Tell me, where is the chieftain's round house?" Colin asked, in Gaelic.

He stood up to face the female slaves. They informed him how to get there. One of the slave women grabbed Colin's arm.

"You can't go unless you have been announced. Only if your presence has been requested," She warned him.

Colin glanced at Rosa and Sasha. His lips were parted as he took a deep breath.

"I'm not to go to the chieftain's place unannounced, apparently."

Rosa stood up. "Amoli is in there with that savage, 'n God only knows what he's done to her."

Sasha patted Colin on the shoulder. "Miss Amoli is not as helpless as you think, Mr. Limmerick. She can be cunning girl."

"Ye 'n Rosa need to blend in with the crowd 'n find those two hunters who took the device. I'll be waitin' here for yez with Amoli."

Colin took his sword and spear as he made his exit. Rosa slowly lay on the wool blankets.

"Sasha, I've got to rest. Please, let me sleep a bit."

"No time for sleep. We must find two hunters."

"What if they put up a fight?"

"I'll blow their heads off with gun."

Colin walked through the crowds. Several women ogled over his grand appearance. The crowd lessened as he walked toward the head chieftain's roundhouse. Colin stood by the doorway and listened in. He could hear the chieftain shouting. Colin stormed in. Amoli was sitting on the floor with her back against the wall.

She stood up and ran to him. Her eyes were glazed with tears.

"Thank the good Lord, yer okay."

Colin tugged at her arm. The chieftain stepped forward with his sword in hand. His sword blocked the exit. Colin shouted to the chieftain in Gaelic.

"She belongs to me!" the chieftain ranted. He whacked his sword against a clay pot on the floor. It shattered into pieces. Amoli screamed and cried. "You are expected to duel with the next Viking intruder, but I will fight you to the death for the girl."

Colin glared at the chieftain and took his time to answer. "She's me own property." He said in English, paused when he realized the chieftain didn't understand. He then, repeated himself in Gaelic.

162

"When I fight you, you will die," the chieftain said.

Colin shrugged his shoulders and tried to show disinterest as well as disrespect. Amoli tugged at Colin's armor.

"Colin, what's he saying to you?"

Colin looked down at her, " He wants ye. He wants ye bad, so he does."

"Well, did you tell him he can't have me?"

"Aye. Too many times I've told 'im."

"Doesn't he understand what you're telling him?"

"Don't think so, lass. He wants ye."

Amoli cried into a fit of hysterics. "Tell him he can't have me. The only man I want is you."

Colin sighed. "He's wavin' his sword. I think we need to make our exit."

The chieftain blurted, *"I will fight you when the sun is brightest in the day."*

"Noon, I think he means noon. These wankers can't tell time. Did ye know that?" Colin grabbed Amoli and rushed to the exit, pushing the chieftain's sword from him. Colin stared the chieftain in the eyes. *"I'll fight yez with me bare hands. No need for swords."*

The chieftain laughed at Colin, as if he pitied him. *"Swords and spears."*

Colin grimaced. *"No weapons."*

The chieftain stood in front of Colin. He ran the tip of his sword along Colin's bicep and pressed it into his arm. Colin watched blood drip from his arm to the floor.

"Swords and spears," the chieftain insisted.

Colin gripped the chieftain's arm so tight his sword dropped to the floor. Then Colin punched him so hard in the face the *thud* made a crashing sound. The chieftain fell to the floor, out cold. Colin took Amoli's arm and they made their exit. Colin briskly walked through the village with Amoli in his arms.

"Colin? Did you kill the head chieftain?" Amoli asked.

"Donno."

"Would it be bad if you did?"

He stopped and held her shoulders tightly. "Can things get any worse? If we don't find Sasha's time-travel device, we'll all surely die here, lass."

"Colin, you're hurting me."

He removed his hands from her. "Sorry, lass." They continued to walk in silence. "We got to find Sasha 'n Rosa 'n get out of this God forsaken century."

"What did you discuss with the chieftain? Why did he cut you?"

Colin glanced at her. "Donno."

"It was more than nothing. He seemed very upset with you. He cut your arm."

"He wants ye, that's for sure, he just wants ye."

"Why does he want me so much?"

Colin stepped closer to her. "'Cause yer beautiful."

Amoli gleamed at him. "Miss Emanuel is beautiful, too. Why doesn't he want her?"

"Rosa looks too much like the other wenches 'round here, ye don't." Colin took Amoli's hand. "We've got to continue lookin' for our mates, so we must."

"Colin? Won't you kiss me?"

Colin sighed with frustration. "I can't."

She ran in front of him, rather than beside him. Sasha and Rosa were in the main square of the village. Colin and Amoli approached them. Sasha smiled and ran his hands through Amoli's long black hair.

"So, Miss Amoli, you survive some days with bad chieftain, da?"

Colin's smile dissipated. "Did ye find the two hunters?"

"It's like finding a needle in a haystack. I'm beginning to think that we're doomed," Rosa said, with distress in her voice.

"Rosa, not to worry, population not so big in this time. Your haystack is thinner than twentieth century," Sasha said.

Amoli glared at Colin. "Colin? You are so very aloof with me, yet I can see that you don't appreciate Dr. Dimitrikov touching me."

"Mr. Limmerick, always so nervous when I am around his woman."

Colin shoved Sasha. "Feck – off, ye wanker."

"Colin?" Amoli crossed her arms in front of her. "You let me be alone with that Celtic chief. You let me spend nights with him. It was so very horrible. All I did was cry."

Rosa shoved Amoli. "Wait a minute, little Miss. Colin was very preoccupied with constant Viking battles. He almost died, you know."

"I almost died as well, Miss Emanuel. How would you like to spend several nights with a smelly and ugly Celtic chief from another century?"

"You can't deal with the fact that Colin ended his courtship with you. You and Colin are not a good match. There is too much of an age difference and your cultures are always clashing. Colin is right, that maybe you would be better off with some younger man from India that your parents approve of."

"If Colin allowed you to spend several nights with that chieftain, you would have been so very horrified, Miss Emanuel."

Colin took Amoli's arm. "Ye can't be havin' a scuffle now; save it for another day."

Amoli stepped closer to Colin. "You threw me to the wolves, the way I see it. You're right, Captain Colin Limmerick. I should be very much better off with someone more humane than you."

"Amoli, calm down. This sure is not the time or place. Just hold yer tongue 'till later, if ye choose to ball me out."

Amoli stepped directly in front of him. "That horrible man could have raped me and killed me. He tried to rape me several times, but I bit him on the arm."

"I couldn't fetch ye, lass. I was battlin' Viking warriors."

"I don't care. I'm tired of your excuses. I'm tired of your silly time-travel expeditions. I'm tired of your stupid boat!" Amoli shouted, so loud that her voice cracked. The people in the village stopped and stared. "I'm tired of your silly research. And, most of all, your heavy drinking disgusts me." She punched his arms. She kicked him in the knees and stepped on his feet. She grabbed his large hand and bent back his fingers. She jumped up and yanked his long hair. "I hate you! You're a drunk! And you're a whore of a man. You have slept with so many women. I bet you have slept with women on this journey."

Rosa tried to focus on something else.

"I never want to be with you. I hate you so much. Whom haven't you slept with?" She cupped sand from the ground and threw it at his face. "Dr. Dimitrikov, please get us home. I can't stand being in the presence of Captain Limmerick any more!"

Rosa shook Amoli by the shoulders. "Get a hold of yourself. We can't go home. Two hunters took the time-travel device, you fool. We've got a big problem."

Amoli looked at Colin and Sasha, and cried, "We're never going home?"

"We're trying to find the men who took it," Rosa said. "Look, I'm glad you're alright, but you have got to understand that this is time-travel. There are no guarantees."

"What are we waiting for? Why aren't we finding them?"

Sasha glanced at Amoli. "Because it was so dark in the night. There are no lamp posts and Miss Rosa was struck so hard by hunters. It was dangerous for her. She not really see who did this to her."

Rosa glanced at Colin. "Don't lose focus. You made your decision to break ties with her. You can't allow yourself to feel emotions now. We have to find those hunters."

"Can't help feelin' like shite, love." Colin's head hung low. "Sounds like she hates me guts, don't ye think?"

Rosa took Colin's hand. "We need to find those hunters. That time-travel device is all we have. You can patch things up with her when we get back to the twentieth century."

Sasha took Rosa and Amoi's hand. "We must not split up. Four of us must remain together at all times. We will go amongst villagers and find these hunters. Mr. Limmerick, you must be our language guide. You speak Gaelic. Miss Amoli should keep herself covered. She is too different than others. Mr. Limmerick and me will carry weapons, including gun."

"Not yer gun, mate," Colin interjected.

"Da, gun is important. I want."

Rosa tugged on Sasha's arm. "Let's just concentrate on getting the device back in our possession. Murdering ancient Celts and Vikings is not what we came here for."

The four time-travelers infiltrated the village. They walked to a roundhouse, where a family had settled. Colin sat beside one of the males. The man glared at Colin and continued to make his tools. Colin smiled at him.

"Excuse me," he said in Gaelic. *"I'm lookin' for two hunters. If ye know of any, can ye direct me to where some hunters may be?"*

The man laughed. He called his relatives over and told them what Colin had requested. They all laughed. Sasha glanced at them, then at Colin.

The man sat closer to Colin. "We are all hunters in this village. How do you think we eat?"

167

Colin stood up and looked at Rosa. "Ye really gotta try to remember what those hunters looked like. Just don't know if we can find them at this rate."

"What they say?" Sasha asked.

"They think I'm a wanker."

Amoli was swaddled in sheets with just her eyes showing. She noticed two men walk behind the family's round house with spears.

"Miss Emanuel, would those two men be the hunters?"

"Maybe they are," she said, as she followed them with the three time-travelers trailing behind.

She got closer to them, while the others hid behind a cluster of trees. One of the hunters recognized Rosa. He stepped closer to her. He muddled a few words to her in Gaelic while his cohort grabbed her. Rosa screamed.

"Mr. Limmerick! They are the men," Sasha said in a whisper, as they hid behind the trees.

"Don't like them handlin' Rosa in such a way, do ye?"

"She knows what she doing."

"Oh my, Miss Emanuel is so brave to do this," Amoli commented.

Rosa squirmed in the man's arms. He let her down on her feet.

"Where's the time-travel device?" Rosa asked. They looked at each other with confused expressions. "Okay, I'll draw it in the mud."

She found a twig and drew an outline of the device. They laughed and one of them picked her up and threw her over his shoulder. They walked away from the roundhouse. Colin, Sasha, and Amoli followed discreetly. They sauntered through the wild brush to a small, partially dilapidated roundhouse. Rosa was roughly placed on her feet. She panicked.

"Where's my device?" she screamed, at the top of her lungs.

Sasha, Colin and Amoli looked at each other.

"I'm goin' in there," Colin said.

Sasha shoved Colin against the tree. "Stop! We must think how to do this. If she so needs us, she will call."

"Ye just heard her, didn't yez?"

"We must think how to get back device."

"They's ninth-century wankers with not a brain in their heads. Can't reason with shites like that, now can yez?"

"We will do what we can. You have bigger fish to fry. If we no get time-travel device, you will be fighting chieftain soon for Miss Amoli."

"Don't bother fighting for me, Colin. You'll probably lose anyway," Amoli blurted.

Colin glanced at her with saddened eyes. "Why ye talk that way, lass? I'll fight to the finish for ye, surely, I will."

"You leave me with very much disappointment."

Sasha placed his arm around Amoli. "No time for this; we must get back device."

The hunter in the roundhouse pushed Rosa to the muddy floor and jumped on top of her. He tugged at her dress. She kicked him in the groin and he fell to the floor. Rosa ran out of the house. Colin and Sasha ran to her. Rosa was out of breath.

"They have our device and they're not going to give it back."

"We will kill them then," Sasha responded.

Some hours later they walked through the dense brush.

"We really should see if our tent is still standing," Rosa said.

"It will be big surprise if it is," said Sasha.

They walked through a beautiful meadow. Amoli slipped on a loose rock and fell down the slope. Colin quickly tended to her.

"Leave me alone. I can get up myself."

169

Rosa glanced at Amoli struggling to get up from the slippery mud. "You don't have to be rude, you little brat. Colin is offering to help you."

"Miss Emanuel, why do you hate me so much?"

Rosa turned away from Amoli. "What's there to like?"

Sasha helped Amoli up and brushed the mud off her dress. "This is no place or time for cat fight. I am tired of all of this, but to fight amongst ourselves is bad."

"Sorry, we are all people with human emotions, I suppose," Amoli said.

"You don't know the meaning of the word," Rosa snorted back.

Colin took Rosa's hand and held it tightly. They continued to walk until they finally reached the remains of their tent.

"It looks as if she got herself a wee bit roughed up, wouldn't yez think?" Colin said, while he gathered some of the scattered pieces of the tent.

"Oh, God, now our tent has been destroyed," Rosa said, rubbing her hands over her tired eyes.

"What do we do now? Amoli asked.

Sasha glanced at his three cohorts. "What you think? We fix it. At least they leave enough material for us to work with, da"

"They left one sleepin' bag, if yez can believe it?"

"We now know what two hunters look like. We now know where their ugly house is too. Tomorrow, I will blow off both heads, and we will get device and go back to twentieth century, da?"

"Not so fast, mate. We don't have any idea where they put the device. Killin' them will only make things worse," said Colin.

"Colin's right, Sasha. As much as they make me want to vomit, we need to play their game so we can get them to lead us to the device," Rosa said.

170

Chapter Twenty-One

The four time-travelers worked relentlessly on gathering tent remains, as well as furs and hides for them to sleep in. Rosa ran her fingers through her long knotted hair.

"Oh, my gosh, why do I agree to go on these historic expeditions with you? My hair is a disaster. I really need a bath."

Colin gathered logs to build a fire. "Ye do it 'cause yer a scientist, that's why."

"Now, we lost the time-travel device to those hooligans. What's next?"

Colin knelt to the logs and lit a match. "We just have to get the device back."

"What if that chieftain finds us and demands you fight him for Amoli?" Rosa asked, sitting on a log.

Colin stood up. "Then, I suppose I'll have to fight 'im."

Sasha walked past them with disheveled tent pieces in his hands. "Miss Amoli is lucky lady. So many men fight for her hand."

Amoli sat on the one sleeping bag inside the patched-up tent. "I don't feel lucky."

"I'm feeling as if the worst is still yet to come," Rosa said.

"The worst was losin' the time-travel device. Nothin' can surely top that, can it?"

Amoli grimaced at Colin.

"Ah, losin' the device is surely the second worst thing that's happened, where Amoli bein' in the chieftain's possession, is definitely the worst."

Sasha opened the tent. "Miss Amoli, we only have one sleeping bag. Spread it out flat, so we can use it as

171

insulation from cold ground. All four of us will have to sleep tight on it."

"They took our sleeping bags, too. What awful people," Amoli said.

Colin lit the fire. "There, this should keep us all from freezin' in the night. In the mornin' I think Sasha 'n I bes' see those hunters, 'n apply force on them, if need be."

"Well, I don't know about all of you, but I'm exhausted and it's getting dark," said Rosa.

She crawled into the tent with Amoli. Colin and Sasha followed. The four of them tried not to touch each other, despite the lack of tent space. Rosa and Amoli fell asleep immediately.

"Mr. Limmerick," Sasha whispered. "You sleep yet? Girls are asleep, da?"

"Aye."

"I need cigarette. I will go outside tent and smoke, da?"

Colin rolled onto his side without bothering the females. "Go ahead."

Sasha crawled over Colin and exited the tent. He sat on the log and watched the smoldering fire as he pulled out a cigarette. He only saw and heard the crackling kindles of the fire Colin built. He sat and smoked almost hypnotized by the silence. His eyes started to close on him. He dropped his cigarette butt onto the damp grass. A rustle in the bushes made a cracking noise, which startled Sasha awake. He grabbed his handgun and made sure it was loaded with bullets. He heard the brush against the trees, cracked twigs and branches cracking and falling to the ground. He poked his head into the tent.

"Mr. Limmerick," he whispered, poking at Colin's leg. "I think Celts or Vikings are in bushes."

"I'm just too tired, mate."

"You must get out of tent, now, or I will shoot them."

"Ye can't do that. Ah, feck." Colin slowly crawled out of the tent, trying not to disturb the women. He sat beside Sasha on the log. "Where are they?"

"Shhh...listen. They are in trees." They heard the trees rustle and the branches break. There was a sound of heavy thumping steps that got louder and louder. "Is there army of them coming to get us?"

A loud snorting sound and heavy footsteps echoed through the trees. Colin glanced at Sasha with a puzzled expression on his face.

"For some crazy reason, these sounds are all too familiar to me, mate."

"Who is it? I kill them."

Colin placed his hand over Sasha's gun. "Wait." The snorting grew louder and a large shadow appeared by the moonlight. Colin's eyes widened. "What the feck is that?" He stood up, and took a few steps toward the large figure. "Oh, feck. Oh, sweet Jesus, tell me this isn't so." Colin took a deep breath. *"It's Megaloceros giganteous.* Rosa didn't dream it. She saw it in the flesh."

"How?" Sasha asked, standing up. "This is 840 AD. How is this possible?"

"The time vortex fecked history, man. We're stupid fecks. We's tryin' to play God, 'n now a prehistoric beast is livin' amongst the ancient Celts. Oh, God."

The large beast backed away from Colin and Sasha. It turned away from them and let out a loud snort. It walked into the dense brush. Sasha stood beside Colin.

"What we do, now?"

"We get the time-travel device from those hunters in the mornin'."

"What if chieftain comes for you? He want fight you."

"I punched him in the face, last I saw of 'im. But, aye, he'll come for me, so he will. I know it."

Loud footsteps made a hard *thwack* on the muddy ground. Tree branches broke and crackled.

"Is it prehistoric beast again?" asked Sasha.

"Sounds like horses, so it does."

Several horses trotted to their tent. The head chieftain sat on his horse peering at Colin with a menacing expression on his face. He shouted in Gaelic as he waved his spear at Colin. His men got off their horses and charged at Colin.

"Run, Mr. Limmerick!" shouted Sasha.

"Too late, they've got me now."

They locked chains around his ankles and wrists. Sasha dodged for his gun. He aimed it at one of the guards and shot. The guard fell to the ground. The other Celts stepped back, startled and fearful. The guard who was shot lay on the ground dead.

"Mate! What ye doin'?" One of the guards pressed the point of his sword into Sasha's belly. "Mate, ye pull the trigger again, 'n you'll get a blade in yer gut. Just lay low. I'll be fine." The guards confiscated Sasha's gun and they locked chains around Sasha's wrists. "Great, mate, now they've got the time-travel device 'n yer gun. *Megaloceros* is runnin' about the woods in the ninth century 'n I've got to duel with the head Celtic chief. Can it get any worse?"

"Nyet. Should I call women in tent?"

"Don't! These Celts don't know they's in there. Let's spare Amoli this time. Rosa will know what to do in the mornin'."

The horses began their slow trot as the guards surrounded Colin and Sasha. They walked in the direction of the village.

174

Chapter Twenty-Two

Rosa rolled over on the sleeping bag to feel for Colin. She slowly opened her eyes and gasped from her sleep state.

"Colin?" Rosa said.

Amoli turned to her.

"Sasha's not here, either. Knowing them, Colin is chopping wood somewhere and Sasha is smoking a cigarette."

Amoli smiled and rolled over.

"You know, you've been unfair to Colin," Rosa said, sitting up.

"Oh, really? He keeps pushing me away. It hurts so very much. I know he still loves you, Miss Emanuel."

Rosa grinned. "I know he does. We should be together again. He made a big mistake choosing you. It's for the best that the both of you are no more."

"But that will never be, because I'm the one he wants to marry. He wants me to be his wife."

"You're his second choice. I'm his first. I was always first for him."

"I don't really think so. His first choice would be me," Amoli said, trying to primp her black, knotted hair. She crawled out of the tent and slowly stood up straight to looked around. "Where are they, Miss Emanuel? I don't see them."

"Take a good whiff. Can't you smell Sasha's tobacco?" Rosa crawled out of the tent. She scanned the wooded area with her eyes. "There's no sign of them. That's not like them."

"Maybe Colin found a beautiful woman that he wished to spend the night with?"

"I don't think he would have done that last night. He wasn't even drinking."

"We're here, alone? I'm so frightened," Amoli said, shaking with fear.

"How did you spend those long nights under the Celtic chieftain's wing?"

"I slept in the corner as far from him as possible."

"I'm surprised he didn't force you into doing something else."

"He grabbed me a few times, but I bit his arm. He bled."

"Good for you. Now, I'm wondering if Colin and Sasha were taken away by those goons. The fire is out completely. If Colin chose to leave our camp of his own will, he would have ignited the fire, wouldn't you think? Knowing him."

"I suppose."

"This is not like him. He was taken against his will and we slept through it. That chieftain wants to fight him for you."

"Everyone is always trying to win my hand. Sometimes it is very difficult to be so beautiful."

Rosa bit her lip and turned away from Amoli. "You're such a foolish girl. If it appears that everyone wants to marry you, it is more likely they want something else from you. You aren't so beautiful, Amoli Sharma. You don't really have much of anything else to offer."

"You're very rude. Colin thinks I'm very beautiful, so then I must be."

Rosa turned to Amoli. "Have you noticed Colin has been wearing his glasses more often, lately?"

Amoli's eyebrows lowered closer to her nose. "You are so very rude."

"Look, Colin and Sasha aren't here. My thoughts are a little preoccupied. We need to get that time-travel device from the hunters. They are both pigs and they will stop at nothing to get what they want from us. We have to be smart."

"What do we do?"

"Maybe I'll drug them. I have a bottle of aspirin with me. Maybe I'll give them the entire bottle."

"Don't you think they would know?"

"I'll lure them with my beauty. Better yet, why don't you lure them with your beauty, since you're the beautiful one. We now know where they reside. We will go there and you will show them how beautiful you are. I will spike their food with the aspirin. Maybe I'll even make them a meal. Colin's slaves could help us with that one."

"Colin has slaves?"

"Yes, and they're beautiful Celtic women."

"They belong to Colin?"

"They sure do." Rosa and Amoli peeked into the roundhouse where Colin was usually held. "Colin?" Rosa said, in a whisper.

"Rosa?" Colin responded.

Rosa and Amoli stepped into the roundhouse.

"Colin, you're chained to the wall?"

"Of course I am. We all knew this was comin', didn't we? Sasha shot one of the chieftain's guards. Don't know where they took him, but I do know they took his gun. We's all fecked for good, I think."

Rosa rubbed her hands over her face. "Oh, God, that's dangerous."

"Maybe not. They've never seen a gun before. They don't know how to use it. Don't even know if there's enough bullets in it to cause a mass killin'."

"Oh, Colin, how could Sasha be so stupid?"

"He's not stupid, love. He tried to help me when they was seizin' me."

Amoli stepped back. "I don't like to see you in chains, Colin."

"I don't fancy the idea meself."

"I've got a bottle of aspirin with me. I'm going to spike the hunter's food. I need a freshly cooked meal. Where's those slave girls?"

"They should be bringin' me the grub any time soon. Aspirin, eh? What would that do to them anyways?"

"Make them ill, of course, " Rosa responded.

The slave women entered the house. They placed several platters of roasted swine on the floor and poured Colin a large flask of wine. The chains locked around Colin were long enough where he could feed himself. Colin asked the slaves to leave.

"There ye go, love. Ye got yerself a home cooked meal. Crush the aspirin 'n mix it in." Colin watched Rosa crush the aspirin with a serving utensil. Amoli sat at the opposite end of the house and smiled at Colin. "Amoli, ye still angry with me?"

She bowed her head. "How can I be? I love you too much for that."

He smiled at her. "I'll never stop lovin' ye, ye know it, lass."

Rosa sat on her knees. "Can you two stop it? I'm in the middle of making a potion for those idiot hunters. I really don't want to watch you two make up."

"Colin, will that chieftain kill you?" Amoli asked.

"I can't let that happen, now can I? But, lass, ye really need to lay low 'n not let any of his guards spot yez. They will keep ye captive again."

"Shouldn't you have the duel with him first?"

"He's the chief. Don't really have a say in this, so I don't."

"Okay, I think I'm just about done with this," Rosa said. "I'm very worried about Sasha. What if they killed him with his own gun?"

Colin smile dissipated. "They don't know how to use a gun. They would shoot themselves before they can shoot Sasha. Sasha is also great with a sword."

Amoli swaddled herself with blankets. "They won't find me dressed like this."

178

"Are you going to lure those two idiot hunters with your beauty, or do I have to do it myself?" Rosa said, standing up.

"I suppose I will. I don't want them to touch me, though."

"Be prepared. They will touch you," Rosa responded.

One of the female slaves entered the roundhouse. *"Excuse me, m' lord,"* she said, with a timid Gaelic voice. *"You will be expected to duel when the sun light is at its brightest."*

Colin nodded his head to her. She sat beside him, and slowly brought her lips to his. Rosa smiled and Amoli bit her lip. The slave ran out of the roundhouse and called for the other slaves. They all entered. It was time for them to dress Colin for battle.

"Rosa, Amoli, it's best yez both leave; they need to get me armor on. The time has come where I have to fight."

Rosa kissed him on the lips. "I'm going to get back the time-travel device right now. I'm not going to allow those two hunters to take control of matters."

"That's what I like to hear, love. Please watch yerself."

Amoli shoved Rosa aside. "If you lose I will belong to the chieftain. You can't lose."

"I can't, nay I can't."

She kissed him on the lips. Rosa and Amoli left.

"I have this food spiked with aspirin. I can't wait to see their reaction to this," Rosa said, with a chuckle.

Amoli glanced at Rosa. "What if it kills them and we never get the device back?"

"Keep your questions to yourself." They hid behind a tree and watched the two hunters enter and exit their dilapidated roundhouse. Rosa noticed the more aggressive hunter enter. "This is our chance. Get his attention, while I place the food in front of him."

"I don't like this," Amoli said, with a nervous twitch.

Rosa pushed Amoli toward the house. "Just do it! We don't have time to waste."

Amoli hesitantly made her way to the house. She faintly knocked on their door. The main hunter answered it. His eyes widened when he saw Amoli. Rosa appeared with the platter of food in her hands. The hunter relished in their beauty and the fine aroma of the meal. He took them inside the house. Rosa smiled at him. She noticed he was alone. She placed the food in front of him. Amoli tried to smile, but she found it impossible. He gorged himself in the food. Rosa noticed a large jug of wine. She poured him a flask.

"Here, this will wash it down much better," she said, with a smile. He didn't understand her English, but he grunted and snorted as he guzzled the wine and feasted on the cooked meal. Rosa tapped Amoli on the shoulder. "Look for the device," she whispered.

"I have been looking. I don't see it."

"I wonder if the other idiot has it with him," Rosa said, as she pretended to be interested in the hunter.

"Would that be bad, Miss Emanuel?"

Rosa stood straight as she faced Amoli. "What do you think? Yes, Amoli, it would be bad."

***

The crowd of spectators gathered. Colin was pulled by chains, locked around his wrists and ankles; so he could follow the chieftain's guards. The chieftain scanned the crowd the best he could. He saw Colin at the end of their battleground.

A guard on a horse trotted to Colin. *"M' lord wants to know where the girl is. She must be here, he says,"* the guard demanded, in Gaelic to Colin.

Colin rattled his chains to make a clanging sound. *"I don't know where she's at,"* he responded, in Gaelic.

"The battle with our lord cannot begin until the girl is found. You must wait here."

"Can ye rid me of these chains?"

"No!"

Colin watched the chieftain command his orders to his men. They rode off on their horses in search of Amoli. Colin's head hung low as he stared at the ground.

***

Rosa watched the hunter eat and drink his last bit. Amoli sat on the floor with unease. The hunter moaned from an upset stomach. He lay back on the floor and rolled around in discomfort. Rosa went through his belongings.

"Where did he put that device?" she demanded.

Amoli slowly stood up. "I don't know," she said, with a whimper.

The door swung opened and the other hunter entered. He was surprised to see the two women. His eyes widened when he saw his cohort wallowing on the floor in agony. He had the device in his hand. Rosa jumped at him and snatched the device.

"Follow me, Amoli!" Rosa shouted.

Rosa ran so quickly she didn't bother to see if Amoli was behind her. They both tore through the dense brush. Rosa suddenly stopped. *Megaloceros giganteous* stood in front of her. Rosa screamed.

"What's that?" Amoli asked, out of breath.

"That animal is Colin's research. That is a prehistoric mammal," Rosa commented, while she tried to catch her breath.

The large animal appeared startled and ran in a different direction. The hard cracking sound of horse hooves hit the muddy ground. Amoli looked up and realized the chieftain's guards had come for her.

"No!" Amoli screamed.

She ran. Rosa stood still with the device in her hands. She watched the guards take Amoli away. Rosa sighed with relief.

"At least I've got the device. But where's Sasha?" She dragged her fingers through her long knotted hair. She walked through the woods back to the village in search of

181

Sasha. She entered the round house Colin was usually held in. Her eyes saturated with tears when she saw Colin wasn't there. "My friend and love, you're probably in battle now. I can only pray for you," she said.

She walked past a different roundhouse. She gingerly poked her head in. Sasha lay on several cotton blankets. There was a spread of food before him with several young female slaves around him, serving him food and wine.

"Rosa, *zdrastvuytye...da...kak dela?*"

"What are you doing?"

Sasha choked on his wine as he tried to sit up.

"Have you forgotten your English?"

"Rosa, I am being rewarded."

"For what? Shooting people?"

Sasha gestured to the slaves that they should leave. "I see you have time-travel device. Good girl."

"Pardon me? Colin is about to go to battle. Amoli has been recaptured by the chieftain's guards and you're sitting here getting pampered by these prostitutes?"

"Slaves, my dear Rosa. These wonderful ladies are slaves, can you not see that?" Sasha stood directly in front of her. He watched the female slaves exit the roundhouse. "I am being rewarded for my magic."

"You sound a little drunk to me."

Sasha smiled. "I have gun back too. They not know how to use it," he snorted, with a cackling laugh. "They think I am magic man."

"How do you know they think this of you? You don't speak Gaelic."

"I am intelligent man. I know."

"Look, we have to save Colin. Can the time-travel device do anything to help him?"

Sasha paced a bit. "Nyet. Not enough time. He has to win fight on his own."

"I don't know if he can do that."

"He do good with past fights."

"You kept blowing off his opponents' heads, that's why. You can't do that to this chieftain character. Colin was just lucky with those past battles."

"Head chieftain deserves to get his head blown off, nyet?"

"Sasha," she said, tugging at his arm. "We've got to at least be present. We need to offer our support."

"Da, we go and cheer on Mr. Limmerick. He is big mountain of muscle, he will win."

Chapter Twenty-Three

The dense crowd stood and gawked at Colin standing in the main circle of the village. The head chieftain made his appearance. His guards escorted him through the crowd. Amoli was held behind the crowd, high up on a surface that overlooked the crowd. The head chieftain glanced at Colin.

"You are ready, my friend?" he called out to Colin in Gaelic.

The crowd mumbled. Colin pressed his teeth together. Rosa and Sasha tried to cut through the crowd. Rosa tripped over a goat, but Sasha caught her in his arms. Colin held his sword in front of him. He peered at the head chieftain.

"I can't use this sword!" he called out, in Gaelic. The crowd's roars intensified. The head chieftain looked at Colin. *"We either fight with our bare hands or I use a longer sword."* Colin took one step back. *"Ye heard me!"*

Rosa glanced at Sasha, who was swallowed by the crowd. "What did Colin say?"

"How should I know?"

"The crowd is reacting to whatever he said to the chieftain. "Do something!"

"You have no faith in Mr. Limmerick? He will win fight."

She stepped back. "Of course I have faith in Colin. He's just not the best swordsman. He's more used to street brawls. He's also too big, which makes him such an easy target."

"Just watch your Hercules. He will win. He is bigger and stronger than all in this land. Have faith."

The crowd roared when two guards handed Colin a long sword. Rosa's eyes widened.

"Oh, I see. That's what he wanted, she said nudging Sasha."

Colin took the mammoth sword and placed his hand on the grip. He held it in position. The chieftain smiled. He positioned his sword with the point toward the ground. "Wait!" he called. The crowd was silent. *I cannot allow you to use such a powerful sword. You would win. I must also use the same.*

The crowd roared. The same two guards also brought the chieftain a long sword. Colin noticed Rosa in the crowd. She waved at him. The long sword was far too large for the chieftain, but rather small for Colin.

The chieftain charged at Colin. He blocked him with his sword and stepped back. The loud clanging sound of the two colliding swords hit with conviction. The chieftain charged again, where Colin blocked him with ease; he had gained better control over the huge sword.

Colin took a deep breath. Sweat dripped from his face. Amoli watched from above. She cried and screamed, which intensified Colin's nerves. Colin took a few steps toward the chieftain. He swung his sword, but his opponent moved out of the way so quickly that it caused Colin to lose balance. The chieftain moved toward Colin and sliced his thigh. The crowd howled. Rosa screamed. Amoli continued to wail with her lamenting cries. Colin felt his blood ooze from his body. He didn't dare look at his wound. He held the large sword high to cut the chieftain, but the chieftain was too fast to move out of the way.

Colin grew frustrated, where he charged again and again, and he cut the chieftain's arm. The crowd cheered for Colin. He stopped and achieved eye contact with the crowd.

"Don't lose focus, Colin!" shouted Rosa.

"I will destroy you, newcomer!" shouted the chieftain.

Colin didn't flinch. He swung the sword above the chieftain's shoulder and knocked him to the ground. The crowd chanted in hysterics. Rosa's eyes widened.

"Colin! Now is your chance! Finish him off!" Rosa blurted with angst.

Colin charged at the chieftain, who was just getting up; and sliced off his finger. Colin stepped back, astonished at what he had just done. The crowd roared. The chieftain howled with agony and anger and lunged his sword at Colin, while he tried to stand up. Colin was fast enough to move out of the way. The crowd cheered. Colin gleamed at the crowd, amazed at their response. The chieftain finally stood up, panting with anger as blood poured from his amputated finger. The opponent charged at Colin and relentlessly slashed his sword at Colin several times; Colin clashed his sword against the chieftain's with enough force to push him over. The crowd stood up and chanted. The opponent was down again. Colin gleamed as he took a deep breath. The chieftain recklessly tried to stand up, Colin pushed him down again with his foot. The crowd howled. Colin had his back to the chieftain, but the chieftain managed to stand up abruptly and turn to Colin to swing his sword with speed and lunge it into Colin's stomach. The crowd wailed and screamed. Colin fell to the ground, drenched in his own blood. He lay flat on his stomach, with his face buried in his large biceps.

Rosa could no longer scream. She was frozen in disbelief. Sasha tried to get her attention, but she could no longer hear or feel. Amoli fainted. The chieftain held up his sword and chanted to the spectators. He placed his foot onto Colin's back. He then stood up completely onto Colin's back. The crowd roared, many cried and they vacated the area. Rosa still stood in the same spot. Sasha wrapped his arms around her.

"I not know what to say."

She slowly looked at him, but remained silent. The guards took a lifeless Amoli away. Rosa held onto Sasha.

186

"Help me," she said. He held her hand and pulled her toward Colin, who lay face down on the bloody ground. Rosa fell to her knees beside Colin. "Tell me this isn't true."

Sasha knelt on the ground and placed his hand under Colin's face. "He is breathing. Not good breathing. He almost dead, I think."

"No! Sahsa, do something!"

Sasha turned him onto his back and noticed the sword had punctured his flank muscle. "He lose much blood, but he still has breath."

Rosa placed her trembling hand over his mouth. "He is breathing. He doesn't seem to be conscious of us being here. I'm afraid," she said, with a gasp of breath. "I'm afraid he'll die on us."

Sasha placed his arm around Rosa's shoulder. "I am so sorry. We are in such primitive century."

"I have a needle and thread." Her eyes bounced everywhere with nerves and emotion. "Sasha, build a fire. We need a fire, now!"

"You have needle and thread? Why?"

"I always have a needle and thread with me. Build a fire!" she shouted, with cracking vocal chords. "I'll sew his wound. I'll make him better. I've got to."

Sasha got up and gathered some dry branches. He lit a match for a small fire. Rosa had her needle and thread tucked inside a cloth bag she had brought everywhere with her. She nervously took the needle and dropped it into the fire.

"Okay, Sasha, now I need you to fetch me some strong alcohol. Did Colin bring any of his whiskey with him?

"He might have some. If I can't find, I will steal some from villagers. If they no have whiskey yet in this time, I will take other strong alcohol, da?"

187

Rosa's eyes were crazed. "Good, good. After you bring me the alcohol, I want you to do something else. Go and fetch Amoli away from that grubby chieftain."

"I have to get past many guards. How I do?"

"Colin would want you to remove her from there. You must do this for Colin's sake." She pushed her hair from her face. "Is your gun loaded?"

"Da, always."

"If anyone gives you a difficult time I want you to blow them to bits."

Sasha stared at her, astonished at her last request. "I will do as you say." He ran off. She sat beside Colin and watched the pin sit in the flames of the fire, until Sasha returned.

"All I find is wine."

Rosa started to shake. "Well, that won't do. I need a spirit of some kind; something stronger."

"You want to clean your hands? I bring lye with me."

"You did?" She jumped up and kissed him on the lips. "Why didn't you tell me? Where is it? I want to disinfect the wound and my hands."

"I put some toiletries under bush over there. I bring straight-razor, lye, something to make me smell nice."

"G-Go fetch it!"

He ran through the brush and saw one of the hunters had got hold of his toiletries. He took a deep breath and approached the man.

"Give me my bag of things!" Sasha demanded, with his hands held out in front of him. Sasha tried to smile, but the man didn't reciprocate the gesture. Sasha stepped closer to him. "Give me bag." The hunter held it away from Sasha. "Give me bag or I kill you." The man appeared puzzled at Sasha's language and laughed. Sasha pulled out his gun. He pointed it at the hunter and aimed. "This is last chance. You will die."

The hunter ignored Sasha's gun and pushed him. Sasha pulled the trigger and shot the man. He fell to the ground. Sasha took the bag of toiletries and saw that the lye was still there. He made his way back to Rosa and Colin. Rosa glanced at Sasha.

"What took you?"

"Forgive me, I run into small complication, but all is better now. Here is lye. Clean your hands and disinfect wound."

She took it. She sat on the ground beside Colin and took the wine and poured some of it on her hands, then rubbed the lye in.

"This should do it."

She took a stick and pushed the pin out of the fire. She had her thread ready. She moved closer to Colin and punctured his skin with the needle and watched the thread filter through his skin. Sasha looked the other way.

"I cannot look. Mr. Limmerick lose so much blood. Poor man. "

"Fetch Amoli while I do this. I don't care who you have to kill. Just get her back here safely."

"If I kill in this century, will I destroy future people?"

"I don't care. This is for Colin's sake."

"I will do my best."

"That's not good enough. Bring her here at once. This is what Colin would want."

Sasha smiled at Rosa in silence. He made his way to the chieftain's roundhouse. Rosa wiped Colin's face with a cloth. She pulled the needle through his skin. He jerked and yelped in agony.

"Shhh! Colin, dear, you must be brave about this pain and let me do this for you," she said, with a soft voice. His eyes slowly opened. He tried to focus on her. His breathing grew heavy. "My love, just take a few deep breaths, relax, and don't worry. I'm going to make everything better."

She ran her hand along his face. He closed his eyes again. She blotted the blood from his wound with the same cloth. She dabbed it with the wine and rubbed over his injury.

Sasha approached the head chieftain's roundhouse. Two guards stood before the house. Sasha casually walked up to the two Celtic warriors. The two warriors pressed their spears against Sasha's chest.

"I go inside house, da?" Sasha said, pushing the spears away with his hands.

The two warriors pressed their spears even harder against his chest. They grunted at him. One of the warriors grabbed Sasha and pushed him to the ground. Sasha rose up and pulled out his gun. He positioned it and aimed. The gunshot was loud and echoed through the trees. The two warriors fell to the ground. Sasha stormed into the roundhouse. He stopped at the head chieftain who was cuddled with Amoli on a heap of blankets. Amoli's eyes widened.

"Dr. Dimitrikov! Get me out of here!" Amoli shrieked.

The head chieftain sprung up and shouted at Sasha in Gaelic. Sasha grabbed Amoli's arm and pulled her toward him. The head chieftain continued to shout and stomp his feet. He grabbed his spear and pointed it at Sasha. Sasha pulled the trigger. The head chieftain fell to the floor. Amoli screamed.

"Dr. Dimitikov, you shot him! Is he dead?"

"Do you care? You like?"

"Well, yes. He wanted his way with me, you know. I was very frightened. But I saw Colin fall to the ground. Is he alright?"

Sasha didn't know where to focus. "Chieftain put sword into Mr. Limmerick's stomach. He could be okay, now, I not know. Rosa fix him up, I think."

Amoli gasped for air. "What are you saying? Is he going to die?"

190

"I not say that. Rosa want you with her and Mr. Limmerick now." Sasha took her hand. "Come with me. I will show you."

They ran through the brush. Sasha led her to Rosa and Colin. As they got closer, they could see Rosa sitting in the fetal position.

"Rosa?" called Sasha.

"Miss Emanuel?" Amoli said, running to her. "Where's Colin? Is he alright?"

Rosa's eyes saturated with tears. "I think he died. He lost too much blood. I'm not a doctor."

Amoli ran to Colin's side. "Colin! Oh, God! Speak to me! Don't go!"

Sasha helped Rosa up. "Did you give him food? He must eat because he lose blood. Did you do that?"

Rosa's eyes widened. "No, I didn't. It never occurred to me. He's not even conscious. How in the hell can I get this man to eat?"

Amoli stood up. "We have got to get him some food. Who has food?"

"Sasha, go to the village and steal some food. Get those slave women to do something," Rosa demanded.

Amoli poured some water over his face. "Wake up, my love." Colin's eyes slightly opened. She kissed his lips. "Colin, do you hear me? Do you see me?" He moaned and sighed. His eyes closed again. She tapped his cheek. "Please, my love, you must wake up. I can't stand any more of this. I love you so much. You will some day be my husband and I will be your wife."

Rosa glanced at Amoli. "I sewed up his wound. He underwent some terrible pain. He is still in pain. He lost too much blood. I'd like for him to eat something, but he's hardly conscious."

Amoli lifted her head from his chest. "Oh, yes. He should eat if he has lost blood."

Sasha returned with the two slave women. They carried platters of food and sat on the ground beside Colin.

They stroked his face. They conversed with each other in Gaelic. Amoli watched every move they made.

"He's my fiancé, so back off!"

Rosa slapped her across the face. "This is not about you, brat! Colin could die and all you care about is your stupid wedding. Grow up!"

Amoli faced Rosa. "If you touch me again I'll break your neck."

Sasha broke both women apart. "What you do? You fight about what? No time for silliness. Allow slaves to help him. They are fond of him. He was good to them."

One of the slave women propped his head up so the other slave could give him water. A few drops entered his throat. He hacked out a rough sounding cough and his eyes opened. The slave broke a piece of bread and fed it to him. Rosa continued to pace. Sasha sat on the grass with Amoli.

Colin sighed a few times. Amoli leaped toward him, but Sasha pulled her back. The slaves continued to feed him and hydrate him. Colin's eyes widened. The slaves spoke to Colin in Gaelic. Colin tried to move his body, "Ah, oh, me dear God. Shite is what I feel just now." Colin tried to move his body, but he winced with pain.

Rosa and Amoli sat by his side. Rosa smiled at him. "You took a hard hit from your opponents sword, my dear."

Colin placed his hand over his wound. "Stitches, I've got stitches, so I do?" The slaves smiled at him. He took their hands and brought them to his lips. He kissed their hands several times. "Thank yez to all."

"How you feel, Mr. Limmerick?" Sasha asked.

"Like pure shite, so I do. I'm exhausted."

Colin looked at Amoli. "Glad to see ye here with us 'n not with the chieftain."

Amoli appeared nervous. "Sasha had to shoot the chieftain dead, so he could free me. Don't be mad."

Colin's eyes widened as he glanced at Sasha. "So, ye did."

Rosa smiled.

"It was the only way to free me. I think Dr. Dimitrikov had no choice."

"I understand, lass. So, I'm not angry in the least. As long as yer safe with us 'is all that counts, hmm?"

Sasha tried to help Colin to stand up.

"Well, Colin, I think Sasha needs to get us back to 1910 A.D., yes, back to our own time," Rosa commented.

"Leave? Yer sayin' we need to leave?" Colin questioned.

"Of course. Don't you want to leave this God forsaken century?" Rosa asked.

"Can't do that just as yet."

"Mr. Limmerick, why you so stubborn? You not find your research here. We must go home and you must see doctor, da?"

"Can't do that just now. *Megaloceros giganteus* is roamin' these ancient Celtic lands, 'n we need to stop this disjointed tamperin' of history. Prehistoric beasts bes' belong in their own time, don't ye think?"

Rosa rolled her eyes back. "What good is your research if you're dead? You're wounded. You have got to see a doctor. I stitched you up, but I'm no medical expert."

Colin stepped toward Rosa and pulled her against him with an affectionate hug. "And, I thank ye for savin' me life, love. I love ye, so I do. I thank ye for that. We's come this far, we might as well deal with this passage of time 'n get the prehistoric mammals back where they belong." Colin tried to walk. He felt pain in his flank muscle where the stitches were. He placed his hands over his wound. "Oh, me dear God. How can I carry on in this way?"

"Precisely, Colin. That's why you need a doctor. A real one," Rosa commented.

193

The two slaves gathered close to him. *"You cannot remain here if you wish to fight the chieftain no more,"* said one of the slaves.

"The chieftain is dead," Colin informed them.

The two slaves glanced at each other in silence. *"Dead? Who killed him? You?"* One of the slaves asked.

"Me friend, here," Colin responded to them.

"Chieftain's guards should be looking for you."

"Where can we go, then?" Colin asked.

"Come, we will show you a place far from here. Nobody goes there. Legend says monsters roam the lands," the slave said.

"Monsters, eh?" Colin responded in English, as he glanced at Sasha and Rosa.

Rosa stepped closer to Colin. "What's she saying? Did she see *Megaloceros?"*

Colin scratched his bearded chin. "Likely."

Amoli tugged at Colin's arm. "Lets go back to our time. I hate it here. You need to see a doctor, so we can plan our lives together."

Colin gently retracted his arm from her. "How ye mean, lass?"

"We need to be married, is what I mean. You're for me and I'm for you."

"Oh, lass, please forget me as yer husband. That can never be. I'm so sorry. I'll love ye always, but ye need yerself a stable man." He moved his body close to hers and brushed his finger along the side of her face. "Yer such a fine lass, so ye are, so, young 'n beautiful. Why on earth would ye wanna waste yer time on someone like me?"

Rosa crossed her arms in front of her. "Here we go again."

"Look at you, Colin. You're a Celtic warrior. What woman wouldn't want to marry a Celtic warrior?" Amoli asked in her timid tiny voice.

"Probably, most women," Rosa interjected.

"I'm dressed like a Celtic warrior, but I'm definitely not a Celtic warrior. I'm a fisherman who's interested in me academic research, 'is all."

"I find you fascinating," Amoli said, with her eyes filled with tears.

"Ye said it yerself, lass. I drink far too much, 'n me research bores ye to tears."

Sasha took Amoli's hand. "Miss Amoli, this is not time or place. You will get Mr. Limmerick back some day. You are determined girl. You will meet your goal."

"Thanks, Dr. Dimitrikov. You've always been so kind to me."

One of the slaves took Colin's hand. *"I can get you some horses, and then you must go."* Colin kissed her on the lips.

The slave smiled. *"Wait here. You must leave in that direction. Go beyond where the sun shines the most. Go down mountain and walk past the trees. You will smell sweet flowers."*

"I reckon ye couldn't draw me a map?" Colin asked in English, but then rephrased himself again in Gaelic.

The two slaves looked at him and smiled.

"We'll be waitin' for yez," Colin said, in Gaelic and in English.

The two slaves gestured for Colin to bend his knees to get closer to them. They both kissed him on the lips and smiled. Colin watched them walk into the dense brush. Rosa stood beside Colin. "What was exchanged between you and them?"

"We need to stay here until they return with horses. They know a place we can go for safe refuge."

Rosa crossed her arms in front of her. "Horses, how nice. Safe refuge? I'll believe it when I see it. You're so hardheaded, Colin. It's your way or nothing, isn't it? You need to see a doctor."

195

"Horses? I can't ride a horse. I don't know how. Do you know how to ride a horse, Miss Emanuel?" Amoli asked in a panic.

"Yes, I do," Rosa responded. It's a way of life in England, but now that there are more and more automobiles, horses are seen less."

Colin placed his arm around Amoli. "You can ride with me. Just hold on tight."

"Better yet, she can ride with me. I am nicer than you," interjected Sasha.

"I don't like this one bit," Rosa said.

"Why, love? Those two slaves have kept us fed. They prepared me for battle; what more can one want?"

"They're ninth-century prostitutes, Colin. They've given you what you want, therefore, they're in your good books. You can be so disgusting at times," Rosa said.

Amoli stood closer to Colin. "Did you sleep with those women?"

Colin rubbed his hands over his face. "Oh, good Lord, Amoli, please."

Sasha nudged Colin in the ribs. "Well, Mr. Limmerick, speak the truth."

"Oh, Sasha, you're the most fiendish of all. You slept with those women as well. You're both disgusting. Maybe this is just the way men are…truly disgusting."

Amoli flopped on the ground and started to cry. Colin nodded his head. He painfully knelt to where Amoli sat.

"Lass, there's no time for tears at a time like this. Our lives could be in danger if we don't get out of the chieftain's territory. If ye wish to give me hell in 1910, I wouldn't blame ye a bit, but lets put our emotions on hold for the time bein', eh?"

The two slaves returned, each on a horse with a horse beside them.

"We have brought you two horses. We will lead you to this place. Hopefully, the chieftain's guards will not come looking for us. We don't have time to waste."

Colin helped Rosa onto the horse behind him and Sasha did the same with Amoli.

***

They followed the two slaves. The sky dimmed and it started to rain. It took time to travel on the rugged terrain. They saw small prehistoric mammals scurry about in the distance. Rosa tightened her grip around Colin.

"Just focus on where we're going and look straight ahead. Don't bother with the wildlife you're seeing," Rosa said.

"How can I not? It's puttin' a pit in me gut, so it is. Feel like such a failure," Colin said.

"There is no time-travel manual available where you can purchase at any book store. Time-travel turned out to be much more complex than you had ever imagined," Rosa said, sitting behind Colin on the horse undergoing a bumpy ride.

"But, I should've realized that the outcome of time-travel would never be a cut 'n dry result. I must be stupid or somethin'."

"Please don't put yourself down. You are an extraordinary man for your accomplishments. I love you for who you are."

"Lord love ye, but tell me how I'm goin' fix this mess?"

Rain continued to spit over the land. It wasn't a raging rainstorm, but a consistent supply of heavy droplets. The skies were gray, and the temperature had dropped.

"Oh, Colin, we've been riding for hours. Ask one of the slaves how much longer. I can barely take anymore of this ride. I'm surprised Amoli hasn't made Sasha crazy with her complaints."

"Aye, she's been quiet, hasn't she? Hope she's all right. Worried, so I am about her."

"Worried? Don't worry about her."

197

Colin sped his horse to be aligned with one of the slaves. *"How much longer?"* he asked one of the slaves.

She glanced at Colin. "Much time is still left," she responded.

"Colin? How much longer?" asked Rosa.

"Still a ways to go, apparently."

"Can't we rest for a bit?" pleaded Rosa.

Colin aligned his horse with one of the slave women. *"Can we rest?"*

"No!" she responded.

"Colin turned to Rosa. "We can't."

"Colin, this is getting out of control. We've been riding through this rough blackness in the rain for hours and we're still not there?"

"It's for the best, I'm sure."

"What are they leading us to?"

"Safety, love, safety."

"If you want safety, we need to get back to our time."

"Can't do that, just yet, love."

Chapter Twenty-Four

After several hours, they finally reached their destination. The two slaves led them to a cave that was hidden behind a dense forest. They slid off their horses to stretch their muscles from the long treacherous ride.

"In this cave, you will be safe," one of the slaves said.

Colin poked his head in. "My, it's definitely not the accommodation we's used to, but it'll have to do."

Rosa stepped forward to peek inside. She winced with disgust. The slave women looked at Colin but were silent. Amoli peeked inside the cave.

"Is this supposed to be our hiding place?"

"It is, lass."

"We're supposed to sleep in this hole?" Rosa asked with a grimace.

Sasha noticed rats scurry about, a few bats hung from the wall, and a small snake slithered out through the opening.

"It is not Grand Hotel, but we be fine."

The slaves hugged and kissed Colin. They climbed back onto their horses and rode off.

"Well, we best build a fire, sprawl out our one sleepin' bag 'n get some rest for the day a head," Colin said.

"So, I wonder why the villagers don't step foot around here," Rosa said, with a sarcastic tone.

"I don't like it here, not one bit," Amoli commented.

"Forgive me, but I really must rest," Colin said, as he lowered his body onto the sleeping bag that was sprawled out.

"I can't sleep here. It's just awful," squealed Amoli.

Rosa stepped closer to Amoli. "Can't you see Colin is still in pain from his wound? Those slaves girls did us a favor bringing us here."

"I don't like them. They're always touching Colin."

Rosa sighed. "Of course they are, they're his slaves. Are you going to tell me you never had slaves in India?"

Amoli sat beside Colin. "Uh, yes. My family did have one or two, I suppose."

"Then keep your thoughts about yourself."

Amoli nestled up to Colin. "Are you going to allow her to speak to me so rudely?"

Sasha laughed. "Please, ladies, we are in middle of hell hole right now. Lets not make it worse, da?"

They unpacked and settled in for the rest of the night. It was early in the morning, when a loud squeal echoed through the trees. Rosa immediately sat up.

"Who's there?"

Sasha and Colin continued to snore away. Amoli sat up.

"What was that?"

"Shhh! Something is outside this cave," Rosa said.

"I'm scared," Amoli said.

Rosa made her way to the cave opening. She noticed the sunlight beaming through. She stepped out of the cave and heard the same loud squealing. She gingerly pushed away the bushes and tree branches. The loud sound continued. She couldn't find what was making the noise. She crouched down and saw two medium-sized reptiles fighting for their dead prey.

"Oh!," she gasped. She pulled her hands in and crawled on the muddy ground back to the cave. She entered the cave and knelt beside Colin. "Colin." He turned toward her on the sleeping bag. "Wake up! Oh, my God, Colin!"

"Aye, what is it, love?"

"Colin, something is outside the cave."

"Of course, somethin' is outside the cave. Wildlife is outside this cave."

"This is wildlife in a new dimension. I saw two dinosaurs fighting for their prey."

"Dinosaurs?"

"Something has gone very wrong with your experiment."

"Are ye sure it was dinosaurs, what ye saw?" he asked, sitting up in excruciating pain from his battle wound.

"I think they looked like *Velociraptors*, but I'm not sure. How can this be?"

Colin rubbed his tired eyes. "Dinosaurs in 840 A.D. Oh, God, I hope ye was havin' a bad dream or somethin."

"Did you say you saw dinosaurs outside this cave?" asked Amoli.

Sasha opened his eyes. "What you say?"

"If we allow dinosaurs to roam in this time, they will surely wipe out *Megaloceros giganteus*, as well as the other prehistoric mammals. We have to get the dinosaurs back in their own time. Sasha, get up! Ye have work to do, man!" Colin said, in a panicked tone.

"Oh, Colin, why do you waste your time with Sasha and his faulty time-travel device? He hasn't a clue how to fix any of this. He's a physicist!" Rosa blurted.

Sasha stood up and faced her. "What you say? I am only scientist on earth who knows anything about time-travel. Name me scientists with time-travel method!"

"Colin, aren't you afraid dinosaurs could wipe out us humans? Amoli added.

Colin chuckled. "I'm not worried 'bout the human species, lass, we're so accustom to killin' anythin' in our sight, don't ye think? Humans can take care of their own."

Amoli appeared worried. "I don't think I would know what to do if I was faced with a dinosaur."

Rosa stepped closer to them. "I think you would know what to do. What did your father always teach you?"

Colin wedged himself between them. "Enough. I'm concerned about the prehistoric mammals bein' wiped out by dinosaurs. Good God, can this get any worse?"

Amoli tugged on Colin's arm. "Are we going to be wiped out by dinosaurs?"

"It's important that we don't retaliate, 'cause we'd be breakin' the evolutionary chain. Surely, Darwin would have had the same concerns, don't ye think?"

"So, are you saying if the dinosaurs want to eat us, we should let them?" Amoli asked.

"Oh, I donno what the feck I'm sayin'. I need a stiff shot of whiskey, that's for sure."

Rosa pulled Sasha's time-travel device from his hand. "You need to bring this device to the dinosaurs and send them back 65 million years. You need to lead them through the passage of time with the device," Rosa said.

"Give me back device! You speak so like woman! You not know my device!"

Colin took the device from Rosa. "She's right. We need to send these dinosaurs back where they came from. If they charge us we need to keep them distracted."

"I don't want to see them!" shouted Amoli.

"Ye don't want to wait here, now do ye?" Colin asked. "By yerself?"

Rosa paced around the cave. "Those dinosaurs didn't look the way they look in the textbooks. They had feathers. They looked like over-sized birds."

"I don't care what they look like. If they charge us I shoot them dead. That is all," Sasha grunted.

"Ye can't do that, man!"

"Stop me."

"Shite! What ye sayin'? Ye can't be shootin' dinosaurs! Ye just can't!"

Rosa paced, as the two men argued. "No, you can't be shooting dinosaurs, but we can divide and conquer." Sasha stepped closer to her. "If we use bait of some kind, the dinosaurs would be attracted to an easy meal. They would fight each to the death for food."

"Where we get this easy bait?" Colin asked.

"You're a fisherman; why don't you catch some fish?" Rosa suggested.

"With what, me bare hands?"

"You can make some sort of net, couldn't you?"

"Gotta see what materials I can find. We's so far from the village now."

"Forget the village. The village has a hot-headed chieftain who isn't very pleasant. We can find something right here," Rosa added.

"We bes' get lookin' to find material. We can't have dinosaurs terrorizin' the prehistoric mammals."

"I have a net. Not the size net you're used to, but I do have a net," Amoli offered.

"Ye do? How ye have a net with ye?" Colin asked.

"My mother always had me carry a net with me so I could gather seaweed. It is what some Indian families do, I suppose."

"Ye have it with ye, lass?"

"I brought it. Here it is."

She pulled it out of her bag of belongings. It was rolled up. Colin held the net in his hands to examine it.

"This may do fine, so it should. It would definitely attract dinosaurs."

Sasha pulled out a cigarette. "I can't believe I still have. I thought I smoked all cigarettes. I am happy man," he said, with glee. "What if fish attracts prehistoric mammals at same time? Then what? I pull out gun and shoot dinosaur in the face, da?"

Rosa continued to pace. "Oh, God, help this man! Sasha you cannot ever pull your trigger on a dinosaur, do you understand?"

"If it bites you, you would want."

"We're not going to get ourselves into a situation where dinosaurs are having us for their late night meal. We are much smarter than them. We can do this. Colin, you need to find water."

"This is ancient Ireland, don't think findin' water would be a problem."

"Since I was the one with the net, can I come fishing with you?" Amoli asked, in her tiny delicate voice.

"Grand of ye to offer yer company, lass."

Colin smiled at her. Rosa stepped closer to Sasha.

"Get your faulty time-travel device to send those dinosaurs back to their era."

"What era is that?" Sasha asked.

Colin scratched his head, as he looked at Rosa. "So, ye saw *Velociraptures?* They lived in the last dinosaur era, didn't they? Don't know, really. Never studied dinosaurs. Me work is on prehistoric mammals."

"Cretaceous, they're cretaceous alright. They were the ones who traveled in groups. We have to be extra cautious, because of their collective behavior. They conquered with their numbers," Rosa informed.

"Now, yer soundin' like such an archeologist, Rosa. Yer a brilliant young woman, an' beautiful at that," Colin said, with his arm around her.

"C'mon, Colin, lets go fishing," Amoli said, tugging on his arm.

Colin and Amoli left. Rosa glanced at Sasha.

"Since we've come on this expedition, you've been a little too trigger happy."

"With good reason. I save Mr. Limmerick's life, did I not?"

"Yes, and I agree with that, but you can't go around thinking if anything gets in your way you're simply going to blow them to bits with that gun of yours."

"Don't care. I hate this journey. I hate Celtic people. They smell."

"Sasha, they are ancient people. Of course they smell; they're supposed to."

"Mr. Limmerick have so big idea to prove impossible, all with my expertise."

"Yes, it's your brilliant expertise that brought us to the ancient Celts rather than the time of the prehistoric mammals. Good chap."

Chapter Twenty-Five

Amoli sat by the shoreline. She gingerly tried to immerse her toes in the icy water. She giggled at the sharpness of the cold waves. Colin was knee deep in the water, working the net to catch a fish or two.

"Colin, how can you stand in such frigid water? You'll catch a cold. Come sit beside me. I promise I'll keep you warm!" Amoli called out.

"I need to catch enough food to make a prehistoric lizard fight for it, wouldn't ye think?"

"I'm just so tired. I wish we were lying in your bed in your comfy flat in London."

Colin turned to her. "Comfy flat, ye say?"

"Yes, of course. Wouldn't ye prefer to be there?"

"Not sure, lass. Can't really say I'd regard it as comfy."

"How can you not be sure? This is a hard life, in this century, and now with these beasts. I'm very frightened."

"I'm sorry for that. Feel like a shite, so I do. I've dragged the three of yez on this expedition."

Amoli watched how Colin worked when trying to catch fish. She noticed how quick and skilled he was. He filled the net with several large fish. Colin had a large bundle of caught fish. He carried it as he made his way out of the frigid water. Amoli tried to dry him off with a towel. He sat beside her. She took his hand.

"Do you still love me?" she asked.

"Never stopped."

She inched her way closer to him. He held her in his arms. They heard a squawking sound in the distance.

"Oh! Colin, what's that?"

"Likely, a dinosaur. Can't believe this shite. Will it ever stop?"

"Dinosaur? Shouldn't we leave here?"

"Is there a place for safe refuge in this God forsaken century? Tell me, lass?"

"Maybe we should go back to that Celtic village?"

Colin chuckled. "Was that a safer haven for ye?"

"Can't we go back to 1910? Our time?"

"Aye, we've only messed things up here. We should quit whilst we's ahead."

"Dr. Dimitrikov has to send us back home. I'm so frightened!"

Colin stood to help Amoli up. They walked through the dense brush and noticed the tips of large reptile combs poking from above the bushes in the far distance. They were extra careful in not making too much noise as they made their way through the brush. They saw Rosa and Sasha sitting by a newly pitched tent.

"Oh, Colin, you caught so much fish. Fantastic! This should work well with those *Velociraptors*," Rosa said, with a smile.

"So, I'm hopin'." Colin glanced at Sasha, and said, "Ye know, mate, I was thinkin' when I was just fishin'. That meteor strike in Siberia, 1908; by any chance, has it done any damage to the passage of time?"

Rosa took Colin's arm. "Yes, Colin! Good man! Sasha's time-travel device probably has had nothing to do with all these displaced species from pre-history. I was thinking the very same thing!" Rosa shouted, as she tugged away at Colin's arm.

"I mean, you can surely send the wenches 'n yerself back to 1910 A.D., couldn't yez? Yez could go back 'n have a good night sleep, couldn't yez now?" Colin asked.

"Yes, you are so correct. You're being sensible," Rosa blurted.

"Well, me first concern is that the three of yez get back to our time safely."

"Da, I will try to get time-travel device to take us to our time," Sasha said.

207

"As for 840 A.D., I think it's a tragedy the Celts may no longer have their chieftain, 'n I feel completely responsible for it."

Rosa's smile dissipated. "Colin, what are you saying?"

"What you going to do? You going to be new chieftain for Celts?" Sasha asked with a grin.

"Colin, I don't think you know what you're saying right now," Rosa said. "Didn't you want Amoli safe from that horrible chieftain?"

"Of course."

"Well, the only way Sasha could achieve your wish was to shoot the chieftain down. This is a barbaric time. We're twentieth century people. We're not used to such disgusting tactics," Rosa instilled.

Colin leered at her. "What are the Boer Wars? Is that not disgusting'?"

"Colin, you can't compare The Boer Wars, which is a modern-day war to the constant barbaric battles of this primitive century."

"Why not? Don't really see the difference, really."

"Colin, you just can't look at history as a duplicate of our modern present time."

"Why not. It's all the same. Humanity keeps repeating' the same actions over 'n over. The human species lives 'n breathes war, so it does. Don't really matter what century, our species will 'n always will be aimin' to destroy. Bunch a fecks, so we are."

"Colin, this is not the time or place for your questions and philosophies."

"Fine, so it is."

"However, Colin, the four of us need to stay together, no matter what. You cannot remain in this dreadful century. Besides, it would break your parents' hearts."

"Oh, yes, me parents. But, I am Celt. They need someone big 'n strong to battle the Vikings. I'm worried

208

for them, now. That chieftain was a hard act to conquer. Not an easy bloke, so he wasn't."

"They also need big and strong leader who is master swordsman. You are not master at sword, Mr. Limmerick," Sasha interjected. "King chieftain could have survived, a?"

"I'm goin' to stay here, so I've been thinkin'. I can't allow dinosaurs to destroy prehistoric mammals, 'n I can't allow the Celts to go on without a chieftain. I can never return to 1910 A.D. with this hangin' over me."

"What are you saying?" Amoli shouted, with a shrill scream. "No!"

"Oh, God, now you're talking nonsense. You need to go back with us," Rosa said.

"You will die here, Mr. Limmerick," Sasha said.

There were hard cracking sounds of branches being snapped in half. The thunder of unfamiliar sounds spewed from the trees. *Megaloceros giganteous* bolted out of the forest. The four time-travelers were still as the watched the large antlered prehistoric mammal run a in a fury. Several *Velociraptors* followed it from behind.

"Sasha, get yer gun 'n shoot those lizards!" Colin shouted.

"You can't be killing off displaced dinosaurs!" Rosa shouted. "What got into you to?"

The *Velociraptors* stopped by the bundle of caught fish. They pulled away at the net with their sharp teeth. The four time-travelers remained still. Sasha loaded his gun with bullets as he kept one eye on the raptures.

"I won't stand here 'n watch creatures from the late *Cretaceous* destroy our prehistoric mammals. I've put too much work into them, I just won't have it," Colin said.

"If I see T-Rex terrorize *Megaloceros* I will shoot it dead, not to worry," Sasha said, with a smile.

Rosa's eyes were wide open. "Sasha, close the pathway to time and there will no longer be displaced prehistoric mammals."

"I not know how to do. If you know how, then please."

"How can we do such an involved operation if we haven't the knowledge to do it, love?"

"We're scientists, not fools; we need to find a way. Isn't that the reason why we came on this expedition in the first place?" Rosa shouted loud enough, her voice cracked.

Suddenly, a cluster of small trees mashed to the ground. The loud cracking sound of broken branches penetrated the air. A large presence of some kind was coming their way. Braches continued to snap and break as the sharp sound of bushes and leaves rustled and echoed throughout the forested area. Amoli looked up to see two menacing fiendish eyes peer through the trees. She screamed and jumped into Sasha's arms. *Tyrannosaurus Rex* pushed over the trees and roared like thunder.

Rosa glanced at Sasha. "Speak of the devil."

"Remain still and silent," Colin whispered.

A lost-looking *Smilodon* scurried in front of the thundering meat-eater. *T-Rex* snatched it into its enormous jaws and clamped down. It was so immediate, that it was difficult for the four time travelers to ingest.

"Shoot!" Colin shouted, with widened fearful eyes.

"Shite, man, can't believe we's seein' *Smilodon* in this picture as well. Did we ever feck things up."

"Of course, I'm not even surprised. We really did try to play God, didn't we?" Rosa commented.

Just as Sasha was about to pull the trigger, an even larger animal stomped over the leafy trees and knocked *T-Rex* over with its long strong neck. Amoli kept her eyes shut as she held onto Sasha tightly. *T-Rex* scrambled to rise back on its feet.

"Did such a large beast ever exist?" Rosa asked Colin, in a whisper. "I'm not as well-versed as you with large land prehistoric mammals.

"*Indricotherium*, so it is. Spectacular mammal, so it was."

The four time-travelers watched *Indricotherium* move closer to the fearless meat eater. *Tyrannosaurus Rex* crouched down to show it's power to strike, which didn't make Indricotherium even flinch. The vicious meat eater stepped forward with the intent to strike, but the mammoth mammal stepped closer as well and showed no fear. *Tyrannosaurus Rex lunged at the large mammal and tried to snap its jaws at it. Indricotherium pushed its way forward to knock T-Rex off balance, where it fell clumsily to the ground. It immediately stood up to face its match, when Indricotherium stood on its two-hind legs, and its front legs landed onto the vicious reptile.* Tyrannosaurus Rex was crushed under *Indricotherium's* legs.

"You see, Mr. Limmerick, prehistoric mammals not need your help. They can do on their own."

Amoli's eyes were closed and her face buried in Sasha's arms. Rosa watched in silence. Sasha smiled as he glanced at Colin.

"Perhaps the prehistoric mammals could fend off the dinosaurs. There's a great time gap between them 'n dinosaurs don't have the brain power," Colin said.

"They're not supposed to coincide with each other," Rosa cautioned. "It's not supposed to be this way," she said feeling frazzled by the episode they just witnessed. "Dinosaurs couldn't adapt, where as mammals could."

"Not these mammals, my dear Miss Rosa," Sasha responded.

"Of course not. Nothing of this size could survive.

"Just don't know how to stop misplaced prehistoric animals from gettin' scattered about time," Colin said with frustration.

Rosa glanced at Sasha. "Can't you block the passage of time some how?"

Sasha looked at her. "You say me how and I will do."

211

The four time-travelers watched *Indricotherium* stomp all over *Tyrannosaurus Rex*. It glanced down at the four time-travelers, made a few grunts and stomped off. Colin looked at Sasha and Rosa.

"Sasha's time indicator has found the passage through time. It's always been there, that's why it's an indicator."

"The meteor strike released the energy to create time-vortexes," added Rosa.

"I know idea!" Sasha exclaimed.

"You have an idea?" Rosa clarified. "You can block the passage of time?"

"I will turn back dials on indicator like this," Sasha said, as he fiddled with his time indicator.

Colin grabbed the indicator. "Are ye mad, man? Ye just can't feck 'round with it like that? Yer gonna send us to *la Bastille* in the middle of the French Revolution!"

"I know what I doing!" Sasha barked at Colin.

Chapter Twenty-Six

The four time-travelers found themselves lying in a field. Rosa lifted her head.

"Sasha, did you just send us through a time-vortex?"

Sasha smiled, as he sat up. "I not know where we are, but maybe I broke passage through time, da?"

Rosa placed her hands on her head. "Oh, my God! Wouldn't that be wonderful."

Amoli lifted her head and started to cry. Sasha sat beside her.

"Why you cry, Miss Amoli? We could be home."

"Dr. Dimitrikov, this has been very disturbing for me. I just wish I was sitting in my aunt's house right now."

Rosa stood up and scanned her surroundings. "Where's Colin?"

Sasha stood up. "He never travel good in time vortex. Mr. Limmerick, where are you?"

Colin opened one eye. "I hear yez, mate!"

Rosa rushed to his side.

"Where are we at, now?"

"It looks as if we're in Ireland 1910. I think we're home."

"With nothin' accomplished except a dead Celtic chieftain," Colin said.

Amoli pushed Rosa over and nestled up to Colin. "I hope we're home. We went through a very bad experience, Colin."

"It was time-travel, lass. This is what time-travel is. It's lousy by nature."

"I never want to time-travel again."

Rosa rolled her eyes back. "Good God, do you think we just time-traveled so we could entertain ourselves? You're ridiculous, Amoli Sharma!" Rosa shouted, as she stood up and paced a bit.

213

"You're so rude, Miss Emanuel. Why is she always so mean to me, Colin?"

Colin rubbed his tired eyes. "Yez two are like oil 'n water. God only knows why."

"You want to have big conversation or you want to take boat to England?" Sasha asked.

"I can't wait to jump in my bathtub and get clean," Rosa said.

***

The following morning Colin sat in his office, at the university. Several students had come to see him regarding their lab reports. He sat back in his chair and noticed Timothy Duncan was standing outside his door.

"Timothy, ye need to speak to me?"

"I have a message for you. Your defense committee would like to meet with you in 15 minutes in the conference room."

"Really? Why are ye givin' me this message?"

"Dr. Cushing asked me to. Don't be late. You know how Dr. Cushing doesn't like to be kept waiting."

Colin lifted his eyebrows. "Really?"

Timothy abruptly left Colin's office. Colin positioned himself to rise from his desk in a way where he wouldn't feel the pain from his stab-wound. He took a few deep breaths and used his desk to support himself so he could stand up straight. He left his office with a briefcase full of notes.

Colin knocked on the door. His second reader answered it.

"Ah, Colin Limmerick, please enter. We all wanted to chat with you regarding your latest time-travel expedition."

Colin straightened his tie. He slowly sat down as he kept one eye on Professor Cushing. He took a few deep breaths and eased himself into one of the chairs. He tried to smile at his committee, while he felt shooting pains run through his abdomen.

214

"I returned from me time-travel yesterday, in fact."

"Colin," Dr. Cushing blurted. "I'd like to know, and the rest of this committee would like to know if you have made any progress on your explorations of the horseshoe crab."

Colin's eyes widened. He slowly felt around his jacket to locate his glasses. He found them and placed them on his face. "Horseshoe crab, sar?" Colin gleamed at each of his committee members.

"Yes, Colin, the Horseshoe crab. Where is your latest data?"

Colin fiddled with the notes he had in front of him. "I was on a prehistoric mission, but not to gather findin's of the horseshoe crab. Yer after me doin' yer research, sar. Me own research is on *Megaloceros giganteus*."

A white-haired elderly man smiled. "What did you find, Colin?"

"There was a slight malfunction when enroute to our destination."

The committee of elderly males glanced at each other and kept their eyes focused on Colin. The dean's representative stood up. "We're having an honorary guest join us this morning. We hope this will be suitable to you."

"Honorary guest, ye say? How lovely is that? Who?"

"Well, it's our first time having the Chancellor of the university join us for one of our committee meetings. Are you familiar with Honorable Evelyn Gordon?"

Colin's eyes dropped to the table. "Oh. I see. Um, familiar? So, I am. I've met her, if that's what yer askin'?"

"She should be here shortly. She is the chancellor, a very busy woman at that," the dean's representative said. "Yes, a female chancellor. Isn't that amazing?"

Colin sat back in his chair and loosened his tie. He removed his glasses. Suddenly, a string of waiting staff entered through the door. They brought chilled wine, trays of hot crumpets, scones, an assortment of preserves, and

215

tea. The chancellor followed. One of the waiting staff pulled a chair out for her. She comfortably sat down as he gently pushed her chair in for her. They bowed to her as they made their exit. The elderly men of his committee stood up, as well as Colin. She remained sitting.

"Please seat yourselves, gentlemen. As I already indicated, I wanted to be present at one of your committee meetings, because I want to know exactly what goes on when a PhD candidate is planning for his final defense. There has been so much said about the dynamic research of Mr. Limmerick that I felt I should hear about his latest time-travels."

"I'm not sure if me research is quite ready for our university's chancellor to sit in on our mundane meetin's, Chancellor Gordon," Colin said.

"What I really admire about you, Mr. Limmerick, is how you play down the magnificent work that you do. I find you remarkable. Please, tell us what you experienced on this recent prehistoric expedition?" she said, as the dean's representative poured her a glass of wine.

The Dean's rep smiled at Colin, then at Evelyn. "Yes, we would all like to know."

"It didn't work out."

There was silence in the room. The defense committee exchanged eye contact while the chancellor buttered her crumpet.

"Didn't work out, Mr. Limmerick?" She said pretending to be more engrossed with her crumpet.

"Didn't go as planned.

The Chancellor sat on the edge of her chair. "What didn't go as planned?"

Colin took a deep breath as he stirred his tea. "Well, um, we didn't exactly time travel to prehistoric times."

"You didn't?" Evelyn asked.

"Well, we did see loads of prehistoric mammals, 'n we even saw dinosaurs, no doubt, but…"

"Dinosaurs? Oh my, this is so intriguing," she said, while sipping her wine.

The rest of the committee slapped mounds of butter on their crumpets and spewed crumbs all over their jackets.

"We mistakenly landed in 840 A.D., Chancellor Gordon. It was a malfunction."

"Malfunction?" Oh, my," she exclaimed.

Professor Cushing stuffed his mouth with as many scones as possible. "Liar! How can a time travel expedition malfunction? All lies, I tell you!"

Colin leered at his professor. "So, yer callin' me a liar, sar?"

The dean's rep placed his hand on Dr. Cushing's shoulder. "Easy, Randolph, lets hear what Colin has to say."

"We mistakenly landed in 840AD, Ireland, if ye can imagine?"

"How absurd!" Professor Cushing blurted, with scone crumbs spewing from his mouth.

"I fought Vikings 'n a Celtic chieftain. I need to get back there, 'cause the Celts are no longer with a chieftain. They need a leader."

Evelyn smiled at Colin. "You feel you would be fitting to be an ancient Celtic leader, Mr. Limmerick?"

"Aye. Not so much that I'm a born leader, but I am a captain of a fishin' vessel'n I kinda look the part, don't ye think?"

"You do look the part, Mr. Limmerick. Of course you do," she said with a grin.

"I was in battle with a Celtic chieftain, who was a bit of a shitehead, so to speak. Don't think he treated the Celtic people with much respect, if ye know what I mean? I even fought Vikings, if ye can imagine?"

"Celts? Vikings? Oh, my," Evelyn said. "A Celtic chieftain at that?"

217

"This is preposterous! Where is your evidence, Limmerick?" Dr. Cushing demanded.

"Evidence, ye ask, sar? How does ninth-century armor suit ye? They made it just for me, so I took it with me."

"Armor? You wore armor?" Dr. Cushing questioned.

"Aye, so I did wear ancient Celtic armor."

The chancellor picked away at her crumpet. "I'm sure you looked absolutely, what I'm trying to say is, you must have worn that armor very well, indeed."

Colin smiled at her. "It wasn't a comfortable fit, 'cause it was armor. Armor was never designed for comfort, yer worship."

Dr. Cushing stood up with his finger pointed at Colin. "Tell me this: did you, by any chance, manage to collect research and data based on the prehistoric time-frame you have been researching? What were you doing gallivanting around dressed in armor?"

The dean's representative faced Dr. Cushing. "Randolph, take it easy. Colin did indicate that there was a malfunction."

"Malfunction? He's an alleged time-traveler. What in God's name could possibly go wrong with time-travel?" Dr. Cushing said, as saliva dripped from his mouth like foam.

Colin stood up. "Forgive me, gentlemen, 'n Chancellor Gordon. I do think it is time for me to make me exit from this meetin'. As I already mentioned, Chancellor Gordon, I have been undergoin' a fair bit of discomfort with me academic advisor. I think Dr. Cushing just can't get past me appearance, me dialect, 'n me livelihood. He's been discriminatin' me from the day he met me, 'n frankly I'm gettin' wee bit tired of it."

"Oh, please don't leave. This is your committee meeting. I will see that Professor Cushing is dealt with using the proper measures. We just started learning about your latest expedition," Evelyn said with a calming voice.

218

"I'm sorry, Chancellor, but I don't think I can sit in the same room with me advisor another minute without causin' some serious bodily damage to him," Colin said, as he frantically gathered his papers. "Also, I was injured on this time-travel. Need to see a doctor, so I do." Colin tilted his head toward Evelyn. "Cheers."

***

Colin sat in the university pub with a glass of whiskey. Evelyn Gordon rushed in. She scanned the pub and sat at the table beside him.

"So, here you are drinking away your sorrows. Did you see a doctor? I don't know how you were injured, but if you need to see my family doctor I'm sure he could fit you in."

"Got amateur stitches, so I did. Saw the doctor just now. He said the stitches was done well."

"Stitches? Ouch. Oh, sounds serious. Should I be concerned?"

"Don't think there's a need. It was just yer everyday sword in the gut routine."

She squealed. "Oh, my! What happened?"

"I've already given way too much information. Ye'd never believe me anyways."

She snickered. "You're so nonchalant about this, Colin."

"I just need to return to 840 A.D., is all."

"Return? Hmm, you speak about time-travel as if you're taking a carriage from here to the other end of London."

"Don't mean to," Colin said, as he took a gulp of whiskey.

"Oh, my, when will you be so polite and invite me to join you at your table?"

Colin took another gulp. "Excuse me rudeness. Please join me at this table."

She quickly sat. "I'd like a drink, as well. Some Italian red would be nice."

"Italian red it is."

He propped himself up and walked to the bar. She sat in the pub observing the atmosphere. Colin waited in line at the bar. Rosa walked by.

"I thought I'd find you here. I haven't seen you all day."

"Sorry, I've been dealin' with me defense committee. They called a meetin' this mornin'."

"Were you aware of this meeting?"

"It was somethin' they decided at the last minute. Surely, Cushing was behind it. I was in no physical state for it, that's for sure."

"Cushing can be such an ass."

"That's puttin' it mildly, don't ye think, love?"

"How did it go?"

"Awful, just awful."

"Sorry to hear that."

"I've experienced worse."

"Sasha thinks he found a way to block the pathway of time. Aren't you excited?"

"Excited? That sounds lovely, but I've got someone with me just now. Can I come by yer place later 'n we'll chat about this further?"

"Oh, you do?" She looked around. "Since when did your social life get in the way of getting those displaced prehistoric animals back where they belong?"

"Since I've run into the chancellor of this university."

"You're with her here at this pub? Wouldn't she prefer to drink Dom Pérignon at one of those places on The Strand?"

"Aye, she definitely would. I've got to see if she can pin Cushing to the wall. He got under me skin this mornin'. If I didn't leave I would've knocked his teeth out."

"Try and keep your time with her to a limit. She's the chancellor of the university. Be careful."

220

Colin put his arms around Rosa. "I know what I'm doin', love." He brought a glass of red wine and another whiskey to the table. "Here ye are, Chancellor Gordon?"

"Call me Evelyn. Tell me something: who was that woman you were talking to by the bar?"

"Me cohort. She's an archeologist. She came with me on two time-travel expeditions. She also stitched me up."

"I see," she paused as she examined her fresh glass of wine. "Pretty."

"Aye, that she is 'n brilliant as well."

"Oh, yes, of course she is."

"Tell me somethin', Chancellor, I mean Evelyn: what ye think of me advisor, Professor Cushing?"

She sipped a bit of her wine and took her time to answer. "I can give you a full discussion on the perils of your academic advisor at my place or yours tonight? Why don't I show up at your place? I'd like to see where you reside."

"Me place? It's a disaster, I'm afraid. I'd be too embarrassed to have ye over. I don't even have anythin' to offer ye.

"Don't do anything to your place. I want to see it as it is." Colin ran his hands over his face. "How's eight p.m.?"

"Oh, God."

"Just be yourself. I'll have caterers bring a little something before my arrival, if that's suitable?"

"Caterers? I've got me mother's chicken soup in the ice box."

She laughed. "You're one of a kind."

"Glad to know there's just one of me." He slid his arm around her and gazed at her. He took a deep breath. "Evelyn, ye can't be goin' about to me flat with caterers."

"They do a lovely job; you'd be very impressed. Don't you think you and I need to spend more time together?"

"We could go to the library, or go out for tea, but ye can't come to me messy flat 'n see me under shorts lyin' about the floor."

"I see." Colin smiled at her, but she did not reciprocate. "We can discuss your academic advisor further in my office, if you like?"

"Aye, I'd like that."

"How's this evening? Around eight?"

"Yer office? I'll be there, so I will."

Later that afternoon Colin showed up at Rosa's flat.

"What took you so long, Colin?"

"Feck, I don't know," he said, as he removed his tweed cap from his head.

"Sasha hasn't arrived yet. I baked cookies. Care for one?"

Colin smiled. "If I could just sit a bit, that would be grand, if ye don't mind?"

"Are the stitches bothering you?" He nodded. "So, what did you discuss with the chancellor? You appear to be all hot and bothered. I know you Colin Limmerick."

He chuckled. "She was interested in coming to me flat tonight. She wants to see what a slob I am, I suppose."

Rosa paced a bit. "You're making a big mistake with that woman."

"Yer sayin' this 'cause ye want to come to me flat tonight instead of her, eh?"

Rosa walked over to where he was sitting. "You never once invited me to your bed."

"Stop it, love. Last time I did that, I got a slap across the face."

Sasha pushed the door opened and stepped inside. "So, here I find Mr. Limmerick on time for once."

"I'm always on time," Colin said, as he turned to Rosa.

"I think if I move dial of my device it will take us to a place in time which is cause of all trouble."

"What time period would that be?" Rosa asked.

"I get reading two times in history that were very great. The year it tells me is 1857, when British took control of India. The other time in history I am reading from device is 840 A.D., when Vikings raped and pillaged Celtic people and most of Europe."

"Why 1857?" Rosa asked.

"Why not?" Sasha responded.

Colin chuckled. "Bollocks, this sounds like. Mate, Rosa asked ye a legitimate question. There are several turnin' points in history. Why 1857?"

"It is because device is reading British land. We are in England and device picks up from soil. Big part of British history is 1857. In order to cross over two years and block pathway to time, you must get someone from India and someone Celtic or Viking to come together and venture to both those years. Device will pick up vibrations from both of you and it will destroy what is around it to block pathway through time."

"Whatever happened to the magnetic barrier?" Rosa asked.

"Miss Amoli and Mr. Limmerick will be crossing through magnetic barrier in exact spot. Not easy procedure."

"Would that then mean whoever ventures to 1857 and 840 will come back safely?" Rosa asked.

Sasha glanced at her with sweat pouring from his face. "This is time-travel. No guarantees."

"Colin, you and Amoli are the only two people I can think of who would be suitable to do this kind of expedition," Rosa said, with concern.

"Amoli 'n I are no longer a couple. I've hurt her so much. I can't ask her to do this."

"Mr. Limmerick, set aside your personal life, for once," Sasha blurted.

"For once? What ye sayin', mate? What ye think I am, some wanker, who goes about regular quests to mess up wenches' lives?"

Sasha and Rosa looked at each other, and answered simultaneously, "Yes."

Colin stood up. "Enough of this rubbish. I've had enough. I bes' get on me way. I'm expected at the chancellor's office this evein'."

Rosa cleared her throat. "I see."

Colin placed his cap on his head. "We's gonna discuss Cushing."

"Colin, don't do anything you'll regret tonight," Rosa said.

"I'm a big lad. I can handle this, love."

"Mr. Limmerick, think about asking Miss Amoli to come on time-travel expedition. It will save world. You and her will be heroes."

Colin saw himself to the door. "I need to think about it. Cheers, mate."

Chapter Twenty-Seven

The evening ripened. Colin knocked on the chancellor's office door.

"Do come in," she said.

He took a giant step in and removed his hat. "I'm glad to see there's no bottles of champagne or caviar present."

She snickered at him. "I was just watering my plants."

"Can I sit a bit?"

"Please do. Remove your jacket; make yourself comfortable."

"Would ye like me to begin?" He watched her scurry around the spacious office, watering each plant with care. "Professor Cushing. Do ye want me to explain me problem with me academic advisor? In fact, I think ye already know 'bout this."

She placed the watering can on the floor and sat at her desk. "Yes, Colin, please tell me more, if possible."

"I don't think he 'n I are a perfect fit. His interests are with his prehistoric horseshoe crab. The horseshoe crab is a species that hasn't really evolved in millions of years. Frankly, I haven't any interest in it."

"Well, that would be a definite problem. But I think there is a bigger problem."

Colin's eyes widened. "Really?"

"Yes, of course. You're sitting way over there and I'm way over here. What are you going to do about it? Tell me something," she said, primping her hair. "Do you find me attractive?"

His eyes focused on the floor. "Uh, I do." Colin's eyebrows lifted. "What's this to do with ---?"

"I find you very attractive, Colin."

He sat back in his chair, until it made a creaking sound. "That's good, I suppose."

"Yes, it is. You see, there never is any graduate students who pass through this university that even come close to resembling a big brawny handsome man like you."

He fidgeted with his cufflinks. "I'm flattered."

"Do you find me irresistible?"

He took a deep breath and crossed one leg over the other. "Aye, yer a gorgeous wench."

"Does it bother you that I have gray hair?" She said trying to cover her grays with her long slender fingers.

"Didn't even notice."

"Well, I only have a little bit."

He smiled at her and ran his hand through his long hair. "I think I have a one or two as well."

"How old are you, Colin?"

"I turned forty-two in February."

"Well, you know what? I'm fifty-nine."

His eyes shifted a bit.

"Does it bother you?"

He took another deep breath but was silent.

"I'm seventeen years older than you, did you know that?"

He chuckled. "I didn't know, nor do I care, really."

She stood up and walked toward him. "I don't think I can take it anymore."

His eyes widened. "I-I'm sorry if I'm distressin' ye. Forgive me."

She stood closer to him as he remained seated. "Forgive you? For what?"

"I don't know what to do, is all."

"I think you should rip off my dress and make mad passionate love to me this very second."

Colin's lips parted. She fell into his lap. "Kiss me."

He smiled. "Evelyn, please. Ye can't mean this."

"Why? I'm human like everyone else."

He cupped his arms around her. "Not meanin' to hurt ye, 'n I don't wish to upset ye."

226

His arms tightened around her body. She brought her lips to his. He kissed her lips. She ran her fingers through his long hair and messed it up. Her kisses were wet and sensual, where he forced his tongue into her mouth. She squealed and panted as his tongue pressed against hers.

He stood up with her wrapped around him. He pressed her to the wall and panted. He pulled at her dress, until it fell to the floor. He loosened his tie and she tore off the buttons of his vest and shirt. When she saw his over-sized pectoral muscles, she screamed with pleasure. Her hands ran along the contours of his huge chest. She tugged at his undershirt and rolled it up to his neck. She kissed his belly until she noticed the stitches.

"Oh, oh, my, what's this?" She expressed with concern.

"Stab wound."

"Oh, how awful. Those stitches are ugly, they don't suit you."

"Aye, that they are. Don't like 'im any more than ye do, but they saved me life."

He fiddled with her intricate corset. He pressed her against the wall with his pants down. His erect penis entered her with her legs wrapped around his waist. He thrust in and out many times. She screamed, and he groaned. She screamed louder and louder, and then his penetration began. He pumped in and out. She panted and screamed. His breathing was deep and heavy, the thrusting and pumping continued. He was drenched in his own sweat. Her make up was smeared along her face. He thrust in and out until the final climax and then he slowly retracted from her.

He panted with sweat beads rolling off his chest. He lowered her to the floor. All he wore was his undershirt. She stood close to him with part of her corset still on.

"Do you think we were too loud?" she asked, with a grin. "Did you like it?"

He ran his fingers along her face. "I did." He grabbed his jacket to pull out a handkerchief. He wiped her body as well as his. He found his under shorts on the floor and put them on. "I think I should get a carriage for ye. Ye need to get home."

"Do you want to take me home?"

He sat down to put his pants on. "It's best that I don't, so I think. I'll get a carriage for ye. Ye'll get home safely, no doubt."

She fiddled with her corset and got her dress on. "I really enjoyed tonight, Colin."

"I did, as well," he said, as he looked for his shirt. She pressed her body against his. "Can't recall where I placed me shirt."

"I would like to do this again someday soon. How about you?"

"Yer definitely a fun wench."

Chapter Twenty-Eight

Rosa sat in the teashop across from the university. She glanced at the clock on the wall only to realize it was only 7:00 a.m. She poured her tea and dropped a sugar cube in her cup.

"It's still so early," she mumbled.

Colin stumbled in. Rosa held her hand up so he could see her at her table.

"Why would ye want to meet at this time, love?"

We have a lot to do if you and Amoli are going to stop the pathway of time," she said, as she nervously stirred her tea.

"I haven't spoken to Amoli. Ye heard her say she'd never time-travel again. And, also, it would be best if we didn't see each other. Just don't want to bring her down any more than I have already, if ye follow me?"

"But maybe for you she would."

Colin rubbed his large rough hands over his face.

"How did it go with the chancellor last night? Is she going to find a way to rid Cushing as your advisor?"

Colin noticed a waitress. "A pot of tea here, please!" he called to her.

"You're not yourself this morning. What happened last night? What's wrong with you this morning?"

"Nothin'. Got meself a headache, is all."

"What is she going to do about Professor Cushing?"

Colin's eyes scanned the teashop. "Don't think that topic came up too often."

Rosa dropped a few more sugar cubes into her tea. She watched the tea splash out of the delicate cup. The waitress brought a pot of tea with a few biscuits on a plate.

"All went well. "

"You slept with her, didn't you? Did you sleep together?"

His eyebrows lifted. "Rosa, stop this. Nay, we didn't sleep together."

"I'm sorry I doubted you. What kind of a friend am I? I'm so embarrassed."

He smiled at her. "We didn't sleep together, for sure, but..." He sighed with frustration. "I just don't wanna discuss it, 'is all."

"You had sex, didn't you?"

His head hung down. "Sex?"

"Yes, Colin, you had sex with the chancellor of the university, didn't you?"

He took her hands and squeezed them. "Shhh! Keep it down!

"Colin Limmerick, you get more disgusting with every day that passes. How could you? You're such a sailor!"

He chuckled. "That's what I am."

Sasha entered the teashop with Amoli. Colin's eyes widened as he chomped on a biscuit. Sasha pulled out a chair for Amoli. Colin gazed at Amoli with cookie crumbs falling out of his mouth. "Sasha, I can't believe ye dragged the little lass to this overly early meetin'. Are ye mad, man?"

"I say her you have something to ask."

"Well, Colin, what is it you wish to ask me?" she said, trying not to focus on him.

Colin clanged his teaspoon on the side of his saucer. "Don't know why Sasha brought ye here, really."

"Before you say another word, I want you to know that I have been getting on just fine without you. In fact, I'm very glad you and I have decided to part. I know exactly what you wish to ask of me, but my answer is no. I'm very sorry for that, but it's the way it has to be."

"Huh?"

"You wish to marry me now and I will have to decline your offer. I'm very sorry."

Colin glanced at Rosa, then at Sasha. He sighed as he tried to smile at her.

"I agree with ye. Yer right, we shouldn't marry, 'cause ye deserve someone much superior than me, don't ye think?" She stared at the table. "You've come to a fine realization, lass. I think yer correct about this, but unfortunately that's not what I was goin' to ask of ye. I'm sorry."

"You weren't about to propose to me?"

Colin bit his lip. He sighed as he smiled at her.

Tears rolled down her cheeks.

Colin peered at Sasha. "Mate, what's the big idea ye bringin' Amoli here without even askin' me?"

"You must ask her, now."

Colin tried to get comfortable on his chair. "Lass," he said, trying to clear his throat. "Would ye be interested in travelin' through time again? We's really need yer help."

"You brought me here so early in the morning to ask me if I can time-travel with you again?"

Colin smiled at her. "We wouldn't be goin' anywhere prehistoric. It would be 840 A.D. 'n 1857 A.D. It shouldn't be that bad."

"That bad? 840 A.D. was very terrible for me. That chieftain was very bad."

Colin bit his bottom lip until it started to drip with blood. "I'd be with ye."

"You didn't really help me before. You had clusters of female slaves around you always. How could you, Colin?"

Sasha leered at Colin. "Miss Amoli have point. What you will do better now?"

"Shut-up, mate."

"I wish you would stop torturing me. You must dislike me very much. What did I ever do to you, except love you?"

231

He placed his hand over hers. "Couldn't hate ye if I tried. Ye mean far too much to me. Problem is, lass, I'm a feckin' arse 'n I keep hurtin' ye over 'n over again."

She pulled her hand away from him. "I've had enough of this for today," she said, trying to suck back her tears. She stood up from the table. "I'm a student at the university again. I'm going to get a good education. I don't need you, Colin."

She turned to the door and left. Colin glanced at Rosa and Sasha. He was silent.

"Oh, Colin, I'm so sorry this isn't going well for you at all," Rosa said. "Where Amoli used to be your biggest fan, she certainly hates your guts."

"Well, it's Thursday 'n I need to get me things 'n be off to the harbor. Me mates need me on the ship. Fish stocks are improvin', so they are."

"Mr. Limmerick, Miss Amoli will come around and she will time-travel with us. You will see."

Colin smiled as he hoisted himself up from his chair. He tipped his hat to Rosa and Sasha and left. Late that afternoon, the crew of *The Atlantic Mermaid* met their captain at the docks.

"Captain, glad to see yaz, how was yar week?" Eddy asked giving Colin a strong handshake.

"Me week was interestin' I suppose, but tell me how business was?"

"No worries, Captain, there's plenty of fish now." Colin smiled.

"Hope ya don't mind we'll be pickin' up Lorelei 'n Tara at Rosslare at the Harbor."

"Fine." Colin greeted his crew as he made his way to the trawling nets. He glanced at the hold and wore a big grin on his face when he noticed piles of fish. "Crew, looks like things are back to normal."

"Captain, tell me something, did you know anything 'bout the fish scarcity?"

"Can't tell ye why our fish was gone."

Colin and Eddy worked relentlessly reeling in the ample catch. They docked at Roslare Harbor. Lorelei and Tara entered the ship. Colin smiled at both the women as he continued to reel in the catch. The wind was cool and damp, but Colin was drenched in sweat. He stopped to tie back his hair when he noticed Lorelei standing next to him.

"So, this is how ya'v turned? Yar too much of a snob to even notice me? I'm supposin' yaz all high class now."

Eddy chuckled and slapped Colin on the arm. "C'mon, Captain, we've got work to do, 'n so does Lorelei. No time to waste." Colin sifted through the catch that was in the hold. Lorelei bent over in front of him. Her prominent cleavage was in his face. Eddy tugged at Colin's arm. "Don't give her the satisfaction, Captain. Mind yar work."

"Aren't I here so I can satisfy the captain of this ship?" Lorelei blurted, with her hands on her hips. "It'll cost ya some quid, though."

Colin removed his tweed cap and brushed his fingers through his hair. "Oh, feck, Lorelei. I've got too much to catch up on. I'm not here four days of the week."

"So, ya'v always managed to fit me in yar busy schedule."

Colin stepped closer to her. "Look, glad to see yez, I am, but I can't be with ye just now. Busy, so I am."

She grinned at him. "Later, I'll be waitin' in yar bed."

"Ed, I've got to rest a bit," Colin said, sitting down by the nets.

"Don't give her what she wants, lad. Ya gotta get that cute Indian lass back in yar life. Don't waste yar time with whores."

"It's over with Amoli."

"It doesn't have to be."

"Ed, I've got much on me mind just now. I reckon I'll be sleepin' with Lorelei at some point today, so don't go about makin' me feel like shite even more than I already do."

"Suit yarself, Captain," Eddy said, and walked off the deck.

Chapter Twenty-Nine

It was Monday morning. Sasha sat in the university lab with his time-travel device.

"Sasha! I've been looking all over for you!" Rosa said, as she stormed into the lab, wearing a long white lab coat. "Where's Colin?"

Sasha glanced at her. "You so loud. I not see Mr. Limmerick. He is coming back from his boat on Irish Sea. Maybe he tired, da?"

"He didn't teach his 8:30 lecture. Timothy Duncan had to substitute for him. Is he ill?"

Sasha cackled. "Maybe he have big drunk?"

"Dr. Cushing always gives Colin the earliest Monday lectures when he knows damn well Colin is out of town every weekend."

"Shhh, I try to work something out on device. No matter how hard I try the year 1857 keep turning up. Miss Amoli is angry at Mr. Limmerick. She must go on time-travel. What we do?"

"Well, she has to go. She hasn't the choice."

"You can't make her."

"Yes, I will." Colin entered the lab. He gave a slight bow to his colleagues as he removed his hat. "Colin, you didn't teach your early lecture today?" Rosa said.

"Had to stay with me vessel another night. There's loads of fish, now. Couldn't have made the 8:30 class."

Rosa sighed. "I thought something happened to you."

Colin slid his arm around Rosa. "Nothin' happened, love."

"So, Mr. Limmerick, now that your b-whale beached itself you are a rich man once again," Sasha said, with a grin.

"Rich man? Let's just say, I'm not thinkin' about sellin' me vessel."

"What are we going to do about Amoli?" Rosa asked.

"I've got to try 'n talk to her again, I suppose. Couldn't we find another Indian lass who could do this?"

"You'd have to make this new Indian lass understand time-travel and why we need to do this. She'd have to come to trust us. I just don't know anyone else from India."

"Would Miss Amoli's father do this?" Sasha asked.

"God, no. He hates me bleedin' guts, so he does. I'd never approach him on this one."

"It has to be Amoli, Colin. I'm sorry," Rosa said.

Colin embraced Rosa and kissed her on the lips. "Cheers, love."

He smiled at Sasha and exited the lab.

"What brought that on?"

"You should know Mr. Limmerick by now."

***

Colin sat in his office. He noticed the piles of lab reports on his desk. He found his reading glasses in his blazer pocket and put them on. There was a faint knock at the door.

"Enter," he said.

Evelyn Gordon stepped in. "Hello Colin."

He lifted his head from his desk. "Pleasant surprise, Chancellor." He slowly stood up.

"I had to see you."

"Ye know, people are goin' to talk. This isn't a good idea, ye comin' to me graduate office."

"So, if people talk. Let them." She sat herself down.

Colin removed his glasses. "Evelyn, I've been havin' a rough go with Dr. Cushing. He just don't fancy me. I needed yer help, 'cause the dean was not interested in me complaint."

"But you've sung for me, and wined and dined me. Despite you came to me with a complaint, you also came to me with your dashing smile. You're such a breath of fresh air from all the stuffy *academe* that I'm so tired of."

He tried to focus on anything, but her. "I'm not a breath of fresh air. Ye just don't know me well. Me younger brother hates me guts, me academic advisor hates the air I breathe, 'n me former girlfriend's father hates the ground I walk on."

"How on earth can anyone dislike you? I think you're just wonderful."

Colin smiled. "Flattered, so I am."

"Perhaps you can come to my house tonight? I'm having a little dinner gathering and you would be an excellent escort."

"I've run into some problems with me time-travel expedition. I really should devote tonight to that. Forgive me."

"Couldn't you devote tomorrow night to that instead?"

Colin took a deep breath. "It's really somethin' that shouldn't wait, I'm afraid."

"You're always running off here and there. I can never get you to remain in one spot."

"Dr. Cushing said the same thing to me. He's not amused with me schedule, either."

"I can see you have a lot of work. I shall leave you be for now and tonight I will see you around half past seven?"

He stood up to see her to the door. "I don't know."

She took his hand. "I hope you like *duck a l'orange*?"

"Can't really say I've had it. Used to Irish stew, so I am."

Colin brought both her hands to his lips and kissed them. "I'll try 'n make it."

She gleamed with joy and exited his office. Colin sat back at his desk and mulled through the stack of lab reports when Rosa stormed in.

"Alright, Colin, I just passed the chancellor in the hallway. What's going on?" Rosa sat down. "This seat is warm and I smell expensive perfume."

Colin placed his glasses back on his face. "Please, allow me to read through these labs."

"I'm worried about you. You're not yourself these days."

He removed his glasses. "Shite, I donno. Maybe I'm going out of me mind. Ye know, when I was on me ship this past weekend I overheard one of me crewmembers say that if he looked like me all his troubles with wenches would be over."

Rosa snickered. "What did you say?"

"I told 'im he was nuts."

"Well, one of your biggest attributes is your appearance."

"So, I look good. How brilliant that I look so good to wenches. It's more like a curse."

"Doesn't every man want to be handsome?"

"Aye, a handsome man isn't the size of a mountain like me."

"I'd say tall with broad shoulders definitely equals handsome."

"Yer not so bad yerself."

She blushed. "Colin, you just need to use your good looks to your advantage."

"What's a gorgeous wench like ye doin' in a place like this talkin' to a fart like me?"

"You never stopped loving me, that I know is for sure."

"I never did, yer right. Ye never stopped lovin' me, either."

Rosa sighed. "Why aren't we a couple?"

"Ye hurt me bad, love. Are ye coupled with Sasha, now? Do ye love him?"

"Not the way I love you."

"Got a secret to tell ye. Sasha's got a wife." Rosa sat back in her chair and scanned the room. "She's in Russia."

"Well, I'm not surprised."

238

Colin stood up and walked to where she was sitting. He rubbed her shoulders. "Are ye gonna be alright about this?"

"I'm fine. What angers me is I lost you because of him."

He pulled her up from her chair and embraced her. "Ye wanna come to me flat?"

Rosa's eyes widened. "What are you saying?" She primped the blue, felt bows in her hair. "I've never been with a man in that way."

"Still, eh?"

She stepped back from him. "Sasha and I never did that much. I suppose he was trying to remain faithful to his wife. Now it all adds up." Colin ran his hand along her face. "Colin, please we're at the university."

"Yer still a bit nervous when push comes to shove, eh? Ye propositioned me once before 'n now yer backin' down?"

"Alright. I think I can do this. I trust and love you with all my heart."

He took her hand and locked up his office. When they arrived at his flat there was a note attached to his door. He took the note, which said:

Dear Colin,

I haven't been happy lately. I'm very sorry the way things turned out between us. I would like very much to meet with you. Maybe you can come to my aunt's house for dinner one of these nights.

Amoli

Rosa took the note from Colin. "Now, you're all depressed about her. Don't feel guilty. Her family drove you up the wall. They never accepted you for who you are."

"Aye, but Amoli definitely did. I need to speak with her about the next time-travel anyways."

239

Rosa folded her arms in front of her. "Please don't let this note from Amoli deter you from our romantic time together."

"Love, it's a Monday mornin'. How romantic is that?"

He opened the door to his flat.

"Colin, your place is a mess!"

"Forgive me, love. Just haven't had the time to keep things in order, I'm afraid." He undid his tie and unbuttoned the vest of his suit. He stood behind her to help unfasten her dress. "I've loads of work that must get done before I'm off to the chancellor's dinner party tonight."

Rosa's eyes shifted. "The chancellor's dinner party?"

"Aye, she wants me there."

Colin continued to let her dress down from her shoulders.

"Then what? Are you going to sleep with her?"

Colin stopped what he was doing as Rosa's dress fell to the floor. He gazed at her in her corset.

"She invited me to dinner not her bed."

"You're a man with no will-power. Of course you're going to sleep with her."

He was in a fixed stare at her standing there in her corset. "C'mon, love, ye wanted to be romantic. I'm melting over ye just now."

"Did you sleep with Lorelei this past weekend on your ship?"

"Why ye bringin' up Lorelei? She's a whore." He began to unbutton his trousers.

"Stop right there, Colin! I don't want to see how huge you are right now."

"I slept with Lorelei. I've been sleepin' with her every weekend upon me vessel. This is since things stopped with Amoli."

"And how many times have you slept with the chancellor?"

240

"Slept with? Didn't sleep with her, but I plowed her pretty good about once, I think. It could be twice."

"You button up those trousers and keep them on for once. You're disgusting." Colin threw his arms in the air and sighed with frustration. Rosa gathered her dress and put it back on. "My word, how could I have ever thought you and I could ever be a couple when you sleep with every woman you meet."

"Forgive me, love. I must be a slut of a man."

"Well put, Colin. You are, in deed, a slut of a man. Disgusting!"

"Forgive me."

"Never!" Her dress was on, but she struggled to primp her messed up hair.

"I haven't been unfaithful to anyone, 'cause I'm not attached to anyone, so why ye doin' this?"

"You are a sex fiend. Sex is like a drug to you. Here I was thinking if we did make love right now that would probably mean marriage. You're not the marrying type, Colin!"

"Don't say that, love. I am very much the marrying type."

"For now on, we're just friends and colleagues!"

She ran to the door and left.

Chapter Thirty

That evening Colin took a carriage to Evelyn's home. He was wearing a black suit and tie and he carried a gift with him. He knocked on the door and an elderly gentleman opened it.

"You must be Mr. Limmerick?"

"Aye. How ye know me?"

"Miss Gordon has described you to me several times. Do enter." Colin removed his jacket and the elderly gentleman took it. "The guests are enjoying champagne and appetizers in the parlor."

Colin entered the parlor. Evelyn was chatting up several of her friends when she noticed Colin enter the room.

"Colin! I'm so glad you could make it," she called, and scampered to his side, while taking his arm. "Tell me, did you run into any complications upon your arrival? You must have met Jacob. He must have seen you in." She pulled at his arm. "Do come in and meet some of my very dear friends." Several couples smiled at Colin. Evelyn remained standing next to him. "Everyone, this is Colin Limmerick, the PhD candidate who is researching prehistoric mammals. He is a time-traveler."

Her guests looked at each other, they stood up and applauded. Colin grinned awkwardly.

"A standin' ovation. I feel so special." His face turned a shade of red.

"You are special, darling," Evelyn said. "Colin is a fisherman, as well. He owns a trawling ship and has a crew as well. He teaches lectures at the university, and he is an avid Darwinist." Her guests continued to applaud him. "Would you like to say something to my guests, darling?"

"I wasn't expectin' this. Um, don't really have much to say after that."

Her guests gave a light chuckle. One of the female guests smiled at Colin.

"Evelyn, you didn't tell us your beau is Scottish. We spend our summers at our cottage up in Inverness. It's lovely."

"Irish, I'm Irish, not Scottish."

"Oh, Irish. I can't really say. I've never been to Ireland. So, you're Irish. Isn't Scottish and Irish the same thing?" the female guest blurted.

Colin's smile dissipated. "The same thing? Hardly, but we's all from the Isles 'n the Scots are Celts just as the Irish. There's similarities for sure. There's a difference between Irish Gaelic and Scottish Gaelic."

"Really?" the woman said, as she sat down beside her spouse.

Evelyn gestured for Colin to sit down. "Colin does speak Gaelic," she said.

"What else makes you different than a Scotsman?" the woman asked. "Maybe you don't wear a kilt as they do?"

"We do wear kilts."

The guests looked at each other and whispered some comments.

"Jacob, pour Colin a tall glass of champagne."

Jacob placed the flute glass in Colin's hand and poured. A few hours had passed and Evelyn was seeing her guests to the door.

"What a wonderful evening this was. What did you think of it, Colin?"

"Maybe I had too much champagne." She ran her hands along his chest. "Not used to it; feelin' a wee bit hung over for me own good. Whiskey never does this to me."

"Whiskey would destroy me," she said with a grin.

"Evelyn, I think I should be goin'. I have another early lecture."

"Oh, no you're not. You're spending the night here."

"It's not wise if I do. Yer guests asked me loads of questions. It looks bad if I continue to see yez."

"What are you implying?" He took her hands and brought them to his lips. "It's really nobody's business who courts me. Stay the night, Colin."

"Ye hold a position filled with big responsibilities, the female chancellor of the university can't be seein' one of the PhD candidates. Don't think it looks right, what ye think?"

She pressed her body against his. "I think I'm falling in love with you. I have that butterfly feeling every time I see your face."

He sighed. "Oh, Mother of God help me."

He paused while her hands remained close to his lips. He swooped her into his arms and carried her upstairs to her bedroom. The following morning Colin stormed into his laboratory class 15 minutes late. The students sat in the lab patiently. Colin wasn't wearing a tie, nor was he wearing his vest.

"Forgive me. However, I'm delighted to see all of yez waited so patiently," he announced to his class.

"Sir, will we be examining the prehistoric soil you brought back from your time-travel expedition?" A young male student asked.

"Aye, this is the day."

"How do we know the soil is prehistoric, sir?" the same student asked.

"When I ventured 40,000 years into the past I collected it."

"But perhaps you're just saying that, sir."

Colin paced a bit. The class noticed his disheveled hair and unkempt appearance.

"Ye don't have to believe anythin' I say. I'm a blatant Darwinist at that. So many have challenged me on his theories of evolution. Ye don't believe the soil I brought back is prehistoric 'n ye think what I lecture is rubbish? So be it.

"Sir, have I offended you?"

"Ye have the right to believe or disbelieve; that's why we's in this university. Skepticism is key."

Colin noticed Dr. Cushing enter the laboratory. The class stood up. Dr. Cushing gestured for them to sit. Colin removed his jacket and pulled out a barrel filled with soil. He began to distribute it into several beakers.

"I see you're hard at work, Colin," Dr. Cushing said.

"Can I help ye with somethin', sar? As ye can see I'm in the middle of a lab with me class."

"I'd like to discuss something with you. See me in my office when you are done with your class."

Dr. Cushing exited the laboratory. Colin's eyes shifted a bit, but he continued to provide his class with what was needed to fulfill the lab assignment. When the class ended, Colin showed up at Dr. Cushing's office.

"Sar, ye wanted to see me?"

"Yes, Colin, sit down. There is some talk going about the university that you are Chancellor Gordon's suitor. Is this true?"

Colin's frozen smile dissipated. "Suitor, sar?" Colin took a deep breath and focused on a tiny spider that hung from its web on the ceiling. "Define suitor, sar."

"There must be something wrong with you if you are unfamiliar with that word. What is your answer to my question? You are a PhD candidate from Ireland at that. Chancellor Gordon is, well, she's the chancellor of this university institution. Do you not see something wrong with this equation?"

"Sar, yer implyin' I'm with the chancellor in that sort of way. I have come to know her. As far as me as her suitor, sar, I would say that isn't the case."

Professor Cushing paused. "I see."

"Sar, a busy man is what I am. I run me fishin' business 'n I'm here from Mondays to Thursdays. I haven't the time to be anyone's suitor, sar."

"Ah, yes, of course. You can go now. I've asked my questions."

Colin stood up and left. He ran down the hall, skidding and turning down the stairs and across the street to the next building. He arrived at his office to notice the door was opened. Evelyn was sitting comfortably as she awaited him.

"How'd ye get yerself in me office?"

"I'm the chancellor. I have ways." Colin sat at his desk. "I had a wonderful time last night. You're such a fabulous lover."

"I'm not."

"Oh, yes you are. Are you ever a fine size."

"Evelyn, stop it. Ye 'n I can't see each other anymore. It's not workin'. Yev got too much quid'n too much power. Not used to this, so I'm not. Yer always tryin' to buy me. Worst of all, I was just approached by Dr. Cushing. He just asked me if I'm yer suitor."

She chuckled. "What was your answer?"

"I told him that I'm not yer suitor."

"Oh, Colin, you lied to him."

"I don't fancy liars. I'm not yer suitor, Evelyn. It's impossible for me to be what ye want. Ye treat me like a prize, or some kind of trophy."

"I don't like your tone. Why are you so upset?"

"Ye want me to be kicked out of graduate school?"

"That would never happen. I'm the chancellor; nobody can go above my head."

"Wouldn't be too sure, so I wouldn't." He took a deep breath. "I'm a workin' class fisherman, whose worked his arse off to get into this graduate program. Don't come from yer world, so I don't. I don't fit in with yer social bracket, nor yer financial bracket."

"I'm not parading you around showing off my blue-collar suitor."

"Certainly feels that way."

"Well, I'm sorry if I've offended you."

"Fond of ye, so I am. Yer beautiful. But I think yer position would be in jeopardy, as well if this continues."

"We're adults. Why can't this continue?"

"Because I have so much more to lose than ye do."

"You're such a troubled man. I'm sorry for that."

"Troubled, aye, that I am. I've got to venture through time again. It won't be an easy mission, so it won't. I thank ye for the fundin', but me fishin' business has picked up since, 'n I'd like to pay ye back."

"I wouldn't take your payment. I gave you that funding because I believe in you as a researcher. I think time-travel is so adventurous and brave. I don't really know what happened on your last expedition, but I'm sure it was marvelous."

"Celtic warrior, so I was."

She laughed.

"I was a Celtic warrior. I had slaves who made armor for me. I had to learn how to fight Vikings 'n Celtic chieftains with a sword." She continued to laugh. "What I do isn't adventurous 'n brave. Stupid is what it is. I received a sword in me gut."

"Oh, yes, of course."

"Almost died. Rosa sewed me up. She's no doctor, but she did what she could to keep me alive. Please don't bother with me anymore. Ye deserve a more stable-minded man. Besides, ye said it yerself, I drink too much for me own good. I thank ye for the fundin', it was brilliant of ye to do."

"Ye know, Colin, I feel as if I've known you all my life."

"Ye don't know me, Evelyn; ye don't want to know me."

247

"I understand that this is not what you want. Then I have to respect your wishes."

He stood up and gestured for her to leave his office. He smiled and kissed her hand. She gazed at him.

"I'm sorry, Evelyn."

She turned away from him and left his office. He placed his hat on his head and grabbed his coat and left his office. Later that afternoon, Colin knocked on Amoli's aunt's door.

"Yes," her aunt answered it.

"Howye. Is Amoli here?"

"Oh, hello, Colin. She's at the university taking courses again."

"Fancy the sound of that, so I do. I'll look for her there. Good day," he said, as he tipped his hat to her and left. Before he made his way to the university he stopped at his favorite pub. He sat at the bar and removed his hat. "Gimme a whiskey, please."

Sasha entered. "I find you here, always. What's wrong with you, now?"

"It's confirmed, mate. No good with wenches, so I am. I give up."

"Why you say?"

"Every wench who enters me life gets hurt 'n ye know what? I get hurt as well. If Evelyn wasn't the chancellor of the university, I would've courted her."

"Evelyn? Who's that?"

"Chancellor Evelyn Gordon?"

"You still see her?"

"Worse. I've been bangin' her."

Sasha pulled out a cigarette and a match. "You bad boy, Mr. Limmerick."

"Awful, is what I am, just awful."

"So, why you do?"

Colin received his glass of whiskey. "'Cause if a gorgeous wench fancies me 'n offers me her affection just can't say nay to it, so I can't."

Sasha got comfortable on the barstool. "So, you are slut man."

Colin chuckled as he drank his whiskey. "Suppose I am."

"You hurt chancellor's heart, da?"

"She's not pleased with me just now."

"Miss Amoli has hurt heart, too?"

"Aye. Am I a brute?"

"Da." Colin lapped up his glass of whiskey. "You speak to Miss Amoli yet?"

"I haven't. She's at the university taking courses."

"You must find her so we go on next time-travel expedition."

"If she agrees upon goin'."

Mr. Limmerick, put your drink down, go find Miss Amoli, and ask her. Also, ask her to marry you. She love you so much. I not know why."

"I've hurt her so much. Couldn't I just go on the next time travel expedition?"

"She is our Indian link to the past. The year came up 1857. I tell you this already."

Colin guzzled his whiskey and swished it in his mouth. "Aye, I bes' find her 'n propose this to her. Aye, aye, so I shall," he said, as he sprung up from the bar stool, placed his hat on his head, and dashed out.

Colin sat in the university courtyard. He watched the over-sized ravens dazzle the students. Amoli walked by with a young Indian man. Colin felt panicked as he walked over to her.

"Amoli, uh, hello."

She shifted her eyes to Colin then to the young male beside her. "Hello, Colin."

"It's good to see ye."

"Likewise, I suppose."

Colin stood tall beside the young gentlemen. "Do I know ye?"

The young man looked at Colin. "I am Kaur."

249

Colin's eyes widened. "Oh, Kaur, I've heard yer name before."

"Yes, I am from India."

"Yes, Colin, how rude of me not to introduce you. Kaur is planning on studying here."

"So, yer not plannin' on returnin' to India?" Colin asked a bit confused.

"Not without Amolia," he said, with a grin.

Colin focused on the ravens. "What?"

"Yes, Colin, my father would like me to be Kaur's wife. He comes from a wealthy upscale caste. He also agrees to accept my dowry."

Colin put his weight on one leg, then on the other.

"Do you have to go to the lavatory?" She asked.

"I don't."

"So, you are Colin? Amolia has told me about you. You are very well received at this university due to your unique time-travel expeditions."

"Well-received, ye say?"

"Colin, Kaur and I are planning our wedding. We even have a date."

Colin's facial expression changed. "Weddin' date?"

"Perhaps you would like to be a guest?" Kaur offered, with a smile. Yes, would you like to attend our wedding? It will last for several days, which is our tradition in India."

Colin stepped closer to Amoli. "Can I speak to ye in private, if ye don't mind?"

"Yes, Colin. Excuse us, Kaur, if you don't mind." Colin yanked her arm and pulled her behind a large oak tree. "Colin, must you be so rough on me? Kaur has a temper."

"As do I."

"What's wrong? You're not yourself."

"I've come to ask ye to time-travel with me, but now that I see yer with that wanker, I think I'm gonna ram me fist in his face."

250

"I'm already twenty years old. I cannot be waiting forever for you to decide on a wedding date."

"Do ye love him?"

"It's an arranged marriage. I will learn to love him."

Colin shut his eyes.

"Yes, Colin, I'm no longer going to wait for you. You've been very unfair to me. And as you said yourself, you feel I should be with a much better man than you."

"Before I beat this Kaur wanker into the ground, tell me somethin': do ye still love me?"

She brought her hands close to him and gently touched his chest. She ran her tiny fingers along the neckline of his vest.

"Despite you stepped on my heart and crushed it. Yes, I still love you. And, yes I will time-travel with you, because I will always love you."

He stepped closer to her. He ran his hands along her full buttocks and rubbed her back. His large hands fondled with her long black hair. He brought his lips to hers.

"I couldn't go on livin' knowin' yer with someone else."

She pulled herself away. "Yes, but how many others have you been with?"

He paused. "Can we start over?" He got down on one knee. He took one of her hands and brought it to his lips. "Amoli Sharma, will ye marry me?"

She gleamed with happiness. "Are you proposing to me, again?"

"Aye, lass. December 25th, love. Aye, we'll be married on Christmas day, if that's dandy with yez?"

She leaped into his arms. Kaur approached them.

"Amolia, what are you doing with this man?"

"Forgive me, Kaur, but the man I must be with is Colin." Amoli remained embraced in Colin's arms. "Colin is who I must be with. Forgive me."

"I will tell your father at once!"

Colin stepped close to Kaur. "Amoli's father already hates me bleedin' guts. Ye won't be shockin' 'm, so ye won't."

Chapter Thirty-One

Rosa, Sasha, Colin, and Amoli sat in the laboratory early in the morning.

"Miss Amoli, are you ready to travel to year 1857? You may go to India, you may remain in England. I not know. Time-travel device never give readings like this before."

"I'm frightened, Dr. Dimitrikov," Amoli said.

"Well, da, you should."

"Don't scare her any more, man," Colin interjected.

"Just get on with this, already, time is slipping by," Rosa cautioned.

"Rosa, are ye comin'?"

"Haven't decided."

"You better decide," Sasha said.

Colin held Amoli's hand. "We's a couple again, thought I'd tell yez."

Rosa rolled her eyes back. "Woohoo, I'm not surprised. When's the wedding?"

Colin smiled. "Christmas Day."

"Oh, Colin, Christmas Day doesn't mean anything to Amoli and her family. I don't know what you're trying to prove."

"It's a date I can remember, so it is."

"I'm wearing my engagement ring again," Amoli said, with a giggle.

Sasha smiled. "Very nice, Miss Amoli."

"Well, I suppose it's time to go," Colin said.

"We not have to go to your Ireland. We can go from London."

"Are ye sure?" Colin asked.

"If it not work, we then go to your Ireland, da?"

***

The four traveled to a remote field outside of London. Sasha placed the time-travel device on the grass and turned the dial. Rosa smiled.

"I think I'll come along."

"You hate time-travel," Sasha said. "You come with no more complaints. I not like woman with complaints, da?"

"Someone has to keep everything in check."

They stood around the device where it indicated the passage through time; using certain colors on how to direct them to the time vortex.

"Really hate this part, so I do," said Colin.

The strange aroma filtered the air with vibrant colors. The time-travelers were pulled into the vortex that led them through the passage of time. Rosa lay on the ground face down.

"Oh, God, I hate this too. I feel as if I was taken apart and put back together again."

Sasha tried to stand up. "Nobody promise you luxury ocean liner."

Amoli's head rested on Colin's belly. "Colin, wake up."

"Amoli, just let him be, he never responds well to the time vortex," Rosa said. "Oh my Lord, I'm sounding as if this is routine for me. How awful."

Sasha found the time indicator wedged between two rocks. "Indicator say we in year 1857. This is good. I not know if we in England or India."

"It's too cool and damp. I wouldn't think we're in India?" Rosa suggested.

Amoli sat by Colin's side. "Please, wake up, my love."

Colin's eyes opened. "Feel awful, so I do," Colin said.

Amoli scanned her surroundings. "I think we're in India. I'm home!"

"Not so fast. Colin thought the same about 840 A.D. Ireland. He soon realized it wasn't home. If we're in India, and it's 1857, we're in the middle of a war," Rosa said.

Sasha grinned as if he had gone mad. "Da, this is what we want. We need war so Miss Amoli can block pathway through time."

Amoli looked around. "Wait a minute. This is not India. The trees are not the same, and the climate is very much different. This is too cold to be India."

Colin tried to stand up. "Aye, lass, this resembles the Isles to me."

"It is not usual for device to take us to different place," Sasha said.

"And, how do we know it's 1857?" Rosa asked.

"Time-travel device say so," Sasha responded.

"As if I'm going to believe that silly device?" said Rosa.

"What you say?" Sasha huffed at Rosa. "This is not silly. It guide us to many time in past. You are only woman; what you know?"

"Oh, get off your high horse. So, now that we're still in England, how does Amoli close the pathway through time?" Rosa asked, with her arms crossed in front of her.

"She must get involved with war. It is year 1857. England is at war."

Two British military officers approached the time-travelers. One of the officers put his arms around Colin and Sasha.

"Excuse men, but I'm surprised to see two healthy men like you both just standing around when you should be on your way to fight for the British East India Company."

Colin smiled. "Aye, so yer right, mate."

Sasha turned toward the man. "I not want to fight for British. I am Russian."

255

"Oh, so you're a foreigner. Too many foreigners in our land already. You either get on your way back home or you fight against Indian Independence."

"I not care about this. My Russia has its own problems."

Colin nudged Sasha. "Shhh , mate, just go along with the gent."

The officer looked into Colin's eyes. "We're fighting against the Sepoy Mutiny, you know this, don't you?"

"I do know this," Colin responded, as he glanced at Rosa and Amoli.

The officer tugged on Amoli's arm. "Is she with you?"

"Aye," Colin responded, as he pulled Amoli toward himself.

"Try and keep her out of sight. India is losing this war, anyways."

"She's me fiancé 'n I'll flaunt her beauty any which way I choose," Colin said.

The other officer tugged on the rude officer's jacket. "C'mon, lets just leave here. I wouldn't want to get into a scuffle with him."

"Enough already. Lets just be gone," the more timid officer said.

"You're British, so you owe this to the crown. Someone your size could be an advantage for our side," the rude officer said, as he walked off with his companion.

Colin turned to Sasha. "Look, mate, don't really want to be a soldier, especially in this war. What does Amoli need to do to create a barrier for the pathway of time?"

Amoli noticed Indian men dressed as British soldiers. "I don't like this, Colin. I think I'm going to cry or scream."

"Lass, ye don't want to know the gory details of this war.

"So, does this mean you and Sasha have to enlist?" Rosa asked.

"It seems we do," Sasha said. "But I am Russian. Mr. Limmerick must enlist. He is British."

"So, what am I supposed to do?" Rosa asked.

"Ye need to watch over Amoli."

Sasha noticed his time-travel device was sending messages. "Wait! Device do things I not ever see. It say we must take something from this time and cross it with other time. Da, I get it now!"

"The other time bein' 840 A.D. the time of the ancient Celts?" Colin asked.

"Of course!" Sasha responded.

"What can we bring?"

"Miss Amoli must bring something from this time and cross it with what Mr. Limmerick brings from 840."

"Aye, but what is appropriate for us both to bring?" Colin asked.

"I not know."

Rosa threw her arms in the air. "Oh, God! This is so ridiculous!"

"The British are fighting India, so India will lose its independence?" Amoli asked.

Colin looked at her. "Aye, lass."

Tears ran down Amoli's face. "But why?"

"The queen's orders. Lass, if this war didn't happen yer family would've never come to England, think of it that way." She buried herself in Colin's arms and cried. Colin glanced at Sasha. "What is it she needs to take with her, mate?"

"I would say not rock or something, but maybe something important like soldier's musket, or dagger," Sasha said, with a serious tone. It is weapon."

"Colin, I'm so very saddened," she whimpered.

"Did ye hear what Dr. Dimitrkov said? Ye need to bring back either a soldier's musket, or dagger. If I end up bein' a soldier in this war, I'll fetch 'im for ye." He held her tightly in his arms. "We have to stay here a bit. We need to get back to London, so I can rent a hotel room for us."

"I really hope we're not going to be here for long, Sasha. Remember, the reason we're here is to put up a barrier through the pathway of time. Let's not lose focus," Rosa instilled.

The four of them checked into one hotel room. Later that evening, there was a knock at the door. Colin opened it. It was the two military officers they saw earlier that day.

"Hello, I think? How did you know to find us here?"

The soldiers entered the hotel room without being asked.

"We followed you, of course," the rude officer said.

Colin took a deep breath. "What ye want?"

"You need to enlist. You're a British citizen, you must enlist."

"Irish is what I am."

"Doesn't matter; you need to enlist. You're British."

"I'm Irish 'n I don't have to fight in this war if I don't want to."

"You and your people must be loyal to the queen. Victoria herself has earned the respect of all British subject."

Colin sighed. "Fine, I'll enlist."

"How about him?" the soldier asked, as he pointed to Sasha.

"I am Russian. I not want to fight your war. It stupid."

"Why are you here?"

"I am scientist. I was brought here by university."

The soldier stepped back. "Oh, I see, you're a foreigner."

"How about her?" The soldier pointed at Rosa.

Rosa stood beside Sasha. "Um, I'm his wife."

"How come you're not Russian?"

"I met him in London."

258

"What about her?" The soldier pointed at Amoli. "She can't stay here; she's Indian."

"Well, if I'm British, she can stay here if she's soon to be me wife."

Sasha walked up to the British officer. "Why you follow us? Why you have so much interest?"

"A British subject should be fighting in this war against Indian independence. All subjects of India are now subjects of our queen."

"Just enlist me, already, enough of this rubbish," Colin grunted.

"What's your name?"

"Colin Limmerick."

"Place of birth?"

"Dublin, Ireland."

"Birth date?"

"February 1st, 1868."

The two officers looked at each other.

"What is your birth date?" The rude officer demanded.

Rosa's eyes widened. "He's had a hard day. He meant to say February 1st, 1815."

The quiet officer filled the information onto an enlisting form. "What is your weight and height?"

"I'm six-four, 'n I weigh eighteen stone."

"When you come in, you're height will be measured and so will your weight."

"Ye don't believe me?"

"Just looking at you, I definitely believe you. Sign here and show up at this address by 8 in the morning."

The officers tipped their hats and left. Colin took a deep breath.

"I can't believe I slipped up like that."

"That was close one, Mr. Limmerick. Cat was almost out of bag."

Amoli sprawled out on one of the two beds. "This has been an exhausting day."

259

Colin scanned Amoli's voluptuous body. Her ample breasts almost fell out of her sari, showing defined cleavage. Colin swallowed a few times. He could feel himself panting with desire.

"Rosa, Sasha, would ye two mind takin' a short stroll about town?"

Sasha laughed. "I get it, Mr. Limmerick. You want woman now."

Sasha took Rosa's hand and they left. There was silence in the room. Amoli stood still with her lips parted. She stared at Colin as he stared at her. A trickle of tears ran down her face. She smiled at him. He fiddled around to look for a handkerchief. He gently handed one to her. He stepped closer to her. She stepped back. He stood still in silence.

"Lass ---."

"Don't. Don't say anything, Colin."

He stepped toward her again. "Lass, I can't tell ye how much I want ye right now."

She turned from him. "That's your problem. You want everybody."

"That's not true, lass. I want ye."

"You didn't care about me when we went to 840 A.D."

"A bit preoccupied, so I was. Had Vikings 'n Celtic chieftains to deal with 'n such."

"I don't want to hear anymore."

He caressed the side of her face with his large hand. He lowered his head to kiss the sides of her neck. She smiled.

He continued to kiss her neck where he moved his face lower toward her cleavage. He removed his shirt, but struggled to unbutton his pants.

"Ye got me too aroused already. How am I gonna remove me trousers?"

She fell forward onto the bed with her breasts hanging out of her dress. He lunged onto the bed beside her. He

260

finally got his pants off. He fiddled with her sari. He lay beside her in his undershorts. She was fascinated at how hard and erect he was. Finally, her sari was off and so were his shorts. They both lay on the bed, naked. She held his penis in her hand and rubbed it vigoursly with both her hands. His panting intensified. He then rolled on top of her. He cupped her ample breasts in both his hands and squeezed both breasts together to create an even greater cleavage. He kissed her breasts several times. "I love ye, so much, lass."

"I never stopped loving you, despite the fact you tossed me aside."

One of her breasts was in his mouth, where his eyes widened and he sat up on his knees.

"Lass, I didn't toss ye aside. I was thinkin' ye deserved better than me."

She sat up, where he noticed her breasts hung almost to the bed. "I think you wanted to experiment with ancient women. You wanted to see what it was like."

"Not true, lass. I'm already over forty years old. I think I've had me years of experimentation, don't ye think?"

"Yes, but you never had a chance to be with an ancient woman. What was it like? Was it any different?"

His eyes shifted a bit. "Lass, we's in the middle of our love-makin' here, 'n ye stickin' me with this, now?"

"Of course I am. If we're to marry, then you have to leave your playboy sailor days behind."

"Aye, I was with the slave wenches, but ye 'n I weren't a couple at that point. Didn't think I was cheatin' on ye or anythin'."

"How convenient."

"If ye don't trust me, hows we gonna ever marry?"

"Because, I know you, Colin Limmerick. If you finally take your wedding vows, you will be true."

He smiled. "I know that yer the lass for me, always."

"How about Miss Emanuel?"

"Don't bring her up, Amoli, please. Lets not do this."

She ran her tiny hands over his penis. "It's still stiff. How do you do that?"

He chuckled. "Me pipe has a mind of its own, so I think."

She got of the bed and picked up her sari. "I'm not in the mood for this, Colin. I think our relationship needs some time to heal. Sometimes, I think you just want me for my body."

"Don't say that, lass," he said as he sat on the bed naked.

"I know you're such a good man and that you would make me happy, but ---."

He slid off the bed and pressed his body against hers. He took her sari and tossed it on the bed. He scooped her up in his arms and carried her to the bed. He kissed her neck and planted himself on top of her. His penis was hard and erect. He entered her.

Chapter Thirty-Two

The next morning at 8:00, Colin reported to the enlisting office in downtown London. His height was measured and he was weighed. He signed a few more forms and was fitted with a uniform and helmet. He stepped outside on the street in his uniform to find Sasha, Rosa, and Amoli by the teashop.

"Well, ye like the way I look in this?" Colin asked, with a partial smile.

"You look dashing, Colin," Rosa said.

"Are you going to India?" Amoli asked.

"I shouldn't be off to India just yet. I should be stationed at the base first, don't ye think?"

"You should not be in India. We should be out of this time period before then," Sasha said. "India will not be possibility."

"Imagine, the English are callin' this a mutiny. How's it a mutiny?" Colin asked.

"Colin, whatever you do, don't politically involve yourself in this. We are here for one reason and that is to close the pathway through time. If you have an issue with Queen Victoria, just keep it to yourself. You cannot change history," Rosa instilled.

Amoli buried herself in Colin's arm. "I love you, but you're now a soldier. The enemy of my people," she whimpered. "My father would be greatly upset at you for this."

"So? He's greatly upset with me anyways. This shouldn't change things, don't ye think?"

"My mother and aunt would cry if they knew."

Colin's lips were parted with no response. He looked around for the carriage that was to transport the new recruiters to their base.

"This is a wee bit different than bein' a Celtic warrior, I suppose."

"Better for you, Mr. Limmerick, no swords."

"Aye, but we get daggers, rifles, pistols, 'n muskets instead."

"Bring back what Miss Amoli needs, don't forget. We will be at hotel," Sasha said.

"It's so strange to be in London just fifty-three years before we departed for this expedition. I mean, London still looks very much the same as when we left," Rosa commented.

"So it does. It's a bit strange, isn't it? Many of the same buildings were where here."

"This is time travel. You are to put personal attachments aside and continue on with journey, da?" Sasha said.

"It does look the same, doesn't it?" Amoli added.

"The only thing, that I surely notice is there aren't any roadsters. Everythin' is strictly horse'n carriage."

"I find this a bit disturbing. Fifty-three years is not very far in the past," Rosa noted.

"It's just shortly before some of us was born. Me parents would've fancied this."

"Colin, I'm worried. I don't want to let you go," Amoli said.

"I'm only goin' to the military base. I should be fine, lass."

Rosa kissed Colin good-bye and Amoli embraced herself in his arms. He hopped onto the wagon and left.

The following morning, before the sun came up, the soldiers heard the drums sound off. The new recruiters had to rise and be ready for roll call. Colin was still asleep in his bunk. One of the other recruiters stood by Colin's bedside.

"Wake up, man! It's roll call!"

Colin opened his eyes and sprang out of bed. "Shite! Donno if I can do this each mornin'."

Rosa slumped on the bed in the hotel room. "I feel so guilty Colin is in the army and we're here in a comfortable hotel room just waiting for his return," Rosa said.

Amoli sat on the other bed and watched Sasha hang out the window to smoke a cigarette.

"I don't like this one bit, no I don't," Amoli said.

"Ye know, Colin always gets the worst of things because of the way he looks. He once said to me that being built big and strong is like a curse," Rosa said.

"Mr. Limmerick can take it," Sasha said, puffing on his cigarette. "He is very tough. I like that I can buy tobacco in this time period. I don't mind 1857 at all."

"I mind," Amoli blurted.

"I suppose. So, as soon as he obtains those weapons he needs to leave the infantry and return to us, correct?" Rosa tried to confirm.

"If he agrees to do."

"What do you mean? Of course, he'll agree, won't he?" Amoli asked.

"Knowing Colin, if he gets too politically involved, he won't leave as soon as he should, but if he doesn't, he'll most likely die," Rosa cautioned.

"No," Amoli sulked.

Sasha slid his arm around Amoli. "Why you scare Miss Amoli? Mr. Limmerick is tough man. He survived Viking attack and Celtic chieftain. He will be fine, but he will not go to war. Mr. Limmerick no like war. He dodged Boer Wars, remember?"

"Colin is not a fan of war, that's for sure. He's always been ahead of his time. I just want to see him back here in one piece," Rosa said.

"He will not be sent to battleground for long time. He has time. He will come back to us, you will see," Sasha said.

***

265

Colin was at the base coping with his morning drills of basic training. He was already well versed with the command structure. One afternoon, he was muzzle-loading his musket rifle when one of the other young soldiers sat beside him.

"Are you getting the hang of this, private?"

Colin laughed. "Donno, really. Never even held a gun before. Just don't think I'll be any good at this."

"Don't think that way. The Indians are already losing."

"That's what I'm afraid of. Me fiancé is from India."

"Oh, you definitely have a conflict there."

Colin smiled and stood up with his musket in hand and walked back to his barrack. He walked to his bunk and placed his dagger and gun in a large canvas sack. He lay on his bunk. His lieutenant entered the barrack.

"Private, why aren't you engaging in your afternoon drills? Are you ill?"

"Aye, I am, sar. Please could ye fetch me some water?"

"Are you burning up?"

"Don't know. Just not feelin' well enough to participate in this afternoon's drills. I'm sorry."

The lieutenant scurried to get Colin some water. He returned with an onsite physician.

"Private, are you ill?" the doctor asked.

Colin lay lifeless in his bunk. "So I am, sar."

The doctor checked him over. "Maybe you need to be sent to a London hospital for further tests," the doctor cautioned.

Colin pulled up his shirt. "It's these stitches, sar. I think I could have an infection."

"Infection? This wound doesn't seem to be infected, but you should be discharged and taken to a London hospital."

***

266

The following week there was a knock at the hotel door. Rosa opened it to see Colin before her.

"Oh, Colin! You're back! It's been weeks! We've heard nothing from you."

"It wasn't easy to be discharged from the Infantry, love. However, I made it."

"Colin!" Amoli screamed, as she ran into his arms.

"You've lost some weight," Rosa said.

"So I have. I feel more exhausted than I ever did. It's a hard life gettin' prepared for battle, especially when I'm such an inexperienced soldier."

Sasha walked up to Colin and threw his arm around his shoulder. "Good to see you. Did you bring back evidence for Miss Amoli?"

"Aye, so I did. Brought back war weapons. Had to learn how to use a musket."

Sasha chuckled. "Poor Mr. Limmerick. I use musket when I was eight years old. You live so soft life in your Ireland."

"That's what ye think, mate?"

Colin handed Sasha a canvas sack of military weapons. Sasha pulled out a musket, dagger, and a pistol."

"You use pistol in infantry?"

"I swiped it from me lieutenant. I feel awful about it, but I just kept tellin' meself that I had to do it."

"We cannot wait for morning, because hospital and army will come looking for Mr. Limmerick. We must go through vortex of time now," Sasha cautioned.

"I agree," Rosa said.

Sasha placed the military weapons back in the sack. "We must quickly go back to same field we arrive and activate time indicator. If we lucky, it will take us back to ancient Celts 840 A.D."

The four time-travelers discreetly made their exit from the hotel and took a carriage to the field outside of London. Sasha turned the dial on the time-travel device to the year 840. The four remained close together. Flashes of

267

color and different aromas filtered the air. The four time-travelers fell into the vortex of time.

Chapter Thirty-Three

They lay scattered in the tall grass. Colin was the first one to lift his head. He stood up and noticed Sasha was wrapped around a tree stump. Colin pulled him up toward himself.

"First time I'm helpin' ye after the vortex ride, eh mate?"

Sasha smiled. "Tell me, does this look like your ancient Celtic world?"

"Don't know yet. The wenches are there. I won't rest 'till their up 'n chattin' about with us."

Colin picked up Amoli into his arms. Her eyes opened. She gazed at him and smiled.

"How nice it is to wake up to my prince."

"Please, lass, don't overdo it. After we's married for a bit, we'll see if ye still perceive me as a prince."

Sasha helped Rosa up.

"Should we look for that Celtic village?" Rosa asked.

"Of course, but we here only to get swords, tools, or maybe jewelry, no long visit."

"You don't have to convince me of that," Rosa said, as Sasha helped her up.

They wandered through the dense brush. Colin and Rosa noticed *Megaloceros giganteus* running in the distance. Colin's eyes squinted with terror.

"Just keep walking toward the village. I know this upsets you, but you can't let it," Rosa said.

"*Megalocers giganteus* shouldn't be here," Colin said, as he stopped to re-adjust his suspenders.

"We've ventured through time again, because prehistoric mammals are roaming around 840 A.D. Stay focused, my love," Rosa said.

"Aye, lets carry on."

The time-travelers entered the same Celtic village. Colin smiled at some of the familiar faces he had encountered before. Some of the women who were skinning fish, threw their arms in the air and cheered when they saw Colin.

"Our chieftain has come back to us!" the people shouted, in Gaelic.

Colin stopped walking and smiled at the people.

"Colin, don't get any ideas that you'll be staying so you can be their leader. We're here for a reason," Rosa whispered to him.

His faithful female slaves appeared and embraced him with gladness. Colin held them close to his body and kissed them on the lips. Amoli curled her upper lip to display her anger.

"Colin, we're engaged, you shouldn't be touching them. Not now, not ever!"

"Save your energy, Amoli, now that he's committed to you again, you need not worry." Rosa said.

The slaves brought them to the largest round house, where the head chieftain used to reside. The slaves worked feverishly to make the residence comfortable for him. They brought in a spread of food. A fresh kill of swine was the main course. Rosa turned her head.

"Colin, we'll eat, but I'm hoping we're not staying the night," Rosa said.

"I already agreed that we will be spendin' the night; hope it's dandy with ye?"

"Tell them to find themselves another chieftain. You can't be their man. You belong in a different century," Rosa said, getting agitated.

"Ye know, one of the slaves mentioned just now that the villagers hated their chieftain. She described him as a tyrant."

"Are you surprised?" Rosa said.

The four time-travelers sat on the floor and watched the slave women pour their wine and entertain them with song and dance.

"How nice, Mr. Limmerick, we make friends during time-travel. Not at all like enemy you make with Neanderthal, da?" Sasha said, as he stuffed a hunk of bread in his mouth.

"Don't think it's going to stop here; the Vikings are a bit blood thirsty. I think you may still be a warrior," Rosa mentioned.

Colin gulped his wine. "Warrior? Why would they want to jeopardize their new chieftain?"

"Sometimes, you can be so naïve. What do you think chieftains do? They fight bloody wars!"

Amoli overheard the conversation. "I'm not letting Colin out of my sight."

"If he has to fight the Vikings, you're going to have to let him do it," Rosa said.

One of the slave women sat across from Colin and offered him sweet smelling wild flowers. Colin smiled at her and took them.

"My lord chieftain, a battle is near," she said, in Gaelic.

Colin's eyes widened. "With the Vikings?"

"Yes, m' lord."

"When?"

"Anytime, M'lord."

Rosa placed her wine on the ground. "Well? What did she say?"

Colin stuffed a piece of fruit in his mouth. "I need to be prepared for battle at any time."

After Colin finished his meal, the slaves cleaned him up and gave him a massage. Sasha lay down in a pile of cotton.

"I want cigarette."

"Not here, not now, mate," Colin said.

Colin lay sprawled out on layers of cotton. The female slaves rubbed his pectoral muscles and ran their hands over his biceps. Rosa tried to ignore it, while Amoli sat in the corner and cried. Colin only wore a sheet around his lower half. He walked over to Amoli and sat beside her.

"Don't cry. I need to play this game if I'm to go to battle any time soon."

"I do not really think that you need to play any game. You're supposed to be my fiancé. These women are slaves from the distant past. Why do you even give them the time of day?"

"Forgive me, lass. I'll send them out."

"Give them to me. I want massage," Sasha blurted.

Colin sent the slaves out of the room. "They said they would return in the morning with armor and weapons."

"These slave women make you jewelry?" Sasha asked.

"Aye. I have some here."

"You can use jewelry when you go into time vortex."

"I will."

It was early morning. The slaves entered the roundhouse to get Colin ready for battle. Amoli nuzzled up to Sasha.

"Dr. Dimitrkov, you won't let those Vikings hurt Colin, right?"

"I've got gun, if that's what you mean?"

Colin turned to Sasha. "I heard that. You think I am such a terrible warrior that I need yer help. Don't bother. I can win me own battles. Don't need yer inference, mate. Stay out of it."

"Colin, you nearly died the last time," Amoli said, with a whimper.

"So, let me die. I should've never got us into this mess in the first place."

"Now you're talking silly. You don't want to die. You'd break your parent's hearts," Rosa said.

"All I can do is give it me all."

"And that's what you will do, Colin," Rosa said, with a fake smile.

The following morning the slaves dressed Colin in his armor. They gave him his sword and shield. They could hear the sound of the musical *loch erne horn* play, as Colin entered the center square of the village. There were many spectators waiting with anticipation.

An angry looking Viking stood there with his sword and shield. He glared at Colin. The crowd cheered when they saw Colin. The Viking took the first thrust with his sword. Colin moved away. Colin swung his sword several times, hoping he would be lucky. The Viking swung his sword and slammed Colin on the shoulder. Colin drew blood. Colin focused on each move his opponent made. He could hear the sounds of the anxious crowd. Colin swung his sword; his opponent stepped back and pierced Colin's bicep. The crowd shouted. Blood poured from Colin's arm. Rosa, Sasha and Amoli stood with the crowd, biting their lips. The Viking stepped toward Colin several time swing his sword as if he had gone out of his mind. Colin kept intersecting, one after the other, so quick each time, that Colin urinated in his pants. The crowd roared. Amoli screamed and kept her eyes shut. Sasha kept his gun handy, while Rosa bit her lip. The Viking waved his sword above his head and chanted to the crowd that he was the greatest warrior. The crowd expressed their distaste for him. While the Viking complimented himself, Colin stepped toward him and pierced his sword into the Viking's abdomen. He fell to the ground. The crowd cheered. Colin was amazed.

"This battle ended sooner than I imagined," Colin muttered to himself.

The crowd continued to cheer.

Amoli cut through the crowd and ran into Colin's arms. "You are a great warrior, my love!"

273

"Feck, maybe. Can't even believe this just happened. I'm fecked over me own head 'bout this, that's for sure, eh?"

Rosa and Sasha approached Colin, as the crowd continued to cheer.

"Mr. Limmerick, keep that sword and shield. We can use it for time travel, da?"

"Aye, so I will."

Rosa tried to blot Colin's bleeding arm with a cloth.

***

Colin sat amongst his band of men and the Celtic people the morning after the battle.

"There are countless Viking ships at our coast," one of his men said, in Gaelic. Amoli remained by Colin's side and Rosa and Sasha sat amongst the people in the roundhouse. *"They are destroying our temples and sanctuaries m' lord,"* the same man cautioned. Rosa stared at Colin and smiled. She gestured that she didn't understand what was being said. She shrugged her shoulders. *"They are killing our chieftains in neighboring villages and towns. The Shetlands, Orkney, and the Isle of Man are being invaded by Vikings. They want to take over and rule with Norwegian and Danish kingdoms."*

Colin wore a stern expression on his face. "We can't allow them to take our women and slaughter our men. I understand we're losin' Irish monasteries to them. We have to fight them to the death and save Ireland."

The Celts cheered their new chieftain. Rosa glanced at Sasha, where they felt as if they were missing out on the conversation. Amoli just remained as close to Colin as possible. Colin looked at Rosa.

"The Vikings are sea-born raiders. They've been occupyin' the Irish Sea 'n filterin' through the Irish lands with mass take-overs."

Rosa looked at him. "Thanks for the information, Colin."

Later that afternoon, Colin and Sasha went to battle the Vikings at sea. Colin's band of men rowed the Celtic boat, when one of the Celts spotted a Viking longboat. Colin was nervous, for he had never battled at sea before.

The two ships faced each other. The Vikings filtered into the Celtic ship and sliced whoever was in their way. Colin slipped on the bloody floor and was faced with a head Viking who was en guard with his sword, ready to kill. Colin was unsteady when he tried to gain his balance. He sliced the chief Viking's head off without trying. It was a victory for the Celts.

Later, the villagers performed music and dance for Colin. His slaves stood by his side and presented him with gold and wine. Colin took them and bowed to his slaves. They bowed to the floor to him.

"You have to tell them that you can no longer be their chieftain," Rosa insisted.

Colin turned to her. "I can't do that, love. Ye, Sasha, 'n Amoli need to get back to 1910. Maybe ye can cross me Celtic sword with Amoli's War of Independence musket 'n close the pathway through time. I'm sorry."

"Colin, have you lost your mind?"

"Aye."

"What is this, Colin? Are you breaking our engagement again?" Amoli asked.

"I just know I can't return to 1910."

"Sasha, can you knock some sense into Colin? He wants to remain here and be a Celtic chieftain."

"I seem to be a fair warrior now. I can do this."

Sasha laughed. "Mr. Limmeick, you were always crazy man. You are twentieth-century man. You belong to modern times. You cannot play God."

"That's all I've been doin' here, isn't it?"

Sasha sighed. "You come back with us, cross over with Miss Amoli, and block pathway through time and maybe later you can go back to 840 A.D., da?"

"Colin, you don't belong here," Rosa said. "I knew this was going to happen."

Colin stared at the ground as the musical festivities continued. "I donno what to do. I don't want to break me engagement with Amoli."

"Then come back to our time and be with me," Amoli pleaded.

He took her delicate hand and kissed it. "I'm sorry."

More wine was poured into Colin's flask. Sasha smiled at the beautiful slaves.

"You want to stay here, because you are like king to them. You can have all beautiful women you want, but you will not be so lucky in next battle."

"I can't imagine meself returnin' to our time, mate."

"You cannot disappoint Miss Amoli anymore. You break her heart too many times. She is just little girl."

Colin guzzled his wine in one gulp. "Please, mate, protect our two wenches 'n see to it they get back to our time safely."

"Da, da."

Amoli nestled up to Colin. "I will not go back without you. I refuse. I think it would be best if I remain here with you. We can have a Celtic wedding."

"Lass, this will be no life for ye."

"It is no life for you, either." She tugged on Sasha's arm. "Dr. Dimitrikov, this is a time far gone in the past, right? Then, if Colin remains here, does it mean everything will be gone?"

"The past is gone, you are correct, Miss Amoli."

"What are you running away from in the twentieth century?" Rosa asked.

"Runnin' away? Not runnin' away from anythin'."

"Colin, it's settled. I'm staying here with you," Amoli decided.

Colin took her hand and kissed it. "Lucky to have such a wonderful lass as ye."

"So now Amoli is remaining in this time with Colin. How absurd," Rosa blurted, with her hands in the air.

Chapter Thirty-Four

It was a rainy morning in London, 1910. Rosa sat in the teashop across from the university.

Sasha entered.

"Hello, my beautiful lady," Sasha said, sitting at her table.

"I don't know how you can even smile."

"It is what Mr. Limmerick wanted. You know how stubborn he can be."

"Things just aren't the same around here. I haven't said a word to the faculty. Amoli's parents are going to have to know about his. Colin's parents are going to have to know. What a burden he has left on us."

"Sometimes Mr. Limmerick not think. He have too much passion."

Rosa took a sip of her tea. "Have you noticed that absolutely nothing seems to be the same?"

"What you mean?" He popped cigarette in his mouth. "You still love Mr. Limmerick. Woohoo, that is what it is; you love Hercules."

"I'm serious. Well, for one, we didn't close the pathway through time."

"We try, but nothing happen. Good we still have 1857 musket and 840 sword, shield and jewelry. Only Celtic and Indian person can do it. There no substitutions for time-travel."

Rosa laughed. "Yes, you're right. But I'm talking about just the way things seem in twentieth century London. It all seems different. You don't think so?"

"I not notice," Sasha said, puffing on his cigarette.

"I find the people I run into are very rude, and almost barbaric in their mannerisms."

Sasha let out a loud hack of laughter. "What you mean, my beautiful lady?"

"I'm not joking about this. I haven't seen one auto on the roads. Everybody is using horses and carriages. Where are all the autos?"

"They too expensive."

"An undergraduate student of mine came to me this morning with a textbook, showing how the Romans and the Vikings didn't rule most of Europe, but the Celts did instead."

"Stupid text book."

"I checked the publisher, very well renown."

"Alright, what else did book say?"

"It said the Celts conquered the Romans. It even said the Celts conquered the Vikings."

Sasha's eyes widened. "I think we must time-travel again to 840 and get Mr. Limmerick. He cause too much trouble."

"Sasha, are you saying Colin changed the history books?"

"He is twentieth-century man in ninth century. Of course he change with his modern thinking. He is smart man. But always drunk man, da?"

"Do you know what this means? It means with him playing God and remaining in 840 he will have changed history forever, and we still have prehistoric species roaming around different times being misplaced. What a mess this is."

"What would Dr. Darwin say about that?"

"Will we even have had a Charles Darwin? I don't know. This is all too strange. I love Colin, I want him back here with us."

"Even if he marries Miss Amoli?"

"I suppose so. I even miss bossing her around. Sasha, we have to go fetch them."

"We go back to 840 A.D. and we must bring them back, because history is changed forever."

"Can we leave now?"

"Da, lets go."

279

Chapter Thirty-Five

Colin stormed through the village delegating his men for the next Viking raid. Amoli sat in the main square of the village watching the women scale the fish. Rosa suddenly appeared before Amoli.

"Miss Emanuel?" Amoli reacted with surprise.

"Hello, Amoli. Dr. Dimitrikov is also with me. He's looking for Colin right now."

Amoli stood up and approached Rosa. "Why are you here?"

"Because something very serious has happened. We need to find Colin and have a serious chat with him."

"He's in that roundhouse with his band of men. He seems to like it here."

"Band of men? Interesting. Colin now has a band of men," Rosa commented.

"Of course, he's the chieftain. He had a band of men before as well. I suppose you weren't paying attention," Amoli said with an irritating giggle.

Sasha approached the women and stood beside Rosa.

"Hello, Dr. Dimitrikov." Amoli embraced him.

"So, Miss Amoli, do you like it here?" Sasha asked.

"Not at all. I want to go home. It's terrible. I can't understand Gaelic. Colin is enjoying this primitive lifestyle. I quite hate it. I miss my parents. I want to go home."

Rosa looked at Sasha. "Has Colin lost his mind?"

"I think Mr. Limmerick lost his mind long time ago."

"I don't know if I would say that, but he's taken an interest in living in the past."

"Can we barge into roundhouse and get him?" Sasha asked Amoli.

"I suppose. I don't really know them. This is a far away time in history. I hate it here. Sometimes I cry myself to sleep. I miss my family and friends. I miss our modern day. I hope both of you can knock some sense into him."

The three time-travelers stood by the door of the roundhouse. Amoli walked in first, followed by Sasha and Rosa. Colin told his men to take a break while he spoke to his friends. Colin approached them as they stood timidly by the doorframe.

Howye, good to see yez both."

"You have to return to 1910 because you've changed the history books," Rosa abruptly blurted out.

"I'm kickin' the Vikings arses is what I'm doin'," Colin said with a laugh. "Thought about that, so I did. Didn't really understand what the impact would be, though."

"Mr. Limmerick you change history so much now, you must come back."

"I'm savin' the Celtic people from those goons."

"Colin, you can't change history. I told you this when we ventured to our first prehistoric journey. You wanted so badly to save *Megaloceros giganteus* when those *Paleolithic hunters* were hunting it."

"Aye, yer right, love. When am I ever goin' to stop playin' God?"

"Maybe it's time you stop. I don't think Amoli likes living in the past," Rosa urged him.

Amoli looked at Colin with her deep-set dark eyes. "I hate it here, Colin. I wish we could go home."

"I hope I've taught the Celts what they need to know to defend themselves against the Vikings."

"Mr. Limmerick, you must allow chips to fall as they will. Celts never defeated Vikings. Let it be," Sasha said.

Colin took a deep breath as he gazed at Amoli. "Aye. Understand ye, so I do. I'm missin' me *Atlantic Mermaid* 'n me crew somethin' awful, so I am. Yer right, this isn't for me."

Rosa stepped back. "Oh, that was easy enough. I'm glad you're seeing it differently now," she tried to primp her messed hair. "Colin, please, you and I both know how much you thirst for this kind of thing. You read too much about Darwin, I think."

"Did yez manage to do the crossover through time with using the war weapons of 1857 and 840?

"Did not work. No substitutions. This is time-travel," Sasha responded.

"Oh. None of this makes any sense," Colin said. "Well, I suppose we should do it now, shouldn't we?"

"We have the weapons with us," Rosa said.

The four time-travelers left the Celtic village and walked to a remote forested area. Sasha pulled out the time-travel device and turned the dial forward to 1910. They stood closely together when colorful smoke and that same smell filtered the air. Amoli clutched onto Colin's arm. Sasha and Colin held Rosa's hands. Amoli winched and panicked. They fell through the time vortex to a magnetic pathway through time. Amoli and Colin linked arms. Amoli held the musket in front of herself and Colin did the same with his Celtic sword.

"Wait, it must be correct time when two time periods cross!" Sasha shouted, but he didn't know if they actually heard him as they were in the process of time traveling.

Sasha looked at the dial of his indicator, which told him it was the correct time. The 1857 musket hit the 840 sword and crossed. A magnetic barrier of some kind appeared in front of them. The four of them flung through a *tachion-flux,* which was the flow of particles associated with time. Colin and Amoli were split apart from each other through the vortex of time. The forces were too strong to stay close together. Amoli's screams penetrated through the vortex of time. Rosa closed her eyes and pretended she didn't hear anything.

The four of them lay face first on a field of much shorter grass. None of them even flinched. The wind blew over their still bodies. A stray cat wandered about and noticed them. It sniffed around and left. Sasha lifted his head.

"Oh, my God. So hard ride. My head hurts. Different time-travel ride than others, I not know why."

Rosa rolled over and faced the sunlight. "So bright, but yet I think I'm smelling the sweet wild flowers of home. I hope we're back in 1910. This was a very different and very serious operation. I'm not feeling very well, either."

"Where's Colin?" Amoli asked, in a panic. "I think I'm bleeding. This was so very terrible. I never want to time-travel again. It's just terrible!"

Rosa sat up. "This was the hardest time-travel we had ever experienced."

Colin lifted his head. "I'm ill, that's all I know."

Rosa stood up. She tried to wipe blood from Amoli's head. Sasha remained on the ground.

"I not feel good. I usually feel okay after time-travel. It is usually Mr. Limmerick who cannot tolerate it."

"God help me. I do feel noxious. I always do. Me lip seems to be bleedin'," Colin said, sitting up. He noticed drops of blood had fallen onto his shirt. Those stitches are definitely causin' me some pain just now."

"Sasha, do you think it worked? Do you think we've seen the last of prehistoric misplaced species?" Rosa asked.

"Time will tell. I not know as yet. Maybe it work and some did not make it back to their time, but maybe only a few. I not know."

Sasha tried to stand up. He staggered over to Colin. He extended his hand for Colin to help himself stand up.

"Thanks, mate."

"Mr. Limmerick, you alright?"

"Aye, mate. Not really sure what happened. Do ye think we did it? We've gone through so much in order to make this happen. I'm wishin' hard these prehistoric species are no longer gonna be misplaced," Colin said, holding a bloody handkerchief to his lip.

"I really hope dinosaurs aren't living amongst prehistoric mammals," Rosa said, as she slowly walked to Colin and handed him a clean handkerchief. "Then Darwin's idea of survival of the fittest would definitely come into play."

Colin shut his eyes. "Wouldn't even wanna think of somethin' like that, love. It just wouldn't work."

"Only time will tell," Sasha said, as he fondled his jacket pocket for a cigarette. He was relieved when he did find one. He profusely popped it into his mouth and lit a match. He scanned the surrounding area and took a deep breath. He blew smoke rings as he glanced at his three friends and smiled. "Only time will tell."

THE END